DATE DUE

MAY 0 9 2005		
MAY 1 8 2005		
JUN 0 1 2005		
JUN 1 0 2005		
JUN 1 7 2005 wD		
JUL 0 8 2005 cD		
JUN 1 9 2007		
JUN 2 7 2007 H/t		
MAR 0 7 2014		
MAR 2 6 2014		
GAYLORD		PRINTED IN U.S.A

Trouble's Messenger

Trouble's Messenger

A Western Story

MAX BRAND®

Five Star • Waterville, Maine

First Edition
First Printing: March 2005

Published in 2005 in conjunction with
Golden West Literary Agency.

Set in 11 pt. Plantin by Carleen Stearns.

Printed in the United States on permanent paper.

Library of Congress Cataloging-in-Publication Data

Brand, Max, 1892–1944.
 Trouble's messenger : a western story / by Max Brand.—1st ed.
  p. cm
 "Trouble's messenger first appeared as a six-part serial under the George Owen Baxter byline in Street & Smith's Western story magazine (9/6/30–10/11/30)"—T.p. verso.
 ISBN 1-59414-138-X (hc : alk. paper)
 I. Title.
 PS3511.A87T78 2005
 813'.52—dc22   2004028107

Trouble's Messenger

Chapter One

Now Louis Desparr was content. For twenty years he had been laboring, trading, hauling, packing, portaging, fighting, and all that he had made from that generation of work was enough to give him one good stock of trade goods. That was when he determined to build Fort Lippewan. Another man would have given up, discouraged. But Louis Desparr was not discouraged. At the very moment when another would have withdrawn from the game, declaring that luck was totally against him, Louis determined to make his greatest fling of all. Louis was not only determined, but he was methodical. He believed in hard fighting, but he believed in generalship, also.

First of all, he decided that he would give up the wandering life of the trapper and select a spot for stationary trading. Then he hunted through the list of possibilities that was stocked in his memory. And, when he came in his list to the Lippewan River, his eyes rolled upward in sudden reflection. He could see the point where the two tributary streams ran into the Lippewan. He could see the point where the rocky bluff advanced well out from the shore, naturally defended by its cliff-like steepness and height, on two sides of its triangular shape. The other side, the base of the little peninsula, was narrow. Sometimes, at high water, a current ran across the neck, and the peninsula became a little island. But in any time or case, the site was eminently defensible. The projecting point was crowded with a heavy growth of timber. Down the river and its two tributaries, the Indians, the half-breeds, and the white mountain men could paddle their canoes with very few portages, and those only on the headwaters. They could follow a natural road down to the fort. For that was where he built it.

He had to do two things. First, since the country was in the land of the Blackfeet, and he was not a great friend of theirs—having taken a Piegan scalp or two in his happy younger days—he must have a way of cementing a friendship between himself and that tribe. This he managed, at an easy stroke, by taking as squaw wife, Dancing Shadow, the daughter of the war chief, Angry Child. There was nothing pretty about Dancing Shadow, except her name. When her features were young and tender, she had been kicked in the midst of them, and they were rather mixed together as a result. One eye pulled down and one eye pulled aside. She was always looking two ways at once. Her face was so deformed that not even the thick-skinned Blackfeet bucks could persuade themselves to take her as a squaw, even as a gift.

Proud Angry Child consumed his heart with disappointment and grew so tired of the sight of his daughter's face that the very bones of his head ached when he so much as looked at her. Then arrived the trader, Louis Desparr, half English, half French. Or was there a little strain of Indian blood already in him? He did not want a beauty. He was past the age of romance, and merely asked for a worker. Dancing Squaw was as strong as an ox, and built very much like one. She stood six feet tall; she was made solidly, and based on huge feet. And when the trader saw her, he could tell at a glance that she would be faithful, and never mysterious. So he took her. Not as a gift. He got together some horses, beads, and guns, and gave the handsome lot to

Angry Child, who was almost persuaded that it had been worthwhile to wait even as long as this.

The gist was a masterstroke. It restored to Dancing Shadow her self-respect. It warmed the heart of Angry Child. And it established in the minds of the Indians that this was a rich and generous white man, apt to be a little foolish in driving a bargain. All of this seed would assuredly bear fruit a hundredfold.

Then Louis Desparr went with his wife down to the junction of the streams, and for a whole year they labored at the building of the fort. The two of them felled, trimmed, and squared trees into logs, and ran a redoubtable palisade across the neck of the peninsula. When a party of Dancing Shadow's relatives and friends stopped by to visit with her, Desparr got their help in the hoisting of the main timbers, and once the skeleton of the buildings that was to compose the fort had been established, it was comparatively easy for him and Dancing Shadow to build up the walls and do the roofing.

They toiled and moiled without a pause until the task was almost completed. Then he left her there alone, with a rifle for company, and went off down the river. He came back with all the trading stock that he could get together by spending his last cent, and mortgaging his future to the hilt. Then word was sent out to the tribes, and presently they began to come in.

They still were coming. They brought in great piles of beautifully tanned buffalo robes. They brought in any quantity of beaver skins. They brought in their herds of horses, too. There were suits worked with colored quills, and others heavily encrusted with beads until they were almost like suits of chain mail. Sometimes they carried in painted robes that were true works of art. Often they had exquisitely deco-

9

rated canoes, carved knife handles, eagle feathers in abundance, necklaces of bear claws, baskets, pottery. Whatever they brought, the careless Louis Desparr always was willing to buy or trade for—at a price.

Having once made up their minds, Indians do not readily change them. If a man is once established as a hero, he may run away from twenty fights and have his conduct attributed to mysteriously bad "medicine". So, when Desparr gained the repute of being a rather foolishly generous price maker, the repute clung to him long after he began to drive the sharpest of bargains. Beaver skins and buffalo robes were what he wanted, but he would take anything he could get and put it in his stores, until he had a chance to trade back with it. He gave the red men beads, mirrors, knives, guns, lead, gunpowder, pins, needles, axes, and hatchets, and he always had tea, sugar, coffee, and trade whiskey. The last was an abomination composed of sheer grain alcohol, afterward compounded with coloring matters and greatly diluted. There was a punch in this liquor that was not altogether that of alcohol. But it was a very popular drink with the Indians. Obviously a liquid that drives a brave mad with half a pint is twice as good as whiskey of which one can consume a quart before beginning to stagger.

Louis Desparr traded every morning from dawn to high noon. Then he closed up his stores. The Indians were invited to wander where they pleased and look at goods that they might wish to purchase the next day, but there was no trading in the fort of an afternoon.

Dancing Shadow took charge of the stock and guarded it with her two-direction eyes that saw all things in a single glance, as it appeared. With such a shepherd, sheep would hardly be stolen.

Louis Desparr was left free to conduct more important items of his affairs. For instance, he could interview the influential warriors and the big chiefs. He could chat with visitors from more distant tribes and invite them to come to this haven of just prices and good stock. He could estimate the importance of the men to whom he must give presents, and hit upon the heart's desire of each one. For a heart's desire is usually reasonably cheap, if it is a red man who is doing the desiring. A strip of red cloth may really, to him, be more than a string of ten war ponies. That was the secret of Desparr's success.

He saw his stores increasing. Marvelously they grew. He began to dispatch boatloads of furs in blunt-nosed, flat-bottomed skiffs that could be poled or sailed downstream. For every half dozen or more of these, a narrow canoe would come nosing up the river, keeping to the shallows, delayed only by a few short portages and tugged by horses up to the fort. There, at Fort Lippewan, the stocks were unloaded, and so the trading went merrily on.

Louis Desparr, beginning almost at bedrock, already had cleaned up thousands of dollars in a single season, and a good part of that season was still to run. No wonder that he was content as he sat on the flat roof of his main building with Henry Lessing, the hunter and trapper, both of them smoking long-stemmed pipes. The tobacco was so good—having just arrived, and being in the height of its unspoiled strength and richness of flavor—that now and again, drawing a long whiff, they half closed their eyes. Henry Lessing was an old acquaintance. Now he looked at the bustle below them, where the crowds of children, squaws, and braves were passing and re-passing, with a few white men of various kinds mixed among them. He looked at this bustle and nodded.

"You're gonna get rich, Louis," he said.

"You'll do this one day," said Louis.

"I ain't a thinker," said the other very frankly. He waved his hand beyond the palisade, where the Indian encampments were spread. There were three distinct sections of three distinct Blackfeet tribes then present. So commodious was the land that there was plenty of space for all of them to have camps where water and wood would be easy to get at, and where there was open country, besides, to race their horses and to play their games. The wigwams, half seen through the trees, shone like snow. Voices came shouting faint and far from the open land. Some young men were flogging half a dozen ponies as they raced out to a rock and back around it. Their long hair streamed out behind them. "I'll keep to that," said Henry Lessing. He shook his head. His skin was white, but his soul was now Indian. The other did not argue. He knew that in his own soul there was a great deal of the same urge. To make money was a very pleasant thing. But to be beyond the need of money was, in a way, a yet pleasanter state.

Lessing again looked down into the yard of the fort. "There's the tenderfoot again," he said.

"Which one?" said the trader.

"The one that can talk the Blackfoot language."

"Is he still hunting?"

"Still hunting." Lessing nodded. "Still looking at faces. Have you found out what he wants?"

"He won't talk," said Louis Desparr. "He'll only look." As though the subject were irresistibly interesting, he leaned forward until he could see the man in question.

Chapter Two

It was not hard to pick out the stranger. In the first place, where all the others were in motion, he stood fast at the corner of the storehouse, with his arms folded. In the second place, their skins were dark. The other whites had lived so long and so much like Indians that they were almost as bronzed as the braves themselves. But this lad was flushed rather than stained by the sun. Besides, the others were robed, or dressed, in neatly fitted deerskins. But the white boy was in a rough, gray cloth.

"What could he be?" said Louis Desparr almost gloomily.

"I dunno," answered Henry Lessing. "He's as straight as an Indian."

"He's as blond as a Swede," said Louis.

"He's got a pair of arms and a set of shoulders onto him."

"When he finds what he's lookin' for, there'll be trouble."

"Trouble for the tenderfoot, I reckon."

"He might be a first-class fightin' man," said the other.

After a moment of reflection, Louis Desparr added: "Look here, Henry. How is it that he knows how to talk good Blackfoot? Not like you and me, but the real lingo, like he was raised with it."

"Maybe he was."

"That's likely, ain't it? You mean in one of the tribes?"

"Why not?"

"All that he knows about the Blackfeet is their lingo."

"Yeah, he's a tenderfoot, all right. Won't he ever talk none?"

"Not a bit to nobody," said Desparr. "He acts like he thought that he was a duke."

They went on with their smoking, still staring fixedly at the stranger.

"He's looking for trouble," insisted Lessing. "One of them Indians is gonna pass half a foot of knife between his ribs, if he keeps on starin' at every face with that sneer of his."

"Maybe he don't mean nothing," said the trader. "He's too young to know much."

"Aye, that's true. He's pretty young. I'd hate to be that young again, Louis. It makes me feel pretty chilly even to think of being such a kid again. Like jumping off into ice water."

"Aye." Desparr nodded. "It's a hard thing . . . in this part of the world."

"Did you ever ask that boy a straight question about what brought him here?"

"No. I ain't a question asker. I listen when I get a chance, but him that asks questions is askin' for lies."

"He needs to have some questions asked," said the other.

"Not by me. He's looking for a man, that's what he's looking for."

"Aye, he's looking for a man. He's got a grudge, maybe."

"Yeah. Maybe he's got a grudge. You remember old Siwash Pete Larkin, that had the grudge ag'in' Cap Mayberry?"

"No."

"Why, it was down on the Columbia, where the fish eaters live, and a low crew they are. And Cap Mayberry come up to a sloop from Portland, Maine. . . ." He let his voice die away, unheeded, for it was plain that Henry Lessing was not hearing a word of what was spoken.

Now suddenly the trapper stood up. He was a tall, lean fellow of nearly fifty, iron gray, hard and tough as bull's hide from constant living in the open. He was dressed in deerskin trousers, but they were old and fitted rather loosely. He wore a blue flannel shirt, which had faded over the shoulders to a meager tan. His hair was clipped off short across the brow and descended in a matted, unkempt tangle to the base of his neck. He wore what had once been a white belt of the skin of a mountain goat, but the original color had become grimy and hand worn almost past belief. On one side it supported a great knife in a sheath. On the other side was a double pouch to contain ammunition and tobacco. On his feet were clumsy but comfortable moccasins. And it was plain that no man in the world cared less about appearances than did Henry Lessing.

"I'm gonna go down and talk to that boy," he said.

"I wouldn't do it," declared Desparr. "He wouldn't thank you, and he wouldn't talk."

"Hold on!" said Lessing, raising his hand.

A party of three or four young braves, at that moment, was passing the corner at which the stranger stood, and one of them, stumbling or pretending to stumble, fell heavily against the tenderfoot. The shock knocked him from his place and sent him reeling several paces. He who had stumbled did not stay to apologize. He went on with his companions, and their grins were very broad, indeed.

"Now what'll the boy do?" asked Lessing, muttering to himself.

"Nothing!" exclaimed Desparr. "He's yellow, Henry. Look at that."

For the stranger, recovering from the blow, calmly resumed his former position at the angle of the building and continued, with a high head, to look at the passers-by.

"Yellow as a dog," repeated Desparr.

"Aye . . . maybe," said Lessing.

"The word of that'll get around," said Desparr. "There won't be any peace for that tenderfoot, from now on. Every half growed-up buck in the tribe will try to step on his toes."

"What's his name?"

"He calls himself Peter Messenger."

"Well, Messenger will have trouble, anyway. He's made for trouble. There never was a man with a chin like that, that wasn't made for trouble. But yaller? I dunno about that."

"You'll see. They'll try the same dodge again on him."

"If I was them, I wouldn't."

"You think he's something?"

"Kind of an itch in my bones, I do."

Desparr chuckled. "It's that worthless Dust-In-The-Sky," he observed. "He's always around raising a ruction. There ain't any peace when that young buck is about."

"He'll lose his hair, one of these days."

"He's got some hair already drying in his teepee," answered Desparr. "Comanche hair, at that. Aw, he ain't just a young blow-hard. He loves a fight, does that Dust-In-The-Sky."

"And maybe he'll get it."

"Not out of the tenderfoot."

"Would you bet on that, Louis?"

"I'll bet. What you want to bet on it?"

"You took a fancy to that pinto mare that I rode in."

"Hey, Henry, are you gonna bet that mare on a green-horn that you never seen before?"

"I been doin' a lot of thinkin' about that greenhorn," said Lessing. "I'll bet the mare. What'll you bet?"

"What do you want?"

"I seen one of those new Colt revolvers down in the store. How about that?"

"It's a mighty expensive gun," said the trader cautiously.

"I'll throw in my saddle, too," Lessing said calmly.

Louis Desparr started and shrugged his shoulders. "This is after business hours, anyway," he said. "The gun ag'in' the mare, if you want to. But you're gonna lose. What do you expect? That he'll follow Dust-In-The-Sky, or that the buck will come back to him?"

"The buck will come back to him. He's got the taste in his teeth now, and he'll try to bully the white man. You'll see, Louis!"

"Aye, I'll see."

"There comes Dust, now."

The same party returned, recruited to seven or eight. They wore an appearance of innocent absent-mindedness. "They mean a lot of trouble for that boy," said Desparr.

"They mean trouble," agreed Lessing quietly. "And now you'll have a chance to see."

Almost the same thing happened. As the group came nearer, one of the other young bucks stumbled exactly as Dust-In-The-Sky had done before, and fell toward the white man.

Then Peter Messenger moved. He side-stepped with a gliding speed like that of a cat, caught the young buck as the latter floundered forward, and turning, by a maneuver that even the sharp eye of Desparr could not follow, he flung the Indian over his shoulder. The latter turned a full half circle in the air and landed with such force that the wind was knocked out of him with a grunt audible to the watchers upon the roof.

He did not rise again, at once. The dust that had been thrown out in a great puff on either side of his body now steamed upward and dissolved in the air. But still he did not rise.

"How the dickens did the boy do that?" asked the startled Desparr.

"That's what they call a neck lock," said Henry Lessing. "And if I ain't badly mistaken, young Mister Blackfoot is gonna have a stretched neck and a sore head for a spell. I never seen that trick done better."

"It was neat! It was mighty neat!" said Desparr in generous admiration. "I didn't expect nothin' like that. But there is Dust-In-The-Sky goin' in to finish up the job."

That young brave stepped straight up before the white man and uttered something in an angry voice, but the white man paid no heed to him at all. Oblivious of his presence, he stared past the Indian toward the more distant faces in the crowd that drifted by.

"Look, look, look!" said Desparr greatly excited now. "Seems to me like a real man has arrived out here at Fort Lippewan!"

"Aye," said Henry Lessing. "I reckoned that before. If Dust-In-The-Sky makes a move to touch him, there'll be another explosion. Is Dust-In-The-Sky that much of a fool that he can't tell gunpowder when he sees it?"

The voice of Dust-In-The-Sky rose higher, with a savage snarl in it. That fighting sound stopped every passer-by, and, from a distance, men came running to enjoy the possible fight.

18

"Stop it, Desparr!" exclaimed Henry.

"Let 'em have it out," said the trader philosophically. "Bad blood needs the air. As long as they don't start fighting inside my store, they can do what they please when the sky is over their heads."

"Well," said Lessing, "if it comes to a pinch, I'm sorry for the Blackfoot."

Chapter Three

So convinced was he of the tenderfoot's superiority that he actually turned his head and looked away from his preferred champion to the flash of the sun on the river and the shadowy forests that walked down to the river's side on either hand. Across the open land to the south, he could see a dust cloud. It had been approaching for some time, and with such incredible slowness that he could only guess at an ox team and at least two wagons in the train.

"There it goes!" gasped Desparr with a chuckle of pleased excitement.

He had been so long among scenes of violence that bloodshed meant almost nothing to him. A man had to take his chances as he found them. After all, life cannot last forever. His own hair had seemed to be very loosely and temporarily fitted on his head several times in his career, and, therefore, he had the less sympathy with others when they stood in danger.

As for Lessing, he glanced down in time to see the glitter of steel in the hand of Dust-In-The-Sky. That flash leaped at the throat of the white man, but again Peter Messenger moved. He stepped just enough aside to allow the gleam of the knife to shoot harmlessly over his shoulder. And he stepped just enough in to bring him to comfortable short-arm distance. Then he snapped a hard fist up to the point of the brave's chin.

Dust-In-The-Sky was a brave young man. He was as tough as twenty-five summers and winters of mountain hunting and mountain fighting could make him. But a bell had been rung in his brain with a dull buzz like a swarm of bees. His wits scattered upon the winds. He went backward, like one who cannot get his balance, and, after floundering a few steps, he sank to the ground in a loose, helpless pile, his head slumping down upon his knees.

"He had the shoulders," Lessing said critically, and apparently unmoved by this victory that he had prophesied. "He had the shoulders, and it looked like he had the arms. But he's got the science, too. He's been trained, old son. And he's been trained well."

"Watch, now," said the trader. "There's something more coming. They're gonna mob him, the red dogs!"

The group had swayed threateningly in toward the white man as their leader fell under that stroke. But now they paused for a moment when Messenger leaned and picked from the ground the knife that Dust-In-The-Sky had dropped. A big, formidable-looking weapon it was, brand-new from the store of Desparr, and with the sunlight appearing to run on it like water and drip from its point.

"Hello!" said Desparr. "Does he mean to tackle that band with a knife? They'll cut him to pieces in half a second."

"He won't tackle them. He's defending himself, and that's all," declared Lessing with perfect assurance. "You watch him, Louis."

The hand of Messenger rose with the knife and then flicked it away with a swift and graceful motion. It turned over once in the sunshine, and then landed just between the knees and an inch from the scalp lock of Dust-In-The-Sky, burying its blade to the hilt in the ground.

Desparr jumped up with an exclamation. "Did you see that, Henry?" he asked, utterly amazed.

Lessing merely smiled as though he were hearing a twice-told tale. "He had the shoulders and the arms. He has the fingers, too," he said. "There's nothing green about that boy but his skin, Louis!"

"There go the Blackfeet. They've had enough of that fellow's medicine, and I don't blame them."

The group of young braves, in fact, had withdrawn a few steps, hastily, and some of them picked up their fallen leader. They supported him as they went off. But he was still in dreamland, his head falling back on his shoulders, his face blank, his mouth open, and his feet trailing.

"What a punch!" said Desparr enthusiastically. "An iron hand, Henry. I couldn't do that with a club, let alone a bare fist!"

"See what the boy's doing now," answered Lessing.

The tenderfoot, stepping back to his chosen place of vantage, had folded his arms again and remained exactly as he had been before—his head high, his eye constantly traveling over the faces of the crowd that, by this time, was closely packed about him.

A white trapper stepped from the semicircle and slapped him cordially on the shoulder. The two on the rooftop could hear the boy being invited to take a drink.

His answer was a mere shake of the head, and the trapper drew back with a black scowl. The crowd, at this, rapidly melted away, only a little half-naked Indian boy remaining to gape up at this newly found hero.

"There you are," said Lessing. "That boy has made three enemies in two minutes, and every one of the three would like to have his blood, especially Beaver Jones."

"Beaver's no good," said Desparr. "I'm glad that the boy

could see through him."

Lessing chuckled. "I'll tell you, old friend," he said, "that the boy wouldn't drink because he doesn't know that stranger. He wants an introduction, before he'll take a drink with a man."

"Aye, or else he don't drink."

"Not drink?" said Lessing, rather startled by this suggestion in a land where all men drank what they could get.

"Maybe," said Desparr, putting out a hand before him in a gesture like that of one who vaguely feels his way toward something of importance, "maybe the business of that boy won't let him fog up his brain with liquor."

Lessing snapped his fingers. "Aye, maybe you've put your finger on it," he said. "I'd guess that you're right, Louis."

"You've won a brand-new gun, Henry."

"I've won more than that," declared Lessing.

"What else have you won?"

"A good time," declared the trapper. "I ain't seen that kind of man in ten years."

"What kind of man? Fighting man, you mean?"

"Why, the land's full of fighting men, Louis. How could I mean that?"

"I didn't know. What kind of a man do you mean?"

"Did you see how he stepped?" asked Lessing.

"He's fast on his feet."

"And light. He's a cat, Louis."

"He's about as fast as a cat."

"He's a cat," repeated Lessing with conviction. "It's been ten years since I seen the like of him."

"Who've you got in mind, Henry?"

"There was that Claud Tamlin, but maybe you've forgot him?"

"Nobody that seen Tamlin ever forgot him. You think this kid reminds you of Tamlin?"

"He moved the same way," said Henry Lessing, "and he held his chin up the same way."

"But Claud Tamlin was three inches shorter, and a foot wider, and six inches deeper. You could've cut three or four of this lad out of Tamlin."

"He's young," said Lessing. "But look at that crowd now!"

"What about it?"

"I've seen people move like that when Tamlin was around . . . because they always gave him room enough."

In fact, the casual passer-by now made a wide eddy at the corner of the storehouse, letting the tall young tenderfoot have plenty of elbowroom. They did not any longer meet the eye of the youth, either, but pretended to be very occupied with their own business, although, all the time, it was plain that they were scanning him out of the corners of their eyes. The young braves came by most slowly of all, stalking with consummate dignity—and, doubtless, they were busily measuring the dimensions and noting down the features of this strange fellow. The few white men sauntered past, also, and the squaws came shuffling, their heads jutting forward like beasts of burden.

Only a few of the children stood bravely up to the white lad and surveyed him with smiling pleasure or with a sort of grim curiosity, moving from side to side to view him more closely, while the sun burnished and shone from their coppery little bodies.

"I remember Tamlin at Bent's Fort," said Desparr at last. "I remember him standin' up, and the crowd flowin' around him like water around a rock. He was a rock."

"Aye, he was a rock, and a wildcat, too."

"He was both them things," agreed Desparr seriously. "What became of Tamlin?"

"They got him at last."

"The Injuns?"

"Yeah. They got him at last."

"Which tribe?"

"There's a good deal of question about that. Some says the Sioux, and some says that it was old Broken Feather and his Comanches that finished up Tamlin. And some says that it was these here Blackfeet, as far as that goes."

"Maybe it never happened at all," declared Desparr. "If they got his death scattered that wide apart, maybe it never happened at all."

"Maybe it never did," agreed Henry Lessing. "But they tell the story of him pretty clear. And how he killed seven men and got seven wounds on that last day's fighting."

"That shows that it's all a fairy story," answered Desparr. "You see how it works out? Seven wounds, seven dead men. They always have numbers like that in their folk stories."

"All right," answered Lessing almost angrily. "But he ain't been heard of for years."

"Maybe he's left the land."

"How could he live away from buffalo and Injuns?"

"I dunno. I dunno. I ain't never able to read the minds of people, least of all a Tamlin. Well, are you gonna go down and talk to that youngster, Lessing?"

Lessing nodded. He took off his wide-brimmed hat and passed his hand through his tangled hair.

"You're just likely to be stepping knee-deep in trouble," cautioned Desparr.

"That's what I've been thinkin'," said Lessing softly.

But, nevertheless, down he went to the ground.

25

Chapter Four

Straight down into the compound Lessing went.

The store itself was thickly crowded, still. Through the open door he could hear a sort of babbling song that went up from the crowd inside. Men, women, and children, they all were handling, exclaiming over, crying out about the articles for sale. But nothing would be stolen, even by their clever fingers, for in the background appeared the face of Dancing Shadow, with her double-direction eyes and her weird ugliness. Yet, her expression now made her almost beautiful. For in her hands was all the delegated authority of her husband. She was in importance like a chief among warriors. She could even make small gifts, here and there, to the wife or to the child of some redoubtable figure of the Indians. And she never gave in vain. With that might to give and to receive, she was richly content, and a strange smile beamed upon her lips.

Lessing went on past the store, and almost fell over a pair of Indian lads who, wrestling violently, tumbled out of the doorway of the store, and rolled over and over in the dust, for the grass of the compound had been worn away by the pounding of many hoofs and many moccasined feet.

Weariness of his kind came suddenly over Lessing. He had been several days at the fort, visiting his old friend Desparr, and now a wave of disgust for men and their ways passed over him. The furnishings of his own life were

simple. A horse and a mule loaded with traps, a bit of tobacco and salt, some tea, ammunition for his rifle, a good
new axe, a pair of knives, and he was ready to start his trek
through the wilderness until, someday, he saw before him
the heads of unknown mountains, like vast monsters
holding up their hands to stop him. There he would settle
into another year of life, sinking deeper and deeper into the
woods, until the voices of the wind and of the rivers
cleansed from his mind the sound of human speech, human
wranglings. The crowd through which he had to elbow his
way depressed him unutterably, but at last he found himself
on the edge of the open space that surrounded the tenderfoot, Peter Messenger.

Lessing did not hesitate. He walked straight up to the
youth. There was an odd feeling that the boy grew as one
came nearer to him. From a little distance, he seemed
slender, light, made for swift activity rather than for the
bearing of burdens. But, close at hand, the dimensions of
the shoulders grew. And, from a distance, it seemed a pale,
meager face, but, near at hand, he saw the noble proportions of the forehead and, deep beneath the brows, the gray
eyes that were both alert and still.

"Come with me, Messenger," said the trapper curtly,
and, turning on his heel, he walked away. He half smiled,
wondering if the boy would do as he was bid. To his deep
surprise and satisfaction, he was presently aware that the
tall youth was stepping lightly after him. He led straight out
through the open gate in the palisade, and through the
woods to the edge of the water. There he paused, and Messenger stepped out of the trees to his side. As he came, he
looked searchingly into the face of Lessing, and then his
glance darkened a little with disappointment.

It was as though he had hoped vaguely that this stranger

might prove to be the thing for which he was searching. Instantly Lessing knew that the boy was hunting, indeed, for a human face. Messenger, halting at the edge of the water, faced his guide and waited.

"We're alone here for a minute or so," observed Lessing cheerfully. "Though it won't take 'em long to get on the trail, ag'in."

"Who?" asked Messenger, his frown deepening.

Lessing watched him, half amused and half surprised. "You mean you dunno who would want to take your trail, son?"

Messenger shook his head. He maintained this aloof attitude of his without effort. It seemed natural for him to act as though he were of a superior race, or a superior class, looking down upon the rest of the world.

"Well," said Lessing, "d'you know the names of the two bucks that you laid out?"

"No," said Messenger coldly.

"The first one is Spotted Deer. He has a father that's still a warrior in his prime. He has two young uncles, as hard as nails. He has a brother and half a dozen cousins."

"He's a lucky fellow," said Messenger with his natural sneer.

Lessing nodded. "Any one of those people would be glad to throw a war spear into you, my lad. Then there's Dust-In-The-Sky. . . ."

"Who is he?" Messenger permitted himself to ask.

"Somebody that you'll be sure to hear of again," declared Lessing. "Dust-In-The-Sky is the second one . . . the fellow that you flattened with that left uppercut. Are you left-handed, Messenger?"

"No," said the boy.

Lessing could not help smiling a little.

"The left is the hand they don't expect," he commented. "The point I'm making, though, is that Dust-In-The-Sky has even more friends than the other lad. He could easily bring out a dozen men to run you down."

"Very well," answered Messenger. "It's plain that I'll have to take my chances with them."

"You take your chances," said Lessing, "and get a knife through your gizzard. That's all it would amount to."

"Is that all you brought me here to tell me?" asked Messenger with his habitual cold sneer.

Lessing was a man who had been through his share of troubles in this world, but now he flushed a little.

"Are you going to stick at that?" he asked.

"At what?" said the boy.

"At being a young, hard-headed fool?" explained Lessing.

Messenger started. His gray eyes, losing some of their indifference, sparkled for an instant, but almost at once they grew dull again. But the trapper felt as though he had seen a wild animal raise its head and look at him.

"I don't know," said Messenger, "what I ought to say to you. I haven't asked for your advice. And I haven't asked to be brought away from the fort, where I was busy."

"Aye, you were busy," agreed the other. "Busy makin' enemies. I never seen nobody make 'em faster."

"How was I making enemies?" asked the boy, a touch of harsh anger appearing in his voice.

"Why, by lookin' over people as though they was horses. Back in your part of the country, maybe it's different. I guess that back there it's good manners to stare at everybody as though they had two heads. But out here, it's different. There's a proud lot, out here, young feller. And if you start to handlin' Injuns and Westerners like that with your eyes, you ain't gonna last long."

"No?" inquired Messenger coldly. "I'll have to take my chances in my own way, as I said before, I believe."

"You won't take 'em long," declared Lessing, "because you'll be dead." He picked up a stone from the bank of the stream and began to juggle it carelessly in his hand.

"Suppose you tell me," asked the boy, "why you're troubling yourself so much about me?"

"You oughta be able to guess."

"No. I don't see what my business has to do with you."

"Well," said the other, "a man can't help bein' interested when he sees a youngster start lookin' for trouble."

"I'm not looking for trouble," insisted Messenger. "I didn't raise a hand at either of those two Indians until they forced trouble on me."

"You hadn't asked for it, either, I reckon?" asked the trapper.

"What do you mean?"

"I mean this . . . that you stand there and sneer and stare at everybody."

"I wasn't sneering," said the boy.

"I didn't have no eyes to see you, eh?"

"I'm going back to the fort," said Messenger suddenly, and in impatience.

"Wait a minute," said the other. "Lemme see what's in the brush over there."

Suddenly he flung the stone that he was holding through the face of a tall, dense shrub, at the same time shouting out. In answer, came several deep-throated, muffled exclamations, and a noise of the bush crackling as people retired through it. "Maybe the other side of the brush is the same way," suggested Lessing cheerfully.

Messenger, in the meantime, stood up in the attitude of

a soldier, stiff and tense, with his hands gripped into fists at his sides. He looked to the trapper as though he were about to leap away into the shrubbery in pursuit of the sounds that he was still hearing faintly in the distance. But, if he had this impulse, he managed to control it. His face worked. He grew a little pale, and this pallor made his eyes seem darker and brighter, at the same instant. His nostrils trembled. His lips pressed together. He looked the very picture of a man about to deliver a savage attack.

This picture Lessing studied with an almost professional interest. Then he rubbed his knuckles across his chin. "Are you goin' after them?" he said.

"What do you think?" asked the boy, snapping out the words suddenly.

Lessing grinned. "Did you ever ask advice in your life before?" he demanded.

All at once the other smiled, and his expression, his whole appearance, were so marvelously altered by this smile that the trapper marveled at him more than ever.

"You're a strange fellow," said the boy.

"Am I?" Lessing answered in perfect good nature. "Somehow, I was thinkin' the same thing about you."

The boy smiled again. "I owe you something," he said slowly. "If I'd gone back toward the fort. . . ." He hesitated. Then he brought the words out one by one, as though his honesty were forcing them through his lips. "If I'd started back for the fort, they would have had me. In the back, I suppose." And he held out his hand toward the older man.

Chapter Five

Our significant moments, as a rule, we recognize by looking backward, rather than forward. The dull day turns, in time, into the great one; the lesson that is at first refused is at last accepted; the great enemy becomes the greatest friend; and the old friend is discovered to be half fool and half knave. But Henry Lessing, as the strange lad held out his hand, recognized instantly that a great thing was taking place before his very eyes. He could not help but see that there was far more in that silent gesture than in a thousand words of gratitude from another man. Yet he hesitated to accept the hand that was proffered. However much he respected this boy, and however much his interest was intrigued by him, yet something made him at the last moment draw back, as though there were a distinct realization that, if he dared to become the friend of the tenderfoot, a thousand dangers would instantly be heaped upon his head. Yet that instinct had only a momentary and hardly noticeable control over him. Then he thrust out his hand and grasped that which was offered to him.

The fingers were long, hard, and cool. They pressed those of Lessing with strength, but not with a foolish use of force. Afterward, Lessing felt as though he had taken a hand of iron in his own.

"Now will you tell me what made you come after me?" asked the boy.

"Because you're young," insisted Lessing, "and because every older man is every younger man's father, in a way."

Young Messenger looked rather quizzically at the other. "Father?" he said, and then he smiled.

The cold insolence of that smile almost made the trapper strike him in the face. "Not meanin'," said Lessing angrily, "that I'm the father of any Duke of What Not, like you."

The youth was not angered by this remark. He accepted it with his accustomed calm. "You've been kind to me," he said. "You've given me some good advice. I've told you that I thank you. Is there anything else that we ought to say?" It was like a machine speaking.

"You've added everything up, and there ain't anything left over, I guess," suggested Lessing, suddenly smiling.

"Why do you smile?" asked the boy.

"Why, because you act like such a thing as conversation never existed."

"Ah, you mean that you want to stand here and talk?"

Lessing conquered his first impulse regarding an answer, and merely said: "There's nothing that I want to do more."

There was impatience, there was contempt, and there was endurance, in the face of the boy. "Very well," he said after a moment of struggle, in which it was apparent that he mastered himself even more strongly than the trapper had done. "Very well, you have the right to ask questions, and I certainly shall answer them. Will you begin, sir?"

"Look here," said the trapper. "Who said that I wanted to ask questions?"

"I imagine that is the ordinary process of conversation."

"Do you?"

"How else can it progress?"

"Why," said the trapper, more and more intrigued, and

more and more irritated at the same time, "you could say that's a whale of a big oak tree, and I could tell you about another I'd seen that was bigger, and with more of a head to it, too. Or you could say how fast the water's runnin' there, and I could tell you the kind of fish that you could catch out of it. If you're interested in fishin'."

"I am not," said the boy coldly.

"Well, I was aimin' to point out what could be said, and no questions asked. You might call that the track of a mule deer, there. . . ."

"I wouldn't," said the boy.

"You wouldn't?" asked the trapper with a sudden glow of interest as the talk turned to his peculiar province of lore. "And what would you call it, then?"

"I wouldn't attempt to name it. It looks like a cow track to me."

"Cow track?" cried the trapper, almost shouting. "That a cow track? Did you ever see a cow track with such toe prints?"

"I've never looked very closely at a cow track, either," said the boy.

"Cow track, my foot!" said Lessing, and even chuckled, rather complacent in that his knowledge surpassed in a least a few details the accomplishments of the unusual lad. "There never was a cow that could make a track like that. Nor a mule deer, neither, for that matter."

"I suppose you know what you're saying," said the boy.

"D'you think that I don't?"

"I don't presume to criticize. I've never seen a deer, not even alone its track."

"Jumping, flopping thunderbird!" exclaimed Henry Lessing. "You've never seen a deer?"

"No, sir."

"How did you ever get this far north, then? Or this far west, without seeing a deer?"

"By keeping my eyes on the road in front of me."

"By daydreaming you mean to say?"

"You can call it what you please. But I've never seen a deer."

"Never seen one! Never shot one! Never taken off a hide with your knife! Never seen how it was fitted under the knees and the elbows . . . never seen a deer?" repeated Lessing. "Why, boy, you ain't lived, hardly."

This made Messenger look quizzically up through the green gloom of the branches that hung above them in tower upon tower. "I don't know," he said. "I suppose I can fairly say that I never have in the sense which you give to the word."

"Sit down," said the trapper. "I gotta talk some more to you."

Messenger glanced impatiently down the course of the river as if he wished urgently to be gone. But again he controlled himself, and slowly he sat down on the edge of a fallen log. Lessing dropped down nearby and, half turning, faced his companion squarely.

"You never killed a deer!" he began, gasping out the word.

"I've never even seen one," said the boy, nodding almost sternly.

Lessing raised his hand and pointed his forefinger. "How come that you could use a hunting knife so slick, then?"

The boy hesitated.

"How come," went on Lessing, "that you took a ten-inch knife and handled it like it was understanding what you talked and wanted?"

"I was raised to understand knives and their ways," said the boy.

"You were?"

"Yes."

"How do you mean that you were raised to understand knives and their ways?"

"That's all the explanation that I care to give," said Messenger calmly.

"I'm kind of interested," said the trapper at last, although he had been halted by this rebuff. "I know a little about guns and gun work, and knives and knife work myself. Why would you get to learn about knives if you wasn't going to learn about deer, I'd like to know?"

Messenger considered this for a moment, as though he wondered whether or not he should answer the question. At last he said: "Well, are knives used on deer only?"

"No, on other varmints. But if you've never seen deer, you've never seen much else that a hunting knife would do you any good on."

"No," said the boy, "I never saw wildlife. Just in a zoo, I might say, and a very small zoo, at that."

"My friend," said Lessing, "I never heard somebody talk like you before." This drew no answering comment from the other. "Lemme find out, will you, what you ever used a knife on before today?"

"Certainly," said Messenger. "I don't see any reason why I shouldn't tell you that. I used it on a strong sack, glazed with tar, and stuffed hard with sawdust."

"Why was that, might I ask?"

"The sack, do you see, was no larger than the round of your arm, and the glazed canvas was so hard and tough that only a knife thrown dead to the mark and thrown hard would cut the canvas and stick in that hard-packed sawdust."

It was time for the trapper to stare again. And he stared in earnest this time. "Which I'd gather that you throwed a knife a good deal at a sack, like that?"

"Yes, a good deal."

"And what the hell was you practicin' for, and what made you so hot to stick a knife into a canvas sack, will you tell me, son?"

Messenger allowed a faint smile to touch his stern, rather habitually compressed lips. "Suppose you had to throw that knife across the width of a room," he said, "and, if you failed to stick it in once in every three times, you got five strokes with a half-inch rattan across the bare of your back at the end of the day . . . would that make you interested in getting the knife into the sack?"

Lessing exclaimed. All his free-born American blood boiled suddenly in his veins. "By the jumping, flopping thunderbird," he cried, breaking out into his favorite oath, "what scoundrel done that to you?"

The eyes of the boy narrowed. He rose from the log. "I've talked long enough, I feel," he said.

Lessing shook his head. "That was where you learned to handle a knife, eh? And the same gent taught you how to use your fists, too?"

"Oh, no," said Messenger. "There was a separate man to teach me that, of course."

"You was taught special! You was taught special!" exclaimed the trapper, highly pleased. "I knowed it when I seen you side-step. You wouldn't learn how to side-step like that without special teachin' . . . steppin' out as though the ground had turned red hot under you. You had a reason for learnin' to step fast, I reckon."

"Yes," said the boy. "Either step fast, or be knocked down." And, with rather an absent-minded look, he touched his chin with the tip of a finger. Lessing noticed, for the first time, a thin white scar that curved along the sharp angle of the jaw.

Chapter Six

The trapper wanted to ask a hundred questions. He wanted to ask who the person or persons were who were responsible for such treatment of a lad, and who dared to teach a boy to box by knocking him down unless he learned the proper maneuvers and executed them promptly enough. What mysterious tyrant forced his will so implicitly upon a child? Whose brain was it that had hammered and hammered and heated and cooled and tempered this lad until he was in his present state of mind and body—like iron in brain and in body and in hand?

But he saw, at once, that such a rude probing into the past would bring less than no result. The youngster knew how to hold his tongue. Only a sudden and overwhelming sense of obligation had loosened it sufficiently to make him communicate as many facts as he had already expressed. He resolved on going about things in a more diplomatic manner.

"I remember hearin' a man by name of Tamlin say that the foundation of good boxin' was a straight left and a side-step."

"And a right cross," said the boy.

"But uppercuts," said the trapper, "they don't grow on every bush."

"Oh, no," replied Messenger. "Let me see . . . I didn't even try them for six or seven years."

He said it carelessly, as if it were a matter of no importance, but it conjured into the brain of the trapper a picture of a spindling lad with tow head, narrow lips, dancing feet, sparring with some dexterous and maturely developed brute—someone whose blow, if not dodged or parried or blocked, would knock the youngster down—aye, and perhaps cut him to the bone, as that blow on the jaw must have done, years before. He could better understand now, the alert, cold calm in the gray eyes of the stranger.

Feeling that he had asked about as much as he could gain by direct query, he went on: "Suppose you tell me, stranger, how you're gonna get back to the fort. Them woods might be filled with Injuns. I got an idea that they are."

Young Messenger looked gravely about him at the shrubbery and at the lofty trees. "I could have a look," he said at last.

"How could you have a look, will you tell me?"

"Why, into the bush, of course."

"You're likely to make a lot of noise, wadin' through that brush."

"I won't wade through it," said the boy.

"What will you do, then, if you don't mind me askin'?"

"Why, I'll look over the top of it, like this." He took two steps, and, jumping up, caught a thick branch with his hands, using the forward impetus of his leap to swing up until his feet were planted on another bough. Still without making a pause, he unbent the bow of his body with a force that threw him up to grasp another branch, and so, in a moment, he was lost to the astonished sight of the trapper. This was done so quietly that there was no more sound than presently a faint rustling, such as the wind might make among the branches.

That thought of a great cat that had first come into his mind as he had looked from the roof of the fort down into the compound at the mysterious young stranger again leaped back into his mind. Like a cat, indeed, perfect master of its body and its weight, and sure as a cat in all his movements. Lessing himself, staring up at the boughs by means of which the boy had thrown himself upward into the heart of the great tree, felt the speed of his heart redoubled. Then all noise ceased at once from among the upper branches. There was a very considerable pause, during which Lessing began to stare down at the water as it rushed and foamed around the point before heading down on the little peninsula on which Fort Lippewan stood.

It seemed to the trapper that his own life and thoughts had been increased in speed, and that they were rushing along like the very river, since this lad, Messenger, had appeared in his life not so many minutes before.

Then a quiet voice said just above his head: "There must be twenty of them in the woods."

Lessing jumped almost out of his boots and, turning, looked up. There he could see the head of the boy, appearing at one side of a huge branch of the tree. Messenger was stretched at ease upon the limb, body down. "How," said the trapper, who was proud of the forest-trained keenness of his senses, "how in the name of heaven did you come down through that tree without makin' no noise?"

The boy smiled a little, and again his face was changed by that unusual expression. "Suppose you had to walk fifty feet over gravel and pick up your rations right at the back of the man who was waiting there, straining his ears to hear any movements, even a breath, or the least click of a pebble under your foot? If you can make the trip perfectly once in three times, you get something to eat. Otherwise, you wait till the next day. That's one way of learning to walk softly."

"Aye," said the trapper, "and, if you're a born cat, it's not so hard to be silent in the trees, either."

The boy swung down from the branch and landed lightly on his feet, with no more sound than a falling shadow. There was simply a flexure of his entire body to lessen the shock of his feet against the ground. Lessing would have asked more questions about that feat, also, but he restrained himself. Sometime, if all went well, he would be able to draw the whole story from the lips of the boy. In the meantime, the explanation would probably be some gruesomely improbable thing such as the silent walk with famine for a teacher.

"There are twenty, are there?" asked the trapper, frowning as his thoughts left the boy and concentrated on the danger of their position.

"Yes."

"Where are they?"

"They're stretched in a semicircle from one bank of the water to the other."

"What will you do, if you're left to yourself, to get out of this?" asked the trapper.

"I might go up into the tree and shoot a few of them. I suppose I have a right to shoot my way out?"

"Start shooting, against twenty Indians?" Lessing opened his mouth to say something more, but astonishment choked him.

"Well," said the boy, as calmly as before, "they have cornered us, I suppose."

"Where's your gun? You ain't got one, have you?"

The boy opened his coat and showed a glimpse of a holster slung from the shoulders and hanging at his left side.

"Is that a pistol?"

"It's a revolver."

"At the first shot, you might get one of 'em, but the rest of 'em would hide in that brush like snakes in long grass, and they'd soon begin stalking you."

"I ought to get three or four of them, I think," said Messenger thoughtfully. "Several of them are quite a few steps from any cover, considering the angle that I'd have for shooting down at them. Three or four, perhaps even more."

Lessing moistened his dry lips. "That is plenty fast snap shooting," he said.

"Fast?" said the boy. "Well, that depends. Fast snap shooting?" He shook his head.

"You wouldn't call it that?" said the trapper curiously, and half wondering if, after all, there was a good deal of the braggart in the youth.

"Well," said the boy, "I've never shot at a man before today. But I suppose I'll have to begin sooner or later, out here. All I know is that when you throw the apples into the air and try to get them all with six shots. . . ."

"Have you done that?" cried Lessing, the hair fairly stirring on his head, and little points of gooseflesh forming all over his body.

"No," said the boy. "I never got more than five at a time. I never could get the sixth one. Something always went wrong. But one shot I was sure to miss, or else I was slow, and one of them hit the ground before I could shoot."

He shook his head again, and his brow contracted. It was plain that he did not relish the memory of that repeated defeat. But Lessing was thinking of six little apples, spinning and winking in the air, and the rapid chatter of shots that must have exploded into the midst of them, smashing them to crisp fragments, one by one, until five of the six were gone. No wonder that the lad was able calmly to estimate that he could get three or four of the Blackfeet from the height of the tree before he was able to stop firing because they were in secure covert.

"Well," said Lessing, "suppose the shooting were out of the question. Could you do anything then, to get out of the way?"

"The river, of course," said the boy.

"*Br-r-r!* It's ice water, and that current is running along this bank like a galloping horse. Look at that!" He threw in a small twig. It shot along for a few yards, and then was twisted under the surface by a downward current.

The boy nodded. "It would be a good hard swim," he agreed. "But I've no doubt that I could make it, all right. I'd have to get my clothes off and make a bundle of 'em. They might get soaked, and the gun along with them, but I'm used to cold water. It wouldn't take my breath. I suppose that's what you mean?"

"Aye," said the trapper. "But I'll tell you this, Messenger. If you can handle yourself in that water, you're as good a water dog as any Indian. However, you won't have to shoot your way out of this corner, and you won't have to swim out. Maybe you can guess why?"

Messenger looked steadily at him. "You wouldn't have brought me out here," he replied slowly, at last, "if you could not get me back again."

"Thanks," grunted the trapper. "No, I certainly ain't that kind of a skunk. Listen, now and. . . ." He raised his head and filled his lungs to shout, but at that moment, oddly enough, a roar of voices sounded from across the trees and the open, rolling ground beyond, at the neck of the Fort Lippewan peninsula. It formed itself into a rolling cry, like a cheer. Wild war whoops accompanied it. And suddenly those shouts were reëchoed from among the very trees in front of Messenger and his companion.

"By the jumpin', lyin' thunderbird!" cried the trapper. "Did you hear that name they're all shouting? It's War Lance himself that's come!"

Chapter Seven

"War Lance?" said the boy curiously. "Who is he?"

"Come, come," said the trapper. "You don't know much about the West, and that's a fact, and about the mountains a pile less, but you've sure heard about War Lance?"

"Not a word that I remember. Is he a big medicine man?"

"His medicine is big, but he's not a medicine man," said the other. "He's a chief, and for once they saddled one of their heroes with a right name. They've a way of calling their best braves something like Speckled Antelope, or Deer-That-Jumps, or some such thing. But War Lance is what this fellow is. Straight as a lance, and as sharp and as strong! You've never heard of War Lance?"

"No. D'you think those Blackfeet in the woods are going to see him?"

"They'll see him," said Lessing, "if they have to swim a river full of floating ice. Of course, they'll see him. He's the main trump, the big card, the great snake in their whole nation. Of course, they'll see him!"

"Good luck and a quick trip to them, then," said the boy carelessly. "I'm glad to do without them just now. I didn't relish the idea of a swim in that water yonder."

"I could have talked you through them," said Lessing. "They know me, and they're not a bad lot."

Here Messenger turned sharply on him. "Not a bad lot?"

he repeated. "Not a bad lot? What do you call badness, when they were out there waiting to stick a knife into me?"

"You'd floored a pair of 'em, youngster!" cried Lessing.

"With my hands . . . man to man!" said the boy fiercely.

"If you kicked one of a wolf pack," said Lessing, "would it surprise you a lot if the whole band came for you?"

"Yes, wolves. That's what they are," declared Messenger.

"And if the wolf used teeth, and you had none half so good, would you blame him for that?" went on the trapper.

"I don't understand what you're driving at," answered Messenger. "A couple of those scoundrels pick brawls with me. They're roughly handled, and then twenty of them come and lurk for me among the trees. And you call them good fellows!"

"They are," insisted Lessing. "I know 'em, and you don't."

"Tell me how I was wrong, and how they are right," asked the boy.

"You were wrong to manhandle them."

"What would you have had me do?"

"Something dignified, Messenger. An Injun has a pile of dignity, and he hates to have it roughed around. You remember that, if you're going to be cut out there long."

"Aye," said Messenger with a quick, deep sigh. "I'll be here the rest of my life, I suppose."

"What? The rest of your life? Without going back to the East?" Lessing stared again. He never had seen, he felt, a spirit so little in tune with the great western land.

"I've got to try a thing," said the boy, half to himself, "that I never can do . . . and it'll take me my life. . . ." He made a gesture at the trees, and then at the river. "Among these eternal, gloomy woods," he said, "and ruffians eating dried buffalo meat, living like cattle, drinking poisonous whiskey, fighting, brawling, stealing, trailing, freezing, soaking, sunburned, mildewed, ragged, miserable every day of the year, in one way or another. That's the life that lies in front of me!" He stopped. He flashed hotly and drew himself up. "I've been complaining like a girl, and to a stranger," he said. "I beg your pardon, Mister Lessing."

Lessing nodded at him with an understanding eye. "It looks all rank and raw to you," he said. "You'd rather be back there where you could have a good, comfortable chair and a flock of books around you, and polite folks in for tea, and dances like a state parade, and all that sort of thing, and so this part of the woods looks sort of miserable to you, don't it?"

"It does. It does look miserable!" declared the boy. "But I've talked too much. I've made a woman of myself. I'm sorry." He strode straight ahead, through the brush, and, as he went, Lessing struggled to keep up, calling out: "Keep an eye about you! You can't tell about these red men. One of 'em might be hanging back around here to shoot an arrow or a slug into your ribs. It'd be like that Dust-In-The-Sky, for one."

"Good fellows! Good fellows!" quoted the boy in disgust. "You say that I should have handled them with dignity. How would you have done it, then?" He paused, and looked haughtily back at Lessing.

"I'll tell you," said Lessing. "I would simply have handled him so that he wouldn't have been made a fool. If I could do what you can with a knife . . . which I can't . . . I would never have put a hand on either of them, but I would have fetched out my knife and driven it into the ground right between their toes. That's what I should have done."

"What would have happened then?"

"That's simple. Only one thing could have happened. They would have seen that you weren't simply a tenderfoot, as they took you to be, but a heap big warrior and brave. Dust-In-The-Sky wouldn't have touched that knife, but one of his friends would have pulled it out of the ground, and he would have brought it to you. That would have been the challenge, and you would name your time to meet Dust-In-The-Sky out there in the plains, in the pink of some morning when nobody was up, except a few friends."

"A few friends to help take my scalp, eh?" asked the boy in his hard, suspicious way.

"You don't understand. You would have been the guest of the Blackfoot nation while that fight was going on. No one would have dared to interfere, except some old war chief, some great man . . . like this same fellow, War Lance. He might have ridden out and gone to see you. He might have made you a friendly speech and declared that young men should not come to blood for the sake of a joke and such stuff. He might have made you a present of some kind . . . even a horse, perhaps . . . and that would have been the end of it."

"I wouldn't take the chance of fighting," answered Messenger most unexpectedly.

"You wouldn't take the chance?" echoed the other, bewildered.

"No. I wouldn't take the chance of fighting. I've no desire to turn into a murderer."

"No question of murder," replied Lessing. "It would be a fair fight and all that."

"How would the fight go?"

"On horseback, with a full equipment. He'd probably come out as if for the warpath, with a rifle, and a lance, and a knife. Perhaps there would be a pistol tucked into his belt."

"Well," said the boy gravely, "if I fought him with a rifle, a pistol, a knife, or hand-to-hand, it would still be a murder."

"What?" cried Lessing.

"I was raised for it, trained for it," replied Messenger. "It would still be a murder. What right have I to fight with ordinary men? They know no more about weapons than babies do about books. It would be simply a murder. That's why I used my bare hands on them. I was sorry I showed the knife at all, but just then I lost my temper. I wanted to go after the whole bullying crowd of them, and I controlled myself just in the nick of time, and shot the knife into the ground, instead." He said this rapidly, his voice raised a little, and there was a ring of true misery and regret in it. That raising and training were not things on which he cared to linger, very obviously.

Lessing rapped his knuckles against his forehead. "Maybe you're right," he said. "Maybe you're right, my lad. But . . . let's get on out of here into the open. You'll forget your troubles if you see War Lance."

They went on rapidly through the woods until there was a light, crackling sound in front of them, and Messenger bounded far to the side, behind a tree. Lessing did not follow the example, but he brought his rifle to the ready and stared fixedly among the leaves before them.

"It's nothing," he said presently. "There's no danger that they'll jump you. Listen to the uproar outside. No Indian could prefer his little revenge to the chance of looking at such a party as they have going on out there."

Messenger nodded, and they went on again, with Lessing biting his lip. He had a sudden feeling that this youngster who walked so lightly beside him was not a man at all, but a mass of gunpowder ready to blow up a forest, a village, in a single flare.

From the edge of the woods they could get a clear view across the rolling grounds at the base of the peninsula, and there they saw that the entire Indian population was pouring out from the distant woods and swirling into a mass that took a certain form and straightened and lengthened before their eyes into a line. This line was made of mounted warriors. To the rear formed a cloud of women and children on foot, and little boys galloped wildly back and forth on their mustangs, the clots of turf flinging high above their heads and hanging in the air like swallows.

Lessing began to chuckle softly, but there was excitement in his face, also. "You're gonna see a real man, even if his skin isn't white, my son," he said. He led on, with great strides, and young Messenger easily kept beside him.

They headed, now, straight across toward the narrow of the peninsula base, where the palisade of the fort was strung, and where the gate opened. To that gate, all the occupants of the fort had come in order to see the procession arrive. Some thronged in the gateway itself. Others were grouped on either side, and on the roof of the fort it could be seen that the tarpaulin had been taken from the little ancient brass three-pounder that stood there. Its well-polished flanks were glimmering in the sunshine, and its mouth was trained straight toward the gate.

"That's loaded with powder only," Lessing said in explanation, "but, if there's a need, it wouldn't take long to slap three, four handfuls of shot into the innards of it and blow a whole lane of those Blackfeet out through that gate and into the happy hunting grounds."

They came up the last slope, hurrying their steps, and, as they arrived at the verge of the fort, they could see that the procession that had been forming on the hillside had begun to move. At the same time, there was a wild babble of shouts, war whoops, thunderings upon drums, and screeching upon tuneless horns. This first blast of outcry ended as abruptly as it had begun, and the procession continued with dignity upon its march.

Chapter Eight

First of all, came eight warriors in two ranks. They were naked to the waist, but their deerskin trousers were trimmed and beaded in the height of Indian magnificence. Their belts supported knives and pistols and, here and there, even a revolver, although that weapon had not yet been extensively adopted among the tribes. They were literally brilliant with paint, streaked upon them in rude designs and patterns that were modified according to the emblems or the personal taste of each hero. They carried long war spears, their rifles being consigned to saddle holsters, or else tied on behind the leg of the rider. These lances were decorated with ruffles, collars, and long streamers of eagle feathers, dyed in the most startling colors. Several had woven the stained feathers together, so that the light banners reached almost to the ground.

All of these men, to judge by their headdresses, were celebrities who had counted many and many a coup, and certainly they had taken many scalps, for the eagle feathers crowned them and flowed down their backs even beneath the ends of their long hair. This garlanding of spear and head and hair with feathers, to say nothing of others that decorated the ponies, gave an indescribably light and graceful air to the troop, for the feathers waved, nodded, and bent with the wind, and the horses seemed to leave the ground and fly in the air, also.

Hand-picked among thousands of their kind, and chosen by experts among a nation of riders, these were the finest war ponies that the riders possessed, and they showed themselves off as in duty bound. They were fresh from good grasslands. They had had a long period of leisure, and their sleek sides fairly dripped the sunshine or flashed it blindingly bright in the eyes of the watchers.

"They're the first half of what War Lance calls the sacred band," commented Lessing to the boy.

"Sacred for what?" asked Messenger in his cold, detached way.

"Sacred for the hell that they raise when it comes to a fight," said Lessing with more appreciation. "He keeps sixteen bucks around him who he gets out of the cream of the nation. He made some big medicine and discovered, with the aid of the chief medicine man of the tribe, that if men would attach themselves to him by a special oath, they would get all kinds of Indian blessings."

"Such as what?" said the boy. "And what's the oath?"

"Why, the oath is that once in the band, they'll never leave it. That they'll fight to the death for each other until their chief calls them away from the battle. That they'll charge home in spite of numbers if the call comes, and that they'll never reveal any of the secret councils of the band."

"That's a good deal of an oath," said the boy. "That War Lance can call on any of them to jump off a cliff, then, if he wants to?"

"Of course, he can, and they'd do it gladly."

"Well, what are the rewards?"

"Tons of them. While they're on earth, War Lance promises that all the members of the sacred band will be rich, have sons, and stack up coups and scalps until they're the most honored men in the tribe."

"How does he manage that?" the boy asked.

"Well, it's not so hard as you might think. What's Indian riches? Well, hosses, mostly. About two thirds of the war parties that the sacred band rides on is to lift hosses from the Crows, or somebody else. They run off three hundred, about six months back, right in the middle of winter. As for the rest of the riches, well, the bucks that War Lance picks for the band find it pretty easy to get all the wives they want, and a buck with plenty of wives can always have plenty of robes manufactured, and turn 'em into axes, beads, guns, ammunition, and all that, so that his hosses are still in the bank, and growing with interest. And a man with plenty of wives is sure to have some sons. So you see how it works out?"

"Yes, but the scalps and the coups they count so much on?"

"That's the easiest part of all. War Lance keeps those fellows up to the hilt in fighting all the time, and they either count coups and take scalps, or else they lose their own, pretty *pronto*. It's easier for them all the time, because they've got such a reputation now that, when a bunch of the Crows hears the special war whoop of the band, they take to their heels and run for it. And I don't blame 'em. The sacred band can come up behind on the best hosses that are rode in these here mountains, and they do about as they please. Look at 'em as they come near. There's two ranks in front of War Lance, and two rows behind him."

They came closer. Suddenly the people at the fort could endure the suspense no longer, for the presence of these celebrated warriors was like a weight on the eye and a flame in the brain. And a wild cheer went up from the watchers.

The sudden shout caused several of the mustangs to try

to jump through a hole in the sky, but horse contortions were nothing to those heroes. They sat the animals without a quiver.

"They've got so famous, that band," said Lessing, "that now and then you'll get a famous fighter coming up from another tribe. See that one on the right, that fellow with the heavy shoulders. That's a Cheyenne. He ain't as old as he looks, but he had his face pretty nigh clawed off in a fight with a grizzly. He killed that grizzly and earned the necklace of claws that he's wearing, but you can see that most of his face disappeared durin' the fight. He was a big name in his own tribe, but he come up here to get a little closer to the happy hunting grounds. You see, the sacred band has a special pass to the sky when it dies."

"A pass to the sky?" Messenger echoed, opening his eyes.

"Certainly. Right up to the sky. The minute that one of them passes in his chips, he's snatched to the happy hunting grounds, and there the Old Man gives him a herd of a hundred hosses, though one hoss would be enough, because they're bred so's they can run all day and never get tired in the fields and the hills of the sky. Then the Old Man walks out a hundred or so beautiful girls, and the hero that's dead, he takes his pick, though there ain't much picking and choosing to do, because each one of them is a little more pretty than the rest, and every one of them is a boss hand at cooking, tanning hides, thinning 'em, making clothes, beading, doing quill work, and sewing teepees, and all the other kinds of talent that a man would want in a squaw. Up there in the sky grounds, there's billions of buffalo that run like the wind, but not so fast as the blue horses. And there's heaps of moose and elk and all kinds of antelope and deer, and the bows and arrows of those Sky People will shoot over

56

a hill and kill you a deer on the other side."

"Do those fighters believe all of that stuff?" asked the boy, sneering.

"Sure they do, because War Lance has told 'em those things, and he can't be wrong."

"Why not?"

"Because after a man has taken ten scalps and counted twenty coups, he can't tell a lie among the Blackfeet. Likely War Lance believes all that rot himself. Probably come to him in a dream, and they believe in their dreams more than we believe in our eyes, you can bet."

"They're either half-wits or children never grown up," Messenger declared.

"If you get to know 'em better, you'll change your mind," said the trapper. "Look at number three in the first line. That's Sinking Bull, and what's hanging from his bridle reins is three brand-new scalps. They don't look as though they had finished drying out yet."

The boy shuddered.

"Yeah, it ain't pretty, but you get used to it," said Lessing. "I've taken a couple scalps in my day myself. One was a Pawnee that tried to count a coup on me before he brained me, and I just managed to run my knife into his gizzard and open him up a mite. I took his hair. Seemed like I needed some kind of a souvenir, that day. Look at them boys go by! Every one of them is ten years younger than he looks, and there ain't a one of them that would trade his place in the sacred band to be President of the United States and King of England, all rolled into one."

"Murderers and horse thieves," said the boy. But he was stating an opinion, rather than asking a question.

"No, sir!" exclaimed Lessing hotly. "Honorable gentlemen, accordin' to their lights. And there ain't any man that can travel by any light better than the best that he knows about."

Like eight paladins, those first two rows went by, sitting proudly, managing their frantic horses as though they hardly knew that the animals were dancing and prancing. Just before the gate there was a shallow ditch made by the flow of the current during the seasons of high water, when the river passed its ordinary banks, and, when the eight leaders reached this place, they reined their horses so that the entire troop vaulted over, bounding high. It was a pretty sight, and they went by Messenger with a whirring of feathers, a streaming of hair, and a flashing of spear points.

Never had he seen, at close hand, such magnificent specimens of manhood. There was one among them who appeared both young and feeble, although a second glance showed any trained eye that the youth was a mass of tough fibers and sinews. But the others were massively strong, and their powerful legs seemed to crush the sides of the ponies that they bestrode. These animals, too, chosen as they were, resembled other Indian ponies no more than did their riders resemble the rank and file of the braves. They were small, few if any of them standing more than fifteen hands, but they were perfect models. The old Barb and Arab blood from which they were descended appeared clear and pure in them now, with their big, starry eyes, and their compact heads, and their greyhound bodies. Perhaps they looked a little insufficient for the human burdens that bestrode them, but perhaps that was because the perfect proportions of the animals disguised their strength.

But, behind the troop, came a horseman and a horse that made the rest vanish even from the cold and calculating brain of the boy. He started. Instinctively he put out a hand to grip the arm of his companion.

"Aye, aye," said Lessing. "There's the king of 'em all. There's the grandest chief and the hardest fighter in the whole length of the mountains. They're all small birds compared to that eagle. Look at the head on him, and look at the arms! He's taken more scalps than I ever took bird eggs. That's human hair that fringes his trousers, and human hair that makes that tuft under his lance. That's War Lance, and that's his hoss."

Chapter Nine

The eight who had preceded had looked, to Messenger, like powerful and graceful predatory animals in their strength and in the fierceness and the wildness of their eyes. They did not need fresh scalps dangling from their reins to prove to young Messenger that they were as savage and dangerous as so many tigers. Something swelled up in him suddenly, hotly.

He himself had been taught all the arts of destruction. He had been prepared through all his life to kill and to avoid death. Those arts he had not practiced. But when he saw these savages, suddenly he was glad with all his heart that his hands had been equipped with uncanny skill.

But although they seemed formidable, there was not one who disturbed his self-confidence in the slightest. Like some champion looking at a group of antagonists, he had measured them calmly, and decided that this man was too heavy for his strength, that one too nervous, yonder fellow too slow. They were the instant judgments that a practiced eye will make in such matters.

Then came War Lance, and it seemed to the boy that the very ground quaked beneath him. For this was, to be sure, a different matter. The very horse beneath the chief was different from those that the others bestrode. It was one of those dappled chestnuts, so dark that dappling, like a faint patterning of leopard spots, was barely distinguishable.

Only when the sun struck the velvet of him in a certain way, the design was apparent. He seemed all silk and steel, supple steel that bends and never breaks, sword steel that a warrior can put the trust of his life in. He was a hand and more taller than the rest of his companions, but size had not taken from him the slightest portion of the same nervous fire that burned in them. Only, in him, it was reduced and subdued to the control of his mind. He went with a sober and easy gait. There was no need to check him in with a stern hand for, at his ease, he regarded the ground before him and looked with pricking ears at the riders in front and at the people upon either side. It was only when he looked at the boy that Messenger could tell that the same wild spirit was in him that appeared in all the actions of the other horses. For, in his eyes, a fire flashed from the stallion. It was like the look of a caged eagle, incomparably fierce, grand, and untamable. One might have said that he submitted to the control of this man because he loved the battle and could endure the matchless valor and strength of his rider.

For so War Lance appeared. Physically he seemed the match, and more, for the most powerful of his companions, although they were the picked men of many tribes. As when a thousand athletes walk upon a field, yet one of them, by something in his bearing and the smooth harmony of his might and the carriage of his head, appears a champion, so War Lance appeared among his chosen men.

There was need of the extra size in the stallion. There was need to support the thews and sinews of that warrior on his back. Although he was massive, he certainly was no sluggard. The tendons behind his knee and the smallness of the knee itself told the accurate eye of Messenger a sufficient story.

There was not a touch of paint on the body of the horse
or upon the body or the face of the master. In his long hair
were set only two eagle feathers. One might well have said
that he disdained adornment, and he had reason. He had
been created to take the eye of every beholder, and to keep
the attention riveted on him.

But those matters of horse and the man's body were
purely secondary to Messenger. He looked to the face, and
dwelt there enthralled. The man appeared forty. Being an
Indian, he might be perhaps ten years younger. He had the
true Indian features. Nose and chin and mouth appeared
inflexible in terrible severity, but the brow was as nobly
made as any white man's, and the eyes were large, lumi-
nous, and thoughtful. Perhaps they were a little over bright,
like the eyes of the horse he bestrode, but he kept all under
perfect control. Suddenly the boy could understand how
the braves had listened to the prophecies or the dreams of
this man and believed in them. Given a red skin, perhaps he
himself might. . . .

Here, as the chief came almost opposite, War Lance
turned his head, and the bright, keen glance centered suddenly upon the face of Messenger, and dwelt there.

It struck Messenger like a blow. It dazzled and dizzied
him, and he was blinking and half unnerved when the brass
howitzer on top of the fort roared with a deep, hollow rever-
beration. He started.

At that explosion, the eight horses that had gone before
became frantic and hardly could be restrained by their perfect riders. But not so the stallion and War Lance. With an
unaltered step, the great horse came to the edge of the ditch
and, seeming merely to stretch out for a slightly larger
stride, was somehow across it—an elastic impulse, rather
than an actual jump, it seemed to Messenger. Fierce, keen,

overmastering desire and envy suddenly burned in his heart and in his brain.

He had had his training on the best of Kentucky and Virginia bred blood horses. On them he had been forced to gallop across the roughest country bareback. On them he had been taught to do foolish circus tricks that he had scorned and detested. He had had to rise and stand at a gallop. He had had to learn to lay himself along the side of a racing, headlong mount. He had fallen to the ground in every possible posture. His neck had been half broken a hundred times. He had been a mass of bruises and of sores, until that dreadful education was finished. As his skill had increased, he had been rewarded with still finer and wilder and more unbroken mounts. He had gained a peculiarly savage pleasure in mastering them, one after the other. He had learned to love some of them—the only creatures in his young life to whom he had been able to give the least scruple of affection. But never had he seen such a horse as this stallion.

It was a storm wind incarnate. It was a hurricane gathered in the hand and at the will of the master. Distance did not exist before its stride. Its courage would never fail its strength, and its strength would never fail its courage.

"Yes, sir," Lessing, at his elbow, said. "Two looks at that one would turn a saint into a hoss thief, I reckon." He laughed a little huskily, as though he himself had had the same emotion that burned in the boy.

But that voice and that laughter brought young Messenger down from the strange height to which he had mounted. He was snatched back to the earth, and he glanced aside at Lessing with something almost like disgust in his eyes.

Then, however, he could look at the rest of the proces-

sion. Rather dimly he saw the last half of the sacred band go
by, and mechanically he told himself that it was a match for
the first half of the same troop. Man and beast were as
good, perhaps better. But they seemed slight things compared with War Lance and his stallion. What else, indeed,
in the whole world, was worthy of comparison with that
hero?

Breathing heavily, as though he had been running up a
hill, Messenger surveyed the procession that followed. All
the warriors of the tribes that were present at the fort
streamed by him. The brass howitzer boomed again, and
yet again in welcome, for Louis Desparr knew when to
spare his gunpowder and when to be lavish with it. That
cannon on the roof was the chief item among his dignities.
Yet it seemed to Messenger like the noise of a silly popgun,
when such a man as War Lance was in presence.

He tried to estimate the men as they rode by him.
Calmly he told himself that they were athletes, nearly every
one. Even the old men rode their horses with a wonderful
skill. But they meant nothing to Messenger. His heart and
his soul were yonder, behind the palisades, where War
Lance was now, perhaps springing down from his charger.

He turned to Lessing. "Let's go inside," he suggested.

"Aye." Lessing grinned. "You wanna have another look
at War Lance, close up. But not too close, son. That's the
kind of a fire that'll burn the hands, I'm tellin' you. The
kind of a fire that'll burn you to the heart in a half of a
second. Besides, there's something else comin' up here.
Damned me if it don't look like Summer Day has come
back here, the skunk! I've told you that I like the Injuns,
son, but there's exceptions, the same as there is among the
whites. And Summer Day is the worst of 'em. The
murderin', stealin', faithless, treacherous hound! How

come that the Blackfeet and the Piegans would make a chief out of him? Yes, sir, that's Summer Day. I can tell by the way he hangs his head to one side, like he was sorry for something. He's got plenty to be sorry for, the scoundrel! That's Summer Day. I'd pawn my hide that it is, and damn' lot of insolence he's got to come back here to the fort!"

"Who is he?" asked Messenger, hardly hearing his own question, so disturbed was his mind by other thoughts and that other great picture.

"Why," said Lessing, "he's the real head chief of the Blackfeet. War Lance has got more fame for fightin', but Summer Day is a good second to him. Besides, Summer Day is a grand, high-flyin' medicine man of the first water. He can wither your face in a night, and bend your back double in a day, the Injuns believe. He gets rich, curin' fools. Hot baths is his main hold, like it is with all of 'em, but his lingo is better than most, and they believe in him. Besides, he's got a terrible long list of scalps and coups, and more hosses than anybody else in the whole nation. Yes, sir, that's old Summer Day. Not old, either, except in meanness. He killed a half-breed at the fort here, right after it was opened, and then he faded out into the open country. What's brought him back . . . unless War Lance done some persuadin'!"

This chief had chosen, oddly enough, to take the absolutely rearmost position in the line of warriors, and behind him began the rout of children and women who poured behind, but leaving a safe distance of respect and fear between them and the great medicine man. His head hanging a little to one side, as though in remorseful thought or weariness, Summer Day came closer. He was a beast of a man. His hair was like that of a horse's tail—as long and as coarse, and some of it tumbled unheeded down across his face. A

65

monster of a man, in his sleekly sloping shoulders appeared the immeasurable power of an animal. He did not have a picture horse, like one of the sacred band. Instead, he rode a shaggy, typical pony, although doubtless it possessed wonderful, although hidden, virtues. As he came by, the chief lifted his eyes and glanced with a glittering look to the side.

Messenger stood, stiff as a lance. "It is he!" he gasped.

Lessing, turning suddenly upon him, amazed, saw that the boy was as white as stone, and knew that he had found the object of his quest.

Chapter Ten

The enclosure within the palisade was now swarming with mounted men, women, and children, and the dust began to rise like smoke around the fort, while Lessing still remained outside the wall, gazing at his companion.

"You want that scalp, son?" he said to Messenger. "You want to get at Summer Day, do you?"

Messenger continued to stare wildly in the direction in which the enemy had disappeared. "I have to have him," he said. "I need him more than I need air to breathe. I have to have him! That would make me a free man!" His voice trembled. To see emotion in that youth was like seeing fire spout from hard rock, and the trapper shook his head in astonishment.

"You might as well," he said, "try to take the scalp of the thunderbird. You might better try to take the scalp of War Lance himself."

The boy looked at him with the same burning glance. He looked like one in a frenzy. "Tell me why?" he said.

"Because," declared the trapper, "War Lance is a great fighter, and he has sixteen chosen men behind him, but Summer Day is really the most powerful man in the tribe. He's the one who makes up the victory medicine for 'em. He's the one that they carry presents to. You could hit at War Lance through sixteen braves. You'd have to hit at Summer Day through the whole Blackfeet nation. I tell you

67

what, even if you got at him, he's a terror. I'd hate to be locked up in a room with him, even if I had four fightin' men with me. He'd be wearin' our hair before the finish of the fight, I tell you! Try anything that you want, Messenger . . . try War Lance, even, but don't go throwin' yourself away on a job like the medicine man!"

Messenger made an abrupt gesture. "Let's see what's up," he said, and he led the way through the gate into the big enclosure.

They got, eventually, to fairly good places for observation of what followed, for the crowd of people were stirring so restlessly that it was not hard to drift a way through them. Louis Desparr had come down from the roof as soon as he made out the nature of his visitors, and now he stood in the entrance to the store with a pipe in his hand and a broad smile on his face. This visit from so great a man as War Lance, to say nothing of the head medicine man among the Blackfeet, assured his future prosperity, he felt. He could not help exhibiting some of his joy.

War Lance and Summer Day, in the meantime, pressing up to the lead of the warriors, with a few motions drove them back until a circle was cleared. Then, dismounting, the two chiefs approached the trader. Their greetings were dignified, although rather cold. Now that the two famous Blackfeet were side by side, the contrast between them was more startling than in the line of march. The high head and the magnificent carriage of War Lance were opposed to the cunning and downward look of the medicine man, who appeared to be swallowing a smile and brooding upon mischief beyond the fathoming of ordinary men. He looked at those about him by sudden flashes. His real attention seemed to be focused upon his own thoughts. Yet he appeared in his own way as formidable an enemy as the great war chief himself. All that trickery and fox-like cunning could do were implied in the presence of Summer Day.

War Lance made a speech at once. He spoke briefly and simply. There are two qualities of voice that an Indian uses at will. One is the harsh tone of ordinary public conversation; the other is amazingly gentle and caressing, and one hears it in a teepee and rarely elsewhere. But the voice of War Lance was, on such an occasion as this, like a deep and mellow thunder, reassuring, but filling the hearers with awe.

He said in the Blackfoot tongue: "My friend, several months ago, the great medicine man of the Blackfeet came to this place and killed a man. Then he went away quickly. He did not run away because he was afraid, but because he felt that he might have been wrong, and he did not want to start a fight between all his people and the white men. When I heard of this, I went to him and asked him if it would not be a good thing if he would come back and make that killing right. The man he killed had a value and a price. Summer Day has come back to find out what the price may be, and then he will pay it, and the Blackfeet will be friends forever with the white men."

He paused, and Summer Day with a single gesture signified his assent to what had been spoken.

Louis Desparr nodded at them in the friendliest way.

"This is the way honest people ought to act," he declared. "I cannot say what the value of Henry Adams was. He was a half-breed, neither white nor black. But his widow is still here. There she stands now."

Mrs. Adams was a full-blooded Cree, and not the most beautiful of her race. She could have vied with Mrs. Desparr, in fact. She was a burly creature, with shoulders like a man and long, hanging arms.

"Here is Summer Day come back like a good man to pay you for your dead husband," said Desparr. "What price do you want to put? You name a price, and let Summer Day name one. I'll see which comes nearest to being honest."

Mrs. Adams raised her long arms to the sky and let out a wail, as the beginning of her price setting.

"Listen!" said Lessing at the ear of Messenger. "She'll want a whole herd of hossflesh for that worthless half-breed of hers."

Mrs. Adams at last reduced her keening to a voice that could be understood and announced that her teepee was desolate, and her children were hungry, and the hunter was gone from her side, and alone and sadly she faced life, which promised to be always winter. She wound up by saying that fifty horses would be almost right, but she added that a couple of good axes and a few pounds of beads ought to be thrown in to restore good will perfectly on all sides.

"You've heard the woman," said Desparr to Summer Day. "Now, what price do you put on the head of the man you killed?"

Summer Day hardly lifted his head to answer, and, when he spoke, he looked neither at Desparr nor at the squaw, but across the palisade toward the distant hills and the blue mist of mountains beyond him. It was as though he saw through everything and found these foolish conferences with ordinary men almost too dull to be worth his speech. Finally he said: "That man was neither white nor red. He was neither weak enough to lie down, nor strong enough to stand up. He had a red face and a white forehead. He was nothing. Besides, he stole from me, or tried to steal. But to make this woman happy, and not because I did wrong, I will give her two horses. That is enough to give for such a half-breed."

"That Summer Day," observed Lessing, "would get fat on thistles, I tell you. Listen to him, will you?"

"Aye," said Messenger grimly, his eyes fastened constantly on the face of the great chief. "I'm listening to him."

The squaw broke into a fresh clamor, but Desparr silenced her with a few words. "You know," he said, "that your husband was a lazy man. He never killed a buffalo in his life, and the only elk meat you ever ate was given to you here, in the fort, or by your friends in your tribe. He would not hunt like an Indian, and he would not work like a white man. Now, then, fifty horses are a great deal too much to ask for him. You know that you have a good, warm home here, as long as you choose to work and behave. Your children are being taken care of twice as well as they were when your husband was alive. Eight horses are enough to pay, if Summer Day will give that many."

At this judgment, or attempt at one, the woman screamed out as though she had been stabbed to the heart. Her babble of noise lasted until she saw the hand of the medicine man raised. No matter what her excitement, the awe with which he filled all the red men and women around him was easily to be observed. Her voice gradually died into a dog-like whining, while Summer Day spoke.

"You can have five horses," he said. "That is enough. Two horses are too much. But I am generous. I give you three more, because you are a foolish woman, and fools need to have plenty of wealth."

She screeched again. She began to roll her eyes and her head from side to side, and a great piercing lament for the dead Henry Adams went up to the sky.

Suddenly the medicine man struck his hands together, and, as the palms joined, there was a loud exclamation and a general shrinking back by all who stood around while the widow was turned to stone. For a brilliant play of blue fire had spurted out as the hands struck home, like the splashing of heavily struck water.

Then Summer Day exclaimed in a harsh and loud voice: "You are wicked and of no worth. Five horses you will take, at once, or get none at all. Do you think that I do not see you and your whole life? I see you clearly. You are not sorry that you have lost a husband. You are glad, and already you have found another man!"

This revelation, for the truth of it she did not contest, made poor Mrs. Adams utterly dumb. She no longer resisted, but nodded her head mutely when the trader asked her if this settlement was satisfactory.

In the meantime, two or three boys had left the enclosure and came back driving before them five little typical Indian ponies with rather lumpish heads and shaggy coats.

The awe that had been inspired in the breast of Mrs. Adams by the bit of parlor magic, and the apparent prophetic insight of the chief, were now diminished a little by her disappointment. She asked some of the bystanders if these really were horses or simply big dogs that would eat her out of house and home. However, she took the five very gladly by the rawhide lariats that were fastened to their necks, and so led them away, and the affair of the murdered Henry Adams was concluded.

This Louis Desparr announced with much satisfaction to red and white, speaking in the Indian tongue, for he said: "Now here this trouble is ended. The woman has been paid. She has taken the price. She will forget that she had a husband. So will everyone else. If there is any more hard talk or threatening about the death of Adams, then I will be the enemy of the men who quarrel. So will all good men."

Here Summer Day put in a word for himself. With his

unpleasantly secret smile and eye turned off toward the horizon again, he said: "I have shown you that I am a good man. I have done this not because I felt guilty, but because I wish to have many friends. To women I give gifts to stop their tongues and fill their minds with sleepy good nature. To men, I give bad magic that is very strong, and also blows. I have paid the woman. If there is any man who has a claim against me, let me hear him speak." He turned his head slowly around the circle until his eyes rested upon the face of Messenger.

"I am here to make a claim," said the boy.

Chapter Eleven

The calm and superior smile of the medicine man went out like a torch struck by wind and rain. He looked at the white youngster, and he looked again.

From the Indians, who were pressing closer and closer, there went up a sharp, excited babbling—instantly followed by deep silence as all ears strained to catch the words. Although Messenger spoke in the Blackfoot tongue, which he seemed to understand perfectly, his voice was pitched so low that those at any distance found it hard to make out what he was saying.

The interruption of the smooth ceremony of the reconciliation, which ought to have called for a feast on the spot, caused War Lance to turn sharply about, also, and to stare at the white boy.

But Messenger endured this battery of eyes with the utmost calm, and his head remained high, his expression almost indifferent.

The medicine man did not deign to answer the stranger directly. Instead, he gestured to some who stood near. "Tell this white boy who I am," he said. "And ask him what he can want from me. Perhaps he wants a horse to ride? Tell him that I never refuse beggars."

He had said this loudly enough for the white man to hear, however, and young Messenger replied, using the same tactics of addressing the nearest people and not the magic worker directly: "I hear that this is the great wonder worker, the medicine man of all the Blackfeet, the famous Summer Day?"

"Yes!" burst out a chorus of voices.

Summer Day allowed the smile of superiority and scorn to return to his features.

"I hear," went on Messenger, "that Summer Day can throw a demon into people. He can make one side of the face thin and the other side fat."

"Yes, yes!" cried out the chorus, sharp and harsh with eagerness.

"He can call the spirits out of the sky so that they chatter to him through the smoke hole of his teepee."

"We have heard the voices!" exclaimed the crowd.

The content of the medicine man grew greater and greater. It appeared as though the white man had come there to praise their great chief of the Blackfeet, not to make any real demand upon him. Only War Lance, standing somewhat apart, head and shoulders taller than most of even those big warriors, dropped his head a little and continued to look in fixed thought at the white boy.

"He can," resumed Messenger in his recital, "take away the life of people who are a long way off."

"Yes. He has done it many times!"

"He can bring back to life people whose spirits are already in the happy hunting grounds and ready to leap on the backs of the blue sky horses."

A perfect shout of exclamation answered him.

"Then," said the white boy, "what I am asking him to do will not be too hard. I am asking him to give back the life of a white man he murdered."

All Indian smiles disappeared suddenly, although War Lance was seen to nod a little to himself, almost as though he had been expecting some such announcement as made the climax of this speech of apparent praise.

As for the medicine man, his smile grew wider than ever, but met with honest amazement. His ugly face had a glint of evil malice.

"I have taken many scalps," he declared. "The Blackfeet know it."

"Yes, yes!" they replied hurriedly, their eyes fixed upon the face of the white boy who dared to say so much before the wonder worker, the flame breather, the dreadful favorite of the spirits.

"I have taken many scalps of Indians, and many of the white warriors, too," said the medicine man calmly. "Which one do you mean?"

"Look back a good many years, to a time when you were a very young man, Summer Day. You were not quite so famous then, but you were already a great medicine man and liar."

Summer Day started with a convulsive fury, but this he controlled instantly. "Very well," he said. "You have called me a liar. I am able to listen before I act. The spirits listen, also. I think that I hear them laughing above my head." He pointed solemnly into the air.

"In that time, a good many great suns ago," went on the boy, "you once went through the woods and came on a white man in a small camp. He was all alone. He had broken his leg and was lying there, trying to get well. His friend who was taking care of him had left camp to go hunting. Now do you remember, Summer Day?"

The medicine man actually smiled again, there was such a demon in him.

"I remember the killing of many white men," he said insolently. "But this one is not in my mind."

"You will remember," said the boy in his usual calm manner. "You will remember that you asked the helpless white man where his friend had gone and when he would be back, and, when the white man would not tell, you tortured him. You pushed splinters into his body and lighted them and let them burn into the flesh. You twisted a cord around his head and tightened it until it cut to the bone and almost forced the eyes out of his head. You cut the tendons of his arms and legs, one by one. But still he would not betray his friend. At last, you brained him with his own camp axe, and you took his scalp. Do you remember those things now, brave chief?"

The assurance with which the boy talked had its own effect, and the medicine man, looking suddenly around him, could not help realizing that the picture was not a pretty one. Torture had its own place in the Indian scheme of things, but it was rather a religious rite than a thing for personal indulgence. After the great battle, when many of the braves of the nation had fallen, it was then of some account to pacify the spirits of the dead by sending some of their recent enemies to a death by torment. But it was a thing to be done by ecstasy and not soberly in ordinary fighting. The sleeping or the helpless had no right of life, to be sure, but this picture, deliberately drawn, of the badgering of a man who could not strike back, made even the toughest of the Blackfeet warriors wrinkle their faces in pain and in disgust.

The medicine man, when he saw that his case was not a desirable one, merely sneered as he looked away toward the hills in the distance.

"We hear many men talk," he said, "but how often do we hear the truth? Truth is like a very fleet deer. It runs away when the white men come near. What has made this young boy think that I, chief among the Blackfeet, have done such a thing?"

"First of all," said Messenger, "I could have guessed it by the beast in your face. But secondly, I had something that was a surer proof. You had tormented the poor white man until his brain was sick. You had blinded him in one eye. You had slashed his left arm and both his legs so that he had only one thing that he could move, and that was his right hand. Then you left him lying there while you went off about the camp to see what would be worth stealing. You did not want to kill him in a hurry, but you wanted him to taste his agony as long as possible. Finally you came back to finish him, but, in the meantime, he had done a thing which you could not suspect. You have your painters and your artists, Summer Day. They can draw a buffalo very well. They can even draw a horse, so that the horse can be recognized. Well, that white man had spent his life making drawings and paintings. Whatever he saw with his eyes, he could make the face of it with his hands. And when you went off to plunder the camp, he found at his side on the ground a broad, fresh, white chip of wood that had been newly slashed off from a log to try the edge of the axe. You yourself had cut off that chip to test the axe, Summer Day. When he saw the chip, it must have made the white man think of clean, fresh paper. He had for a pencil the tip of his finger. He had for paint his own red blood. On the chip, then, he drew the face of the Indian who had murdered him, and under it he scrawled one word . . . *Blackfoot!* Very well, now you shall see the face that he drew!"

The crowd, hardly breathing during this recital, now muttered swiftly one to another. There was a general swaying of heads and shoulders as those on the outer rim tried to press in closer.

Messenger took from an outside pocket a strong wallet, which he opened, and took from within it a flat package wrapped securely in silk. This he undid with the greatest care. As he worked, he went on gravely and almost gently: "As the chip grew older and dried, it became less white. It bent. And finally it cracked in two in the middle. However, it can still be put together, and the picture can be recognized, I think."

With this, he put the silk into his pocket, and, fixing the two halves of the chip together, he raised into the air, with both hands, that extraordinary picture, and turned slowly around to let all about him observe the thing. It was no more than three inches wide and perhaps five or six in length. The red blood of the pigment that had been used for paint long ago had blackened with time. The strokes were in themselves very gross and heavy, for a fingertip cannot be expected to make delicate lines. But as an expert worker with charcoal will rough in the most striking likeness, using a broad and blunt-ended piece of burnt wood, so that tortured and dying man had worked with his own blood and with his finger, subduing his pain, making his eyes and his brain clear while he sketched. Underneath it was clumsily written, as though with a failing strength, the word **Blackfoot**. But that word was not needed now. The face was enough. Rough as the work was, the likeness was there. The straggling of the hair across the face, the forward and sidewise cant of the head would in themselves have been almost enough, but, in addition, the leering smile appeared there, and even, as it seemed to the excited watchers, the brilliant, brutal eyes of the medicine man staring out from beneath his straggling forelocks.

So great and startling was the likeness, and so much had even the toughest of the braves been worked up by the scene that went before the showing of the picture, that, as the boy finished turning, the pent emotions burst out in one deep and general exclamation from children, women, and men.

"Summer Day!"

The boy returned the chip carefully to its wrapping of silk and replaced it in his wallet. As he put this into the pocket from which it had been taken, he said: "Now, Summer Day, tell these people that you've been a liar as well as a murderer."

Chapter Twelve

An old fox is hard to corner. Summer Day, even now, failed to look at his accuser. Even now he maintained his smile, and his distant look toward the horizon. Then he raised his hand. "The spirits," he said, "that told me to kill that man, they are with me now. They are just over my head. They are laughing, and glad that I have done what I have done. Yes, my friends, and the good scalp still hangs in my teepee. My wives admire it. The hair still shines like gold. They brush the soot from the smoke out of it. They say that it looks like the white man's money. I killed that man, I remember now. I counted three coups on him."

There was a single murmur. It came from the throat of War Lance, but there was no speech in the sound. It was simply a deep-voiced note of disapproval, and, a moment later, it was echoed by a sort of groan that passed through all the throng.

At this, Summer Day actually put back his head and laughed. He turned a bit, and his odd, shifting glances went over the faces. "You think I have done wrong?" he exclaimed. "Is there a man of you who ever has seen or talked to spirits, except the ones I have sent to you? Why do you frown at me? I am only two hands for the Sky People to use, two ears with which they hear, two eyes with which they see and . . . remember!"

This last cunningly implied threat had such a force that

Messenger, who was watching all things and faces like a hawk, actually saw the bravest and the greatest of those warriors drop their heads a little—even War Lance half turned away, shaking his head, apparently baffled by disgust and yet controlled by the awe with which the chief medicine man always fills a tribe.

The women were naturally more impressed than the men. Some of them hastily turned their backs, lest their faces should be seen and remembered by the terrible medicine man who might straightway put a curse upon them and upon everything in their teepees. Their horses might take strange diseases and die, or the enemy might scoop them up during a raid, or the children might begin to pine and dwindle, and the manhood be stolen from the youths of the family. All of these things might occur. But that was not all, for the whole future might be cursed by the terrible wizard, and a spell cast that would effect even the memory of the great dead, making the minds of the tribesmen a blank to what had been done before. These fears worked so violently that some of the squaws were now seen hastily scurrying away from the edge of the crowd, herding their children before them, or hauling them along by the hands.

Summer Day had struck a subtle but a telling blow, and now he could afford to pay direct attention to the young white man. "Now this boy comes to talk to me," said the chief. "Perhaps he wants more horses, also? Well, I have plenty of them in my herd. Let somebody ask him how many horses he would like to have. I still have horses . . . for beggars!"

Behind the boy, the eager, hasty voice of the trapper said almost on the ear of Messenger: "Take the horses. That's honorable. That will keep your dignity in the eyes of the braves. Don't you worry about that."

"I don't worry about that," the boy assured him. Then, staring directly at the medicine man, he raised his arm and pointed toward the green, rolling lands beyond the gate and the palisade. "There is plenty of room there," he said. "What I want to say to you about that murder, I would like to say out there. And anybody who wants to, can watch my words."

He had caught the true Indian idiom and their manner of talk. And the idea of "watching" words tickled the Blackfeet fancy so intensely that there was a stir among the warriors and a sudden flashing of light across their faces.

As for the medicine man, he now brought his glance back from the horizon at which he had been sneering and smiling for so long. He allowed that glance to rest burningly upon the face of the boy before he said: "This is a young man. This is only a boy. Someone should tell him who I am. Or perhaps he will have one or two friends who will go along with him to fight me?"

This supreme self-confidence was not surprising to the Blackfeet. There were no three of them, with the possible exception of War Lance, who would have dared to confront the miracle man in any sort of a battle.

But young Messenger tipped back his head a little and laughed. It was not forced laughter. It flowed out with a clear, sharp, ringing sound that made one think of the chiming of the cold waters of the mountain streams as they fall among the winter hollows and caves of ice. So freely laughed young Messenger, keeping his bright, gray eyes on the face of the medicine man. "Summer Day, Summer Day," he cried out, "you are going to die! You are about to die! I have waited and worked for years for you. I am going to kill you, and that will make me a free man. Shall I give you a sign of your death?"

The medicine man kept his face fairly well, although in the presence of this easy laughter and this taunting, confident speech it was not altogether easy to do. He waited for an instant, as his wrath gathered, and into that moment of pause dropped the *caw*ing of a crow that was wheeling above the yard of the fort, insolently near.

"I shall give you a sign of your own death!" exclaimed the worker of wonders, the fire dealer. "I shall kill you with fires from the sky!" he shouted, losing his calm like a robe and standing in unconcealed rage before the crowd. "I shall kill you with the blue fires of the sky!" And, striking his hands above his head once more, before the eyes of all men, blue flames were seen to spurt out from between them. There was literally a groan of awe. Even War Lance, striding back half a step, had to brace himself and set his teeth to endure the sight of this sudden miracle.

The heart of the medicine man was comforted, but only for a moment. Then he heard Messenger laughing again.

"That's your sign, and a very poor sign," said the boy. "That's a trick that half a dozen cheap little hired medicine men do every day among the whites. But here's a sign that's worth ten of that. Look over your heads!"

Every eye suddenly glanced up, as though they expected that the sky itself might be opening. They saw there the heavy-winged crow that had jumped itself half a dozen yards higher in the air at the gesture and the shout of Summer Day, and, since they stared earnestly, expecting some sort of a great thing to happen, only two or three of those nearest to the boy saw his hand flash up with a gun in it. The others merely heard the revolver explode and saw the crow, high above them, tip suddenly over to the side, stagger, and then slide slanting downward toward the ground, leaving above him a black puff of feathers that

84

shone on the sun. A moment more and death made the wings of the bird limp. It tumbled head over heels and landed on the ground with a *thump* that was audible in the dead silence that followed the report of the weapon.

There was no shouting and there was no groaning afterward.

This was no miracle. It was simply a case of snap shooting that made the eyes start in their heads.

They began to mumble and mutter. No matter how extremely clever the magic of the medicine man might be, this outright exposure of shooting skill was enough to make them all shake their heads. Certainly it wiped the sneer off the face of the chief.

In the eyes of War Lance appeared suddenly a glint of hope and pleasure that barely glimmered there before it was gone again. He said solemnly: "This young man has asked you to go out and fight with him, Summer Day. You have given him a sign that the Sky People are with you. Everyone knew that before. He is a rash young man, but he does not seem afraid. He is standing there and waiting for your answer."

Summer Day favored the speaker with a sudden, dark glance, but then he smoothed his expression again. He pointed, in his turn, through the open gate of the fort and across the green plain. "Do you see, my friends," he said, "where the river makes the bend, and where it cuts away half the hill and leaves the high red bank?"

They could see. It was the plainest landmark in sight. Here, the narrow, swift river, leaving the hills and its own deep cañon, leaped out into the plain with a snowy face covered with froth. On the right of its mouth, there stood a round-headed hill, the top of which was covered with a tall growth of trees, and darkened with shrubs toward the edges. There was a sort of dark dignity to that hill. It was like a crowned head in the green of the plain.

"There is Thunder Hill," said the medicine man to Messenger. "Go out and ride into it from the left. I shall ride into it from the right. At the top of the mountain I shall meet you and pull down the blue fires and the red fires out of the sky to burn you." He turned to the others. "You, my children, will be able to see the play of the flames, if you look closely against the line of the sky. Shade your eyes and look carefully, for such a thing never has been seen before."

"Don't take that challenge," said the old trapper anxiously, at the back of the boy. "You must not take that challenge!"

"Why not?"

"You know guns. You may know hosses, boxing, wrestling, and all of that. You may climb trees like a cat, but you don't know hunting. And Summer Day does. He's one of the greatest stalkers that ever pulled the whiskers out of a mountain lion and cut his throat when he woke up. Don't be a fool, boy!"

Young Messenger made no reply; there was too much truth in what Lessing said for him to turn the advice aside at once.

The trapper went on: "You most likely could shoot the eyes out of his head in an open fight, and he knows it. But in there among the trees, it'll be the best stalker that wins. Mind that, Messenger."

But here the loud, taunting voice of the chief and medicine man broke in: "What does the young man answer? If his heart is growing cold, let him go away. I have already so many white scalps, what does one more mean to me?"

"Summer Day," said the boy through his teeth, "I offered to fight you in the open. But if you prefer the dark, I'll meet you there. Perhaps it's as well that no one should see what I intend to do to you."

Chapter Thirteen

Not for a moment did Lessing leave the side of his protégé, and he poured out good advice to him constantly. "Messenger," he asked, "tell me . . . you never stalked a deer in the woods?"

"No."

"You never hunted so much as a squirrel?"

"No."

As he talked, Messenger was looking over his weapons. He lacked a horse, and Lessing had sent a half-breed boy to saddle and accouter his own pony. The Colt revolver had to be cleaned and reloaded in all its chambers to make sure that it was in the most perfect working order. In the meantime, they stood aside from the crowd, close to the palisade. The medicine man, also, had withdrawn with a circle of companions, behind the shelter of whom he was donning his war paint and looking to his own fighting tools.

"You've never been out in the wilderness?" asked the trapper with more and more anxiety.

"No, never before this trip."

"You don't know how to walk over dry leaves, and over twigs?"

"No."

"Then fetch off those boots and put on these moccasins. They're old, and that makes them all the better. They ain't got soles, and that means that they'll let you feel the ground with the palm of your foot like the palm of your hand. Look where you step, but keep feeling the ground like you were feeling for diamonds. Put your foot down, toe first, and then roll forward on it . . . like this."

Messenger, without a word, pulled off his boots and put on the moccasins, as directed.

As he stood up again, the trapper continued: "Them that get into the woods where there's trouble ahead of 'em make the mistake of glancin' around too many times. That ain't the way. Notice a deer or a wildcat when it's out in danger. It don't jerk its head around. It gives a good long look at anything that's interesting. Give them the same long looks. Sink your eye right down into the green of the branches and maybe you'll find something that's worthwhile. Keep markin' the things that are around you . . . a tree that you can jump behind . . . a log that you can drop behind . . . a bunch of brush that would shelter a growed-up man. And always remember that an Injun knows how to fade himself out into the grass and make himself as small as a snake, because they got a lot of snake in their natures. And an Injun can hide all of himself behind a sapling that would hide a baby, two years old. Remember them things. Get yourself on a hair-trigger . . . and heaven help you."

As the horse was brought up, Messenger suddenly held out his hand. "You're a friend, Lessing," he said.

The trapper shook the extended hand with warmth.

"If I had a week in the woods with you," he said, "I could teach you something worthwhile. But even then, I couldn't teach you what the Injuns are born knowing."

"If he gets me," said the boy, "he'll probably take the horse that I've ridden on up to the edge of the woods. If he does, it'll be your loss. Here's my wallet. You'll find enough cash in that to make up to you for the loss of the horse and the saddle. . . ."

"I don't want your money, son."

"You don't want it, but you'd better keep it for me."

"I won't touch it. It'd bring you bad luck. If there's any message that you'd like to send out by me. . . ."

The youngster raised his head and looked thoughtfully straight before him. "No," he said at last. "There's nothing that I want to say. There's no message. Those who are interested, they'll hear about the end of me, in time. Good bye, Lessing." He shook hands once more, and, turning, he leaped into the saddle.

Lessing's pinto, a tough little bronco with the look of an over-wise speculator, greeted the stranger with a leap straight into the air, scattering those who stood curiously nearby. As they fell back, shouting in alarm, they saw the moccasined feet of the lad find the stirrups as if by instinct, and, as the pony landed, its ribs were in such a crushing grip that it decided straightway that it had met its master. Off it jogged through the gate of the Lippewan Fort as though it expected to have a long journey before it.

There were mutterings of praise for this feat of horsemanship, simple though it seemed.

"Aye," said the trapper to those who were gathered about him, "a hoss can tell a hand of iron as quick as a man can. Heaven help Summer Day if that lad ever comes to grips with him."

The white lad had actually finished his preparations first. Summer Day, on his long-haired war pony, followed a moment later. He was stripped to the waist. His face and body were fairly glistening with war paint, and a number of fresh feathers had been crowded into his hair. Now, prepared for battle, and with his body erect in the saddle, he looked far closer to the beau ideal of the perfect warrior. As he went out from among the Blackfeet, they gave him a rousing cheer.

They had been moved by the tale of the white lad and the sight of the picture painted in blood, but now their sympathies were strongly drawn back to the side of their champion who was to represent them with red magic against white, and with equal weapons against the white man.

That the latter was likely to prove a worthy foe in spite of his youth, the bit of wrestling and fist fighting, to say nothing of the shooting of the crow, had amply testified. It began to look like a worthy contest, and now it was the old race of the soil against the race of white intruders.

The wild eyes of the red men shone with excitement, and, mounting their horses, they streamed out over the grassy plain and the rolling hills to come as close as possible to the place of the encounter. The people of the fort left it, also—Louis Desparr riding at the side of his friend, Lessing, while the two champions, diverging to the right and the left, came up to the opposite sides of the hill, as had been planned.

On the verge of the green gloom of the woods that covered the height, Messenger drew rein and dismounted. His rifle he was about to take with him, but, on second thought, he abandoned it. In that dense forest, it was highly unlikely that he would have a chance to shoot at a greater distance than that which his revolver covered with accuracy. The rifle's weight and length could be little more than a sheer handicap. Therefore, he left the hunter's treasure behind him, and, about to step into the woods, he looked back at the hills beneath.

There were still a few stragglers coming out from the fort, dashing their horses forward at full speed; the fort itself looked small and dark against the silver flash of the river that almost surrounded it. Nearer at hand, in a long, loose semicircle, were gathered every man, woman, and child of the tribes who were present at Fort Lippewan. They were watching, no doubt, with their hearts in their mouths.

And he himself? There was an odd chill in the pit of his stomach, and a feeling of lightness in his brain, which he knew was fear. But he merely smiled at it. Life, after all, had not been a thing so sweet to him that he should make any desperate effort to retain the spark of it. He could not help shuddering when he thought of the mutilation that would befall him if the medicine man should win the battle. He shuddered still more at his mental picture of Summer Day, issuing from the edge of the woods and galloping his horse down into the plain with the triumphant screech of the war cry bursting from his throat, and the new scalp, dangling from his bridle rein.

Then he put these pictures resolutely behind him, and entered the forest. He had made up his mind on the way to the scene of the battle. No matter what the advice of the old trapper, no matter how well he counseled, he could not expect to match the woodcraft of the Indian. Therefore, he charged almost blindly for the center of the battlefield. That is to say, he ran—as softly as he could, but, nevertheless, making a sufficient crackling noise as his feet fell on dead leaves and twigs—straight up the slope of the mountain until he came to the crest of the hill.

It was very broad, and the growth of trees here was fairly open, far more so than had been the case along the lower slopes. There were plenty of hiding places and stalking places, however. There were clumps of shrubbery through which not even an eagle's eye could have looked, and there were nests of rock, also, outcropping here and there. In the maze of possibilities, it was almost beyond doubt that the Indian would have the best of him. He could not expect to outwit that natural hunter. Therefore, he had to resign himself to being the hunted.

He had decided that on the way across the open ground to the side of the hill, and, for that reason, he had hurried up to the crest. It was barely likely that the cunning Blackfoot would follow the same tactics, and, therefore, he probably had a moment or two in which to prepare for the encounter. He picked out for the purpose a good, stout tree that grew a little east of the summit, although almost upon the same level. To this he went, and, as he approached, he studied the branches with a good deal of care. They were by no means as thick as he had hoped to find them, and the foliage was not impenetrable to the eye. Yet, at least, the upper limbs were fairly well lost in the green mist of the leaves. He decided, after a glance around, that he could hardly do better with the means at hand, so up the trunk he went, cat-like, sure of hand and foot.

He was glad of the light gear on his feet now. It made the grip of his feet almost as secure as that of his hands. So he went upward swiftly to a fork well toward the upper middle of the tree, and toward the western side of it. There he stretched himself out along the fork and the branch beneath it, and waited.

Chapter Fourteen

He was facing the trail that he himself had made coming up the hill. Through the spray of the branches and the leaves, he could keep a fairly good look-out on the lower slope, and his hope was simply that the clever Indian would find the trail and, coming up it, expose himself to the fire of the revolver. He did not ask for more than one fair glimpse of Summer Day. A .44-caliber slug would tell the rest of the story, so far as Summer Day was concerned.

There were other chances that might tell against him. Situated as he was, he could not easily turn and look behind him. To either side his view was also hindered, and even looking straight ahead and down, the little branches and the leaves before him impeded his sight. However, by moving his head up and down and to the right, he could command all the landmarks that he had passed during the last of his journey up the hill, and, if the Indian came up along that trail, it would go hard if the boy did not see him.

The branch was not the most comfortable resting place in the world. The hard, narrow round of it bit into his body, but he was long used to discomforts and he endured this with the calm of a Spartan, and maintained his watch.

The minutes went on very slowly. What amazed him, at first, was the utter silence. There was not a touch of wind to stir the leaves or raise a whisper from them. There was neither bird nor beast to be seen. There was only the pale sheen of the birches down the slope toward the river and, beyond the birches and their broken foliage, the dull red glow of the bank of the opposite hill. To his left, he saw the sleek, polished trunk of a sycamore, growing very far north for its species, although this he did not know.

Otherwise, at first, he heard nothing. But, after a time, this was altered. The sound of his own breathing and the beating of his heart, after the run and the climb, to say nothing of mental excitement, had served as a blanket to muffle the noises that, as he presently perceived, filled the air. Above all there was a soft, dull, droning sound that he now made out to be the booming of the river between its hollow banks. Before, that noise had seemed to be coming from the far edge of the horizon, like a distant, musical thunder. Now it moved nearer and nearer till it was in his very ear, mixed with distinct crisp rustlings of spray. The leaves, too, were not entirely motionless, not entirely silent, but they kept up, here and there, hushing sounds of secrecy. Next, in a pine tree, he saw a squirrel that ran out on a branch and chattered with amazing loudness at something on the ground. He craned his neck to see what this could be, but he distinguished nothing.

A moment later, a hawk flew over the wood, skimming the tops of the trees and dipping up and down over their heads without a perceptible motion of his wings. He uttered a scream that sounded hoarse and distant, although the bird was only a few rods away. Then it disappeared beyond the treetops. Next, a blue jay flew like the streak of a dazzling jewel in motion across the clearing just before him. It whirled up into the air. It hung above his treetop and uttered a harsh cry. Still it hung about that tree, flashing its gaudy body in the sun, so near that he distinctly heard the whirring of its wings. This, if he had known enough of woodland creatures and their ways and what these tell to the observant, would have worried him, or actually driven him out of the tree. But he did not know. He was even rather glad to have that bright, noisy bit of scolding feathers near him. It raised his heart and occupied the corners of his attention, while he still watched the back trail.

Long moments still dragged slowly by, and then he had sight of his quarry. It came suddenly. Clearly in view, Summer Day stepped out of the covert of a group of saplings, standing closely, shoulder to shoulder, and, with his body drooped forward toward the ground, he made long, silent strides for the next cover.

The heart of the boy leaped. He leveled his revolver— and then found his finger stiff and unwilling upon the trigger. He had thought that, being committed to the ways and the tricks of Indian warfare for this combat, he could fight as the Indians fight, subtly, secretly, without mercy when an advantage fell into his hands. But his heart spoke in him, and he could not fire. The next instant, before he could rally himself to the necessity of the thing, the form was gone.

At this, he gritted his teeth and told himself that he was a fool. But it hardly mattered, for the man, since he was coming up the trail, was sure to steal closer and show himself for a surer shot.

Here the blue jay swerved again above his tree, circling, and uttered his cry. But to this the boy paid no heed. There was something else to occupy him, and freeze his mind with attention. He stared at a nest of rocks, from behind which the skulking form of Summer Day was sure to step the next instant. But Summer Day was apparently taking his time.

The minutes went by. No Indian appeared. A vague restlessness and doubt came to the boy. For it might be, after all, that through the imperfect screen of the branches and the leaves he had been seen. He began to look hastily from side to side, until he remembered what the trapper had told him. Hasty glances are worth very little in the thick of the wood. A long and penetrating stare is the proper thing. So he began to use the lesson carefully, as one who knows how to follow instructions. Still he could not pierce the screen of the foliage, or of the trunks, and the scattering rocks. Nothing moved, so far as he could see, except a flight of several bees that rose with a sweet humming noise from the flowers in the sunny clearing, where they had been gathering pollen for their honey-making.

Then something flew crackling, snapping, through the branches, cutting off a twig an inch from his nose, and the ringing report of a rifle *clanged* in his ear.

He looked to the right and down. There was just the hint of the gleam of steel beside the trunk of a great tree, and he knew what it meant. Somehow, the Indian had received a warning in time, and, circling the tree in which Messenger had his covert, he had had his chance to draw a careful bead, and to fire. What could have made him miss, at such point-blank range unless, making deadly sure, he had insisted on a head shot, and some slight movement of the green branches had diverted his aim. Those wonderings and that observance took a fifth part of a second for the boy. In the next instant he was off that branch, and swinging by his hands.

As he looked down, he saw that Summer Day had dropped his rifle and was running forward. It was too late to change his own plan, but easy enough to see the wile of the medicine man. He would not waste time in trying to reload his gun. Instead, he would rush out and, as the white lad dropped to the ground, spring on him with his knife. Already it was prepared in his hand, a long curve of glistening steel. That very knife, perhaps, might have been used to torture the helpless man those years ago.

Releasing his hold on the bending bough, Messenger shot down. He held the revolver straight above him with his right hand. With his left, he caught strongly at bunches of twigs and at small boughs, and these brief handholds, broken almost as fast as they were made, slowed up the force of the fall so that he descended with a heavy shock, to be sure, but on his feet.

And Summer Day, as he lunged in, found himself looking into the eye of a leveled revolver. He was no coward, however. The same wild spirit that is in every true red warrior was in him, and, with a screech of frantic battle exultation, he flung himself at Messenger.

Twice, the latter, in that final instant, pressed the trigger, and twice he could not shoot down a man unequally armed. All his detestation of the red murderer could not force him to the act. Finally, with a groan, he struck at the armed hand of Summer Day with the barrel of the heavy weapon. Right across the knife blade, held rigidly forward, the blow fell, and, with a tinkling sound like that of broken glass, the knife blade snapped.

It was almost too late, but the medicine man sensed instantly what had happened and bounded to the side. The useless hilt he still grasped in his convulsed hand, the murder that he had been foretasting was still making his face horrible as that of a wild beast, and, with his legs planted wide apart and his body stooped forward, he confronted the white man with no surrender in his bearing.

It was the end, however. He knew that magic, the *real* magic, lay in the revolver that Messenger carried. He himself had neither revolver nor even pistol to fall back upon, now. He had his bare hands and the useless knife hilt. It would give weight to a blow, but it could not parry a flying bullet.

Messenger smiled as he looked on the medicine man.

The latter, frenzied by the knowledge of his helplessness, actually stamped upon the ground, and a thin bubbling foam formed on his lips. It was ghastly beyond belief to see a human creature so transformed, so thoroughly masked with fury and with despair.

"Now, Summer Day," said Messenger, "the time has come for you. You are no more, now, than a one-day-old calf with a halter around its neck. You are no more than a twig in my hand. I can break you when I please. Do you understand?"

Great shudders passed through the body of the other. His chest labored with the great breaths that he drew into it and that came out whistling through his teeth. But suddenly he drew himself up. The battle mask dropped from his features. He cast the worthless knife hilt behind him.

"My friend," he said, "what you say is true. Summer Day is no more than a child before you, so long as that gun is in your hands. But you will see. The spirits still help me. They will not let me fall before a bullet."

Chapter Fifteen

To Messenger there came a desperate and deep satisfaction. He now had accomplished his work. The end of the long trail was at hand. A touch of the trigger made him a free man in every sense of the word. The slavery of this imposed duty was ended, and he could go where he would in the world, and be what he was able to make of himself.

These thoughts, streaming through his mind, almost obscured the words that the medicine man had spoken to him, but he was able to smile coldly, and say: "Tell me, Summer Day, what will your spirits do to help you? How will they step in between us? How will they turn aside the bullet that I am about to shoot into your brain?"

"How can I tell?" said the medicine man. "Am I one to read every thought of the Sky People? No, now and then, when I pray, they reveal themselves and the future to me. Who am I to command and direct them? Their thoughts and their ways are better than anything that I could invent."

The white man smiled again with an infinite cruelty. "You talk very well, Summer Day," he said. "You have a good many words to speak, but I don't think that you have anything that will outweigh the little bullet inside of this gun."

"The bullet," said the medicine man calmly, "will never be fired."

"Ah? Never fired?" Messenger said, tightening his grip a

little upon the handle of the Colt.

"No, for you will not do a murder, my friend of the iron hand."

"Murder?" cried the white man through his teeth. "You detestable scoundrel, what was it that you did when you found the helpless white man in his camp and killed him slowly?"

"Look!" the Indian exclaimed, and pointed over his head.

Messenger was not foolish enough to be tempted into an unwary gesture. But he could still look up and keep the Indian somewhat vaguely within the range of his vision. This he was glad to do, because he really was hoping that the Blackfoot might make a sudden rush at him and supply the motive for pulling the trigger—a thing that he still found very hard to do in cold blood.

So up he stared, and he saw before him a small bird flying hastily across the blue of the sky and, above it, a hawk stooping with folded wings. Down at the little bird the hawk dropped, but, as the quarry shifted, footing lightly to the side, the hawk missed his stroke and plunged sheer down for 100 yards or so past his mark. Then his wings exploded, and the force of his downward drop caused him to jump up again into the blue almost to his former height of place. Again he dropped and again. Each time he missed, but the fugitive was forced to descend closer and closer to the earth, instead of circling up to a superior point of height.

"Is that murder that the hawk is trying to do?" asked the medicine man.

"Why," said the boy, "he's acting according to his kind."

"So was I when I killed the white man in the camp," said Summer Day. "I was acting according to my kind. I inquired of the spirits, but they did not tell me that the thing was wrong. They would not speak. Therefore, I did what all my kind would do."

"You lie," said the other sternly. "There are generous Indians as well as white men."

"A generous Indian is a generous fool," said the other. "A scalp is a scalp to a red man, whether it be the scalp of a woman, a child, or a man . . . an old man, a boy, or a warrior in his prime. And a coup is a coup, even if it be counted on a toothless old man who is in his second childhood."

"Do you think," asked the white man curiously, "that you can talk me out of killing you?"

"I do not have to talk," said the other. "Either the spirits will help me, or else they will not. But I think that your hand is already helpless to slay me."

"You will see," Messenger said, and raised the gun.

The medicine man crossed his arms upon his breast and did not reply. Straight he looked into the muzzle of the ready gun, and Messenger vainly gritted his teeth together. He could not shoot the defenseless man. He lowered the gun again and began to curse softly behind his teeth. Summer Day merely smiled.

"You have a knife and a gun," he said, "but, after a moment, you will throw them both away, and you will fight me evenly, with your bare hands."

"Do you think so?" echoed the boy. "Almost one and a half of me could be made out of your bulk, Summer Day. You are almost as big as the horses you ride."

"However," said the Indian calmly, "there is something that makes you even bigger."

"What is that?" asked the boy, half smiling. "What is it that the spirits have told you about me, Summer Day?"

"That you are proud," replied the medicine man. "And pride is like wind in a bladder. It blows up a man till he thinks that he is as tall as a tree. That is what you think, my friend."

At this, Messenger laughed aloud. He could not help it. The combined frankness and insolence of the Blackfoot tickled him profoundly. "Very well," he said, "and you think that I'll actually throw aside my knife and my gun in order to fight you on even terms?"

"You will," said the medicine man.

"Would I not be a great fool, if I did?"

"Yes. But white men are often foolish."

"What would I gain, except a chance to fight a much bigger man?"

"You would gain the one thing that you really want."

"Tell me what that is, Summer Day."

"You would gain a chance to feel me dying between your hands, and that is the thing that you pine for."

"That is true," answered Messenger.

"Yes," said the Indian. "For that is both tasting and eating food, to have a man die in your grip."

Messenger drew in a great breath. "Suppose that I do this insane thing, Summer Day."

"Oh, you will do it, my friend. Your eyes are turning red this moment."

Suddenly Messenger hurled the revolver far from him. The easy trigger, lightly hung, exploded as the weapon landed, and the bullet went crackling and whirling off through the trees. After the gun, he threw his big and heavy knife. Then he made a gesture with both of his empty hands. "Are you ready, Summer Day?"

The latter, grinning from ear to ear, looked after the knife and the gun and measured the distance. Then, disregarding the white man for the moment, he lifted his head and raised both his palms to the sky. Very plainly he was praying to the spirits that, he must have felt, had delivered him from the hands of an implacable enemy. He lowered his head again, and his eyes glittered triumphantly out at Messenger through the dusky hedge of hair that dropped over his face.

"Are you ready, my young friend?" he asked.

"I am ready," Messenger said, alert as a violin string in tune.

"And so am I," said the other, and suddenly, passing a hand inside the belt that pinched his hips, he drew out not a big hunting knife but one with a slender blade. It might have been the blade of an Italian stiletto, needle sharp, and hardly more substantial, but it was certain to puncture brain or heart with the ease of a bullet, and to kill as surely.

Messenger, with an exclamation, sprang back. Horror and disbelief filled him. "Is that your good faith and your truth, Summer Day?" he exclaimed.

The latter, maneuvering to the side, had placed himself instantly between the white man and the weapons that the latter had just discarded. Now he grinned with hideous satisfaction.

"You still can run, white man," he said. "Fool! Young brainless fool! You still can run like a deer out of the forest and let the people in the green hills see you coming while the great Summer Day follows you, laughing, scorning such a child."

The face of the boy turned crimson. "I shall never do that," he said. "It is true that I have been a fool. I deserve to die for it."

"Die you surely will," said the medicine man. "Like a proud young horse, too proud to carry a master, but just proud enough to have its neck broken and to be eaten at a feast. Tough meat, but the Indians have strong teeth." He leaped suddenly forward as he spoke the last word. He had been in the very midst of a triumphant gesture that he broke off to jump in savagely, his lips stretched tightly back across his teeth.

The white boy, leaping aside and back, appeared to stumble. In any case, he had moved, it seemed, too slowly to avoid the knife thrust. But that sudden down sway of his whole body caused the knife to shoot harmlessly across his shoulder. Instantly he straightened. His movement was as swift as that of the dropping and rebounding hawk in the sky above them. With his right hand, he caught the knife arm of the medicine man at the elbow. Then, partially turning, with his left hand he gripped the knife wrist of the big fellow.

These actions, described in slow words, were performed almost simultaneously, like the deft fingering of a juggler who keeps half a dozen balls dancing and floating in the air, although what his hands do is a mystery to the beholder.

One would have said that Summer Day was standing like a statue to allow the other to do as he pleased. But, as a matter of fact, Messenger was moving with the speed of a leaping tiger, but Summer Day's arm was caught in a grip that ground the flesh against the bone. The tendons of his right wrist rolled and ground against the wrist bone, sending shooting, fiery pains along his arm. His fingers grew numb, and from them, as they loosened, the knife fell to the ground.

Messenger completed his maneuver by jerking the arm down over his shoulder and bending forward and down. Impelled by the weight of his own forward rush, the Blackfoot was lifted swiftly up and heaved in a great, clumsily flopping somersault through the air. He would have broken his neck if he had landed on his head. But twisting in midair, like a great cat, he landed on hands and knees. As he looked up, bewildered at what had happened, he saw that the white man stood smiling before him, with the little icicle of a knife glistening in his hand.

Chapter Sixteen

In the greatness of his despair, the medicine man gripped both his hands full of the turf. He had lost the battle, he saw. It seemed to him that a magic as great as any that he had seen practiced in an Indian camp had been used against him. But great as his own fame and reputation were, his love of life was still greater. He did what any sensible man would have done. He bounded to his feet, and, turning, he bolted for liberty in the direction of his horse. He had not taken half a dozen strides before he knew that he was lost when it came to a matter of speed. He threw a glance over his shoulder and saw the white lad coming like a flung stone behind him, gaining with a terrible ease. As he looked back, he saw the other smile and throw the borrowed knife away. A ghastly panic streamed like ice through the blood of the Blackfoot.

He could see that the picture that he had himself suggested was, indeed, a charming one in the eyes of the white man. Now Messenger would be contented with nothing but throttling him slowly, bit by bit, moment by moment, allowing him enough breath to linger out the hour of his dying.

But the battle pride of Summer Day was not yet exhausted. He had fought arm to arm and hand to hand against some of the greatest warriors of his day. In his boyhood, he had learned the complicated tricks of Indian wrestling until they were in his mind by rote, and still he had not forgotten. He was in the prime of his powers. His strength had hardened upon him. He told himself that, if the white lad had known one amazing trick, he could not know much more. He was too young to have mastered the mysteries of the whole craft. Besides, although Summer Day might run from a naked knife, he would not run from the empty hands of any man in the world.

Suddenly he flung himself to the ground. He skidded through the grass. His speed made it seem greased. But, digging in his heels and turning on his face, he checked the slide instantly and started to lurch up to his feet. It was a very skillful stopping trick. It was as though a vastly powerful brake had been applied to a weight that was not, after all, very great. Three times he had used this very same idea on the battlefield, and twice it had brought him scalps and coups that were the foundation of his fame as a warrior. It seemed to work now, for he actually succeeded in getting to his feet without being taken at a disadvantage by the younger man.

Then, throwing back the hair from his face by a backward jerking motion of his head, he saw that the boy stood three strides away, at ease, smiling. His hands were resting lightly on his hips. His head was high, and the first thing that the wary eye of the Indian noted was that these efforts had not made the breast of the youth begin to heave. For his own part, he was panting heavily, but the other seemed to have the wind of a well-trained greyhound.

"That was a bad fall, Summer Day," said Messenger. "Take a moment now to get your breath. Set your wits in order. You'll need them all."

Summer Day, glaring at him, could well believe what he had heard. All the cords of his right wrist were still burning, and shooting pains were still passing up his arm. Never had he felt such a grip as this that had been put upon him. But there was something in the religion of his fathers. There was something, too, in sheer weight and bulk in a hand-to-hand encounter. Besides, he was himself as cunning as a fox. So he struck his broad, painted breast with both hands, and his deep chest sounded like a drum.

"To you, spirits, my friends!" cried Summer Day, and went in to crush his foe. He did not go in blindly. He and War Lance were of an age. As children, they had been almost evenly matched at racing and at wrestling, although perhaps the spirit of the coming warrior was a little keener than that of the coming medicine man. Yet he had held his own very well, and he hardly doubted that he could do as well with this slight creature. A trick had been used upon him before, and he would beware of foolish, headlong charges.

He leaped forward, halted, and then, with a half step onward, he struck with all his might and a closed fist at the head of the other. The white man barely drew back. It was an inclination of the body rather than an actual step, and yet the fist of the Blackfoot missed, whizzing by a fraction of an inch away. Again, and yet again, the medicine man struck, following in, getting his weight well behind the punches. Still he merely labored against the thin air.

He was instantly aware that he was no match for the slender boy at this game of fisticuffs. He strove to dive straight in for a wrestling hold, and, as he did so, the poised right hand of the other dipped over and down, and a hammer stroke went home behind Summer Day's ear. There was no ponderous weight behind it, but the stroke was like that of sharply swung metal. It knocked a wave of crimson and of black through his brain and pitched him down on hands and knees. There, as his brain cleared, he found himself wavering and swaying helplessly. But he was in good condition; his mind cleared almost instantly; he lurched to his feet, looking wildly about him.

Messenger stood a little way off, and the cold, deadly smile was still on his lips. "Wait a little, Summer Day," he said. "There'll be no more dancing, now. You'll have your way with me, but first let your head clear, and get your breath again. You'll need it all before the end." As he finished, he flexed and unflexed his lean fingers, as though already they were tingling for the throat of the Indian.

Summer Day shook his head like a bull. "There was something in your hand. No hand is so like iron," he said. "But now you have exhausted all your tricks. Now I shall be the master, young man. You have fought well. But you have thrown away all your weapons, and now you are mine. The spirits give me the glory. I hear them speaking over my head. I laugh. Your scalp is already drying in the smoke of my teepee fire!"

He made his stature greater as he talked. He went forward with short steps, one hand raised. More than once, before this, he had overawed his red-skinned enemies by these direct appeals to the spirits.

But Messenger continued to smile. Then he walked straight up to Summer Day and held out one hand. "Here," he said. "You may have the first grip. You are like a child or a woman. You are only a soft mass, without any tendons strung in your puppy fat. Now do what you can, Summer Day."

No appeal to spirits could have the force of this calm contempt, this overbearing self-confidence. Summer Day looked up at the bright green of the trees, and it seemed to him that the blue of the sky above them was swirling before his eyes. He stared at the extended hand, suspecting some new trick. But what trick could there be? He stepped in close. Still the white man did not flinch. His breast struck the breast of Messenger. He was glaring down from his superior height into the eyes of the stranger, and those eyes, he thought, were as gray as iron, when strong new iron is fractured across and lies glittering in the sunshine.

A sudden shout of exultation burst, sharp and short, from the throat of Summer Day, like the bark of a dog, and he flung his arms around the comparatively frail body of Messenger. The strain of his might, he felt, could crush in ribs of steel, even if the white man were so provided. He felt the meager back of the youth under the grip of his hands. But though the body of Messenger gave, it would not break. And suddenly all was not well with the chief.

The extended arm of the white man had passed under the pit of Summer Day's left shoulder. Now that arm whipped up and over the shoulder, and the hand of the white lad gripped the Indian beneath and around the jaw. Like a bulldog's was that jaw of the medicine man. A trainer would have picked him for the prize ring on this specification alone. But once more the gripping hand of Messenger seemed to the chief like five constricting bands of iron—cold iron that shrinks and shrinks inexorably, crunching the flesh against the bone. He felt his cheeks ground in against his teeth. His own blood was flowing. At the same time, with the leverage of the hold across his shoulder, the head of Summer Day was being forced up and back. His left arm was locked close and helpless with the pressure. He raised the right like a club to beat in the skull of the enemy—and that poised right hand was caught by the wrist in the same dreadful clasp with which he had become familiar. The muscles were already bruised and sore, and

111

now the renewed pressure caused an exquisite agony. He could have shouted with the pain, but pain cannot find its way up the throat of an Indian brave to the lips.

With all his might, then, he strove to wrench the imprisoned hand free so that with its aid he might drag away the hand that held him by the jaw and was threatening to break his neck. He gnashed his teeth in his fury. His breath began to come with a wheeze, like the wind in a broken bellows. But nothing could avail him to force that grasp to relax.

Then, like a desperate creature, he hurled himself to the ground in order that his weight might crush the body of the smaller man. But, at the moment of impact, a snaky twist of Messenger twitched him away from the danger, and it was the Indian who fell undermost, bruising and half stunning himself.

For one instant he lay still, without struggling. He was striving to think, and his brain was failing him. Far away above him, he could see the same hawk that he had noted earlier sweep now into sight over the head of the very same bird that had been fleeing from it before. The pressure of the chase, no doubt, had made the fugitive circle. Now it was heading for the trees and their sheltering tangle of branches with a desperate speed. Still faster came the hawk above it. It turned over in the upper air. It gave several strong strokes of its wings, and then down it came, bullet-like. The quarry dodged, almost as alert on the wing as ever. But this time it was outguessed. The hawk struck. The feathers flew in a little cloud, almost like a puff of smoke, and then away sailed the tyrant of the air, with a limp form trailing down from its talons.

Was not he, Summer Day, in like manner to become a weak, helpless thing in those murdering hands of iron?

Chapter Seventeen

That, in the first half second, was what he saw. In the next, he was aware that by sheer physical might he could do nothing. So superb was the cunning of this trained wrestler, so magical were his arts, that the harder the Indian struggled, the more his own weight and might of hand and arm told against him. The more he struggled, the harder the grip bit against his jaw, the farther back his head was thrust.

A little more, and he knew what would happen. The right hand of the white man would shift down, in a lightning slip, to the soft, exposed throat of Summer Day, and that would be the beginning of a quick end. For then, as surely as a wolf's grip ever cut off life at the throat of a quarry, just so would the hand of Messenger cut off the life that flowed in the bull throat of the medicine man.

In the second half second, that was what Summer Day fully realized. If, then, no force of hand could beat off this frightful wild catamount of a creature that clung to him, what could he do? His mind wildly passed over the ground on which they were struggling. He remembered that, to the right, the ground ahead sloped off very sharply toward the brink of the bank that hung above the river, far beneath.

There was a roaring in his ears. Was it the sound of the blood struggling through his own arteries, or was it the voice of the river itself, calling to him? A desperate resolution came into the mind of the medicine man. He looked up in agony to the wide blue arch of the sky.

Sky People, he prayed in his mind, *give me strength to kill myself and take this white fiend with me to the same death!*

He heard the voice of Messenger hardly broken by panting, cool, cold, collected, saying: "Like a great soft bulk, without any force. Are you ashamed, Summer Day? Where is your strength? Where are the coups you have counted, and the coup stick that you have counted them on? Where is the last scalp you have taken? They are all gone, Summer Day. You will die and rot in shame. Your soul will dissolve with your unburied body. There will be no dead horse to carry your spirit away on the hunting grounds of the Sky People. You are dying, Summer Day. Now, remember the white man in the camp, and how his eyes watched you. Remember how he screamed, Summer Day. Are you screaming now yourself? Scream again, Summer Day! Scream again. Remember the white man, and the slow death."

For, as he listened to the calm, sure, cruel voice, the utter horror of his position, the maddening helplessness of his mighty body, made a mighty wild cry rise up through the teeth of the medicine man. That same horror gave him a new and sudden strength. It enabled him, floundering, to rise to his knees, and then to his feet. Still, the white tiger clung to him, and the grinding power of the hand beneath his chin forced his head back until he was looking sheer up at the zenith of the pale-blue sky.

The end was almost there. Aye, that moment it began, for the terrible grip of Messenger shifted that instant downward and closed into the cords and the knotted, straining muscles of the chief's throat. Blackness swirled before the eyes of the medicine man. Universal, whirling clouds took the place of the sky. In the greatness of his laboring, his lungs could not spare the fresh, vital air for a single second. He no longer could breathe, yet it seemed to him that he was breathing, and that what he drew down deep were living flames.

All sense of direction was gone from him, so that he could not tell in which direction he was walking. He made two or three steps. It seemed to him that the slope went up before him. He turned about and struggled back in the opposite direction, and, as he walked, he heard the dreadful, exultant laughter of the man who was taking his life. Then suddenly the ground pitched down before him, and more sharply, more sharply.

With all his might he hurled himself forward. The white man, snake-like as before, twitched his body aside from the fall, but the force of the toppling bodies and the angle of the slope made them roll over and over again. They gained momentum. They were spinning forward and down like a ball. Suddenly the frightful grips of the other relaxed, and Summer Day found himself whirling like a wheel down toward the giant voice of the river.

All things, as he dragged down the first life-giving breath, seemed to be mixed, like madness, before his eyes. The sky lay like blue water beneath him, and the trees danced like sparks in the sky overhead. Then his battered wits came back, and he found that he was tumbling toward the verge of the riverbank. It was the thing that he had planned, but he had expected to take the white destroyer with him. Both of them would go whirling over the edge and be dashed to death on the rocks and among the grinding currents of the stream. That hope was lost to him. Still, as he turned, he cast out his arms widely upon either side and one hand gripped a bush.

The power of his hand was such that the grip held, and

the bush held him. It was half uprooted by the first wrench of the halt. It left the body of the medicine man dangling over the edge of the precipice, with the white face of the water dazzling beneath him. When he strove to pull himself up, he could hear a telltale ripping sound, and knew that the last of the roots were breaking. So he swung between life and death like a bubble that must soon burst and be nothing more than a drop of rain.

Then, looking up, he saw Messenger running down toward him aslant on the slope, and with a face that reminded the Indian of the face of a hunting wolf. There was no mercy in it. There was only the most savage thirst for vengeance.

At the same moment, the final deepest root of the shrub gave way, snapping like pack thread. And Summer Day dropped down.

He had no hope, but he struggled for life with the instinct of a wild beast. White men can despair easily. The Indian will struggle even if he be in the middle of rapids, and death be surely before him. So Summer Day, even as he fell, looked wildly beneath him and was aware that it was not a sheer drop, but that the cliff shelved out a little just below him.

Then as he struck a patch of straggling brush that clung somehow to the face of the bank, he spread-eagled, and arms and legs served as friction makers to check the impetus of his fall. Rapidly his fall turned into a reasonably slow descent. He gripped a handful of little branches here. Leaves, dirt, and broken branches and whole shrubs, uprooted, showered down upon him. And next he plunged over his head into icy water.

Straightening, he found that there was no pull of the watery hands of the current against him. Instead, he was in almost quiet water that lay under the hollow shoulder of the bank.

There he stood, and, taking a great breath, before he stirred a step, he looked up at the narrow road through the sky that the ragged tops of the cañon walls fenced in across the heavens. To it he lifted his hands. If piety never had come to him before, it came to him now. With his great arms stiffly stretched above him and with his head thrown back, he uttered the first truly sincere prayer of his life. Hypocrisy and sham were stripped from him. He offered a naked soul of gratitude to his invisible maker. Then he looked about him for a means of completing his escape.

But he was calm. There seemed to be in the soul of the medicine man the divine assurance that he would not die on this day at the hands of the white man or the white water. Then he saw what was to him as good as a great broad boulevard—a six-inch ledge well above the top of the stream, a ledge chiseled there by the superior force of the higher water in the spring of the year when the mountain snows are melting the most rapidly. He was upon it at once and found, presently, that it broadened.

Still breathing hard, but every moment with a lighter step and with a more joyous heart, he went up this narrow path, and found that he was rounding the side of the hill on which he had fought with the white man. He must not break out into the open. For one thing, he would rather have walked into the living fire than to show himself with empty hands, beaten, and a fugitive before the white youngster. On the other hand, he dreaded more than the fire itself, or all the ridicule of his sharp-tongued fellow tribesmen, to face Messenger once more.

His throat still ached, and was bruised by the last grip. The blood still oozed inside his mouth, and his wrist ached and was swelling as though a bear trap had been closed over it.

There was no other man in the world like this. The Evil One himself lived in Messenger, surely, and the Evil One was to be avoided. Later, the Sky People would tell Summer Day what to do, but, just now, he must secure his life. What better than to hide in the very woods where he had fought the youngster? The latter was no cunning woodsman to find him out. How clumsily he had hidden, before, in the top of a tree, leaving himself helpless, with a telltale blue jay dancing about in the air to betray his hiding place. No, there in the woods the medicine man might hide himself and, afterward, perhaps work some fire miracle on the height, to restore the faith of his tribesmen.

So, with vague hopes before him, uncertain of mind, but desperately bent on keeping his life, Summer Day climbed the bank, found himself among the trees near the edge of the woods, and instantly began to slink up the slope. His mind steadied more and more. He felt that he had come to a turning of the ways in his life. It might very well be that this day would so shame him that he would be cast out from among the warriors of his tribe. He would be degraded and despised as a maker of magic, if he could not command enough miracles to protect his own life. And what of the coward who fled from the foe?

But, looking up toward the blue through the tops of the trees, he placed his blind trust with the greater powers, and went his way.

Chapter Eighteen

Walking or running, skulking softly from tree to tree, and from brush to brush, the medicine man kept his eye sharp and his ear keenly attuned to all that passed around him, for the very thought of the young white man was now to him colder and more depressing than the chilliest water in a January river. Death was a frightful thing, but the panic in the very bones of the Blackfoot would have made him leap another precipice to keep away from the hands of Messenger. Therefore, like a noiseless shadow he progressed, and dead leaves could hardly have been crushed under his cat-like step.

Twice and again he dropped to the ground, weak with fear and desperate, as he heard a faint whispering among the trees that, for a moment, seemed like the indrawn breath of a man about to make an effort, as for attack. Again there was a sudden swaying of the shadows as a wind, which was rising, touched and bent the trees of the wood.

The horror of his situation was chiefly in this—that once his terrible young enemy discovered him, he had not sufficient speed of foot to escape, and, once overtaken, he would quickly be destroyed by the craft and strength of Messenger.

This panic, rising in him, several times almost made him burst out from the rim of the trees and take refuge among the massed numbers of his tribesmen who were scattered there. But he did not follow the impulse. He went on, instinctively trusting in the dimmer light.

Now, through the branches of the trees, he could see the spectators on the outer hills, waiting. Sometimes they stirred, riding their horses back and forth. Many of them sat motionless in the saddle. The strengthening breeze fanned the manes and tails of the horses to the side. Weapons glittered—lances, and rifles balanced across saddle bows. It seemed to him that these restless creatures—who were his blood kinsmen, many of them—were like phantasms blown into the pages of a dream. Glimpsed briefly through the procession of the tree trunks, he seemed to see them for the first time, impermanent, unrooted, and changeable as clouds. But they were his people, his place of power, and the thought of losing that place tormented the very soul of the medicine man. What scorn they would heap on a coward and a fugitive.

Still, he was not prepared to die. Not the sort of a death that he must meet at the hands of the white lad. He told himself that he wanted a fighting chance, and no more, against a human being. This man was a ghost, and not a normal creature.

Such were the thoughts of the Blackfoot as he slipped along through the forest, and then suddenly came upon the sight of the pinto of the trapper, Henry Lessing.

The boy had ridden that horse. At the sight of the pony, the dazzled eyes of Summer Day conjured up the form of the boy, again, seated in the saddle. His heart stopped. Gooseflesh puckered his face and his brow. Then, his eyes clearing, he discovered that the white man was not there. What had become of him? For that matter, had he had time to come to this place from the site of the combat?

Another explanation, the true explanation, a moment

later jumped into the mind of the medicine man. Messenger, seeing him fall down the almost sheer face of the cliff, and looking to the roaring, white face of the water, would have taken it for granted that the stream had devoured his enemy. His first impulse, then, might very well be to go take possession of the horse and the arms of his foeman. And when he had found and mounted the little wild Indian pony, he would slowly ride around the edge of the wood, enjoying the plaudits of his friends, and greeted by the amazed and gloomy silence of all the disappointed Blackfeet.

No sooner had this thought come to Summer Day than he grew jubilant, and with reason. For he saw before him a clear path toward the reclamation of his name and fame. War Lance, who detested him, he knew, would not be able to exult on this day over the downfall of his hated rival for the leadership of the tribe. No, not if the slippery wits and wiles of Summer Day could help him to the great end that he saw.

He paused only to slick the water from his leggings with both his strong hands. Then he bounded into the saddle on the pinto. He unsheathed the long-barreled Winchester—a beautiful weapon and worthy of the hands of a chief. He gathered up the reins, and then delayed only an instant to re-plume the feathers in his hair, for they had stuck safe and fast in spite of the turmoil of the fighting. These preparations done, he whirled the pony about. He straightened himself in the saddle. He took in a great breath that threw out his chest. He gathered his spirits like an animal about to leap, and with a ringing war cry, a shout of exultation, he burst on the horse from the edge of the woods where the boy had left him and into the open light of the afternoon.

All before him, as he appeared, the long line of his

people greeted his appearance with a stunned silence, and then with an upgoing, jubilant yell. They swept forward. But he dashed straight on, heedless of their greeting, and, with the rifle held stiffly, straight above his head, he plunged through that line of would-be questioners, and raced on across the hills toward his own camp.

They streamed before him, those anxious, delighted braves. They yelled. They disturbed the air with the chorus of their shrill yippings. Fast as he went on this good horse, the young boys, light as hawks on the wing, darted and hovered and swayed before him, the hoofs of their rushing ponies casting up clots of the soft turf. So into the camp they came.

What was happening on the farther side of the hill where the battle had been fought, they could not tell. They only knew that their own shouts had drawn away toward them all of their tribesmen, and that these were streaming after them across the hills as fast as they could flog their mounts along.

Straight through the camp dashed the medicine man, until he came to his own teepee. There he dismounted.

The strong sun, and the wind of the gallop had dried his clothes almost entirely. The warmth of the fire within the tent and the heat of his own body would soon finish the job. So he threw the reins to his youngest wife—he had taken three squaws, being a man of great Indian wealth—and retired within the flap of the lodge.

They would leave him alone. No one would intrude rashly upon the chief medicine man of the tribe. For a few moments, he would be left entirely to himself. In the meantime, he made a little medicine. He burned some sweet grass and purified himself with the smoke. He picked up a handful of earth and blew the dust away from the few little pebbles it contained, and then threw these up into the air several times, letting them fall back upon the flat of his stiffly extended palm.

It was a very simple way of making medicine. But his oldest wife—a bull for strength and a calf for wisdom—watched him with the same frozen interest that she always showed when permitted to overlook one of the rites that he performed. Most of the pebbles bounced off his hand. There remained, finally, only seven.

"Seven," he said aloud in a deep and sepulchral tone. "Seven," he repeated, and enjoyed the shudder of awe that ran through the body of his wife.

She, poor soul, looked as though she would gladly have been in any other place.

"There are people at the entrance," he said. "If any of them are chiefs, or famous warriors, let them come in."

There were, in fact, four men worthy to fill this description. She knew them at a glance, for no newspaper reporter today knows the influential figures in the government of his city better than an Indian of the old days knew the celebrated men of his tribe. To those four she gestured, and they entered hastily.

There was no impatience shown by the rest of the auditors. They were well disciplined in the matter of giving way before the important men. So they remained in a well-closed semicircle, waiting patiently. The boys, the youngsters who were barely able to toddle, began to gather. There had been no event of note for some time. Now all ears were hungry to hear something extraordinary.

The four inside the teepee were being gratified and fed fat with marvels. The instant they had entered, they had smelled the scent of the sweet grass that prepared them at once for hearing strange things—obviously medicine had been made.

"We must move our camp," said the medicine man. "We must move at once. Go out and tell the women to begin rolling up the lodge skins. Load the horses! The spirits have called to me, and we must go at once. Seven days . . . seven days . . . seven days we must march into the west."

He closed his eyes. He swayed his head as he spoke. He assumed a look of pain, and still with extended arm he pointed toward the west. It made a good, solemn effect, such as he nearly always achieved, for he was one of those consummate actors made more perfect by half believing in their own inspiration.

"And the young white man?" said the medicine man, recovering from his brief trance and shrugging his shoulders. He made a gesture as though throwing something away. "The young white man! The young leaves of the forest, fallen and dead before their time. The young white man! What is he to me? What is he to Summer Day, or to you . . . who are real warriors? I was about to take his life while he begged for my mercy. I was about to take his life, when the spirits. . . ." He raised his head and his glance and seemed to forget his auditors, lost in his semi-divine contemplation.

"And then?" asked his oldest wife softly.

"As I was about to run the knife over his throat . . . for I held him by the hair of the head, and his throat was tight, like the throat of a young calf about to be slaughtered . . . just at that time, I heard the spirits calling to me strongly, and so loud that I thought even the poor white boy must be hearing the cry. They called. They had their thin, cold hands like winter wind upon my arms. They told me to spare the life of the white boy. They said that I must return at once to the lodge, and there make medicine, and ask them what I must do. What was the scalp of a white child compared with the command of the spirits? Instantly I threw him from me. He fell down in a heap on the ground and made weeping noises of joy."

Chapter Nineteen

Young Messenger had planned to do exactly as the Blackfoot surmised, but he had not hurried to put his plan into execution. He had looked over the edge of the cliff and seen the man, as he thought, fall to as sure a destruction as though he had been plunged from the height of a tower toward a pavement. He almost thought that, a moment later, he had seen the glimmering body of the Indian hurled among the teeth of the rocks, instantly drawn under and disappearing forever. And, for a time, he remained there on the lip of the ravine, meditating and half sad.

When we know that great moments have come, the greatness of them is apt to dull our minds, but for this instant he had been preparing almost so long as he could remember. His soft young body, when he was a child, had been schooled to endure cold, heat, pain of all kinds. His mind, too, had been tormented. He had dreaded the dark with an instinctive horror, and he had been forced to spend hours in utter blackness, with strange sounds approaching and receding. He had gone almost mad with these trials, and yet they were as nothing compared to others that were to come. Until at length he had begun to tell himself that nothing could really happen to him. All was a part of his mere schooling, and there was no reality in the world, so far as he was concerned, except that brute-faced creature that had been drawn in the blood of a tortured man. This was shown to him two or three times a year, and the death scene was carefully described again, until he knew it by heart. The words never varied, for they were conned by rote by one whose inflexible mind would not alter a syllable.

More than a pugilist for the ring championship, more than a runner for the great race, he had been trained for this battle. Now it was over, and the burden dropped from his mind. One cannot give up the habit of years all in a moment. The youth needed time to allow the truth to sink home, slowly. As a fatigued man lies in warm water while the ache departs from his muscle and delicious, drowsy comfort runs through body and mind, so now Messenger, sauntering back through the woods, smiled vaguely, looking straight before him. He was no intimate student of nature, but suddenly she was beautiful, and the wood upon the mountain was a terrestrial paradise more charming than Dante's meeting place with Beatrice.

His eyes, running quietly over the big, strong trunks, and following the more liquid running lines of the upper branches, were soothed and enchanted. It was a treasure of form, a thesaurus of exquisite images. These were the first trees he ever had truly looked upon since the days of his youngest boyhood, before the iron had entered his life, and before bitterness of labor gave the chief savor to every hour. In those early hardly remembered years, there had been a casual joy in mere living. Time had its own taste. Every morning's freshness was a separate and unstaled cup of joy. Every afternoon was full of the sleepy pleasure of the summer. These half-remembered thrills began to run through him now. They stirred in his pulses as sap stirs in spring through the body of a tree and causes it to flush with a sudden color. For so Messenger flushed.

He ran a hand across his face. It seemed to him that his

very features were altered. The texture of his skin was smoother, softer. A tension passed from his brain. He stood more freely, and the rigidity passed from him. He began to laugh suddenly, and the sound of that laughter, flowing, strange and free, under the trees of the wood, startled him, but not unpleasantly. All was beauty and all was friendliness in this world. His thought ran back to the figure of the old trapper, and hung there gently.

But there was goodness in all men, more or less. Only the Blackfoot, Summer Day, was the exception. No, hardly even that. For as he remembered the grim desperation in which the big man had struggled for life, and then if not for life, to destroy himself with his conqueror, admiration for the red man came up in the heart of the boy, and a certain unexpected pity.

He was in no haste. He even sat down for a time beneath the very tree in which he had lain along the branch, foolishly ambushing his enemy. The same blue jay fluttered above him, sailing back and forth across the clearing. Smiling up at the bird, he could understand now how it was that Summer Day had been able to detect him in his place of concealment. Nature, through the bird, had pointed a bright finger at him. Nature could do other things yet more marvelous, he had no doubt. Nature, from which his life had been abstracted, made penurious with labor, was now the treasure that he meant to unlock. The nature of man and bird, beast and tree.

He put out his hand and passed the fingers through the short, thick grass, reveling in the touch. He lifted his young head and sighed deeply with delight. Then he saw the revolver that he himself had cast away. It recalled him to the moment, and he stood up. Yonder, too, and close by, the broken blade of the Indian's knife glittered faintly among the blades of grass. With a sudden care for the next man or beast who might walk that way, he picked up the heavy sliver of steel and cast it from his palm, hard flung, into the trunk of the tree. There it stuck, quivering and humming wickedly, and the vibrating light at last steadied and grew still. It seemed to watch the boy with a glittering, wary eye.

He gathered up the revolver, then. He took up his own knife, which he had so foolishly discarded. He took up, as well, the little stabbing weapon with which the treacherous Blackfoot had delivered his second attack. Reflecting upon that, he remembered what the trapper had said about vice and virtue in an Indian. It was natural, was it not, that a red man should take as many advantages, through strength or through deceit, as a wildcat or a hawk in the air?

It was impossible for him to feel displeasure, or disgust, or scorn, at this moment. Finally, after he had done so many things, he was surprised to hear a loud shouting, and then a frantic yelling from the people who waited lower down on the mountainside, eager to get the first news of the battle. What could have set them shouting so fiercely? Or was it with joy that they yelled. He tried the same high-pitched notes, silently. He let them swell in his throat, un-uttered. It was joy and sheer excitement, he told himself, that made them yell so. Then what had happened? What had they seen?

He was in no haste to find out. When one feels that all the world is filled with doors that open only inward upon happiness, there is no need for a man to be in haste to make his choice. The happiest home makes the most casual wanderer.

It was some time after this that, making up his mind to start back, he decided that he would first of all pick up the pony that the unlucky Summer Day had ridden. Then, mounted upon this, he would round the side of the hill and get the trapper's pony. This he decided upon, and walked leisurely down the slope until he came to the outer verge of the trees, pressing through a dense thicket and out into the rather startling light of the open day. There he stood for a moment, warming himself, relishing the very strength of the rays that soaked like hot water through his clothes and comforted his flesh.

But he was surprised. He had thought that the whole wood was surrounded by observers. So it had been when he came in from the farther side. But now he could see not a single form upon the hills—only a few horsemen, in the distance, were making off toward the gate of the fort, and some of them were at this moment actually riding through into the enclosure behind the palisade. He was surprised, but he was not worried.

The old trapper surely would be somewhere near, no matter what had drawn off the rest. Yes, surely Henry Lessing would not be far to seek.

He was right. As he started to saunter along the edge of the trees, he met Lessing coming in the opposite direction, riding a borrowed mustang, and leading the Indian's shaggy pony behind him.

At the sight of the boy, he uttered an exclamation, and reined in his horse. It was an odd greeting, for he stared at young Messenger with a sort of horror that was almost like fear.

"What's the matter?" asked the boy. "You see that I'm out of it, safely enough?"

"Aye," said the trapper bluntly. "I see that you are out of it, right enough." There was no pleasure in his tone.

A bluff old fellow, the boy thought to himself. *He won't show how glad he is that I'm the winner, but he's tickled pink, inside.*

He sprang onto the back of the Indian pony that was led behind. The seat was very uncomfortable, for the stirrups were so short that, to be at ease in them, he would either have to ride high up, just like a racing jockey, or else sit awkwardly back on his spine.

"This is a silly rig, eh?" he suggested to the trapper.

Lessing made no reply. He was turning back toward the fort, slowly reining his horse like a man in the deepest thought.

"I'm going around this side to pick up your horse, Lessing," said the boy.

Lessing started and looked hastily around. There was both amazement and scorn in his face. "What horse?" he asked shortly.

"Why, the pinto that you lent me, of course," said the youngster.

"The pinto that I lent you?" repeated Lessing. "You didn't know that Summer Day rode that one off to his camp?"

"Rode it off! Summer Day will never ride a horse again," said young Messenger.

"He won't? Was it his ghost, then? Or whatcha think happened to the Blackfoot?" Eagerness and more kindliness appeared in the eyes of Lessing.

"He's down yonder in the teeth of those rocks," Messenger said, pointing toward the direction in which the angry dispute of the river roared after them.

"Boy, boy!" exclaimed Lessing with an angry impatience. "Didn't I see him, and with my own eyes, riding off yonder on my hoss? Didn't I hear with my own ears what the Injuns say is his story of the fight?"

Messenger drew the shaggy pony to a halt. "What's his story of the fight?" he asked.

"That he got you down. That you begged for your life. That he promised to let you wear your scalp, and even that he wouldn't shame you, out of pitying such a young kid that had dared to fight him. And that he said he would let it go that you and him had changed weapons and horses, like friends, and that then he turned you loose. And. . . ." He halted.

For Messenger was laughing freely, easily, cheerfully in the sun, his very eyes closed with mirth.

Chapter Twenty

"He got away, after all," said the boy. "Summer Day managed to get down that bank and through the water? Well, if you saw him, of course, it's possible, and he managed to do it. But it's pretty hard to believe, all the same."

"I suppose maybe it is," Lessing affirmed, dark of face.

"Summer Day is still alive, and the job to do all over again!" exclaimed Messenger. "Well, there's no hurry. I've had a taste of that business, and it'll never be hard to finish, of course. But wherever he went, I'll wager that he went fast."

This made Lessing stare with a wider eye than ever. He remembered the flash of the warrior like a thunderbolt flying across the hills. "Aye," he said. "He went fast enough. He went as fast as that hoss could carry him."

The boy nodded. "He won't stop," he said. "He'll keep right on going. He'll keep right on traveling for a considerable time, I suppose."

This time, the trapper actually gaped. "As a matter of fact," he said, "they've struck camp and moved on . . . that whole section of the tribe. The same spirits that told the old liar not to cut your throat, they told him to move the tribe along."

"Ah, did they? They'll keep moving, too, for a time, if he has his way," said the boy, and he chuckled. The kindness left his face, and a sort of careless cruelty came there, instead. In his voice, there was a purr like the contented sound that a great cat makes by a fire.

"What it sounds like to me," said the trapper, "is that you never was put down by the Injun, after all . . . that he never had a chance to cut your throat at all."

"He missed his stroke, the sneaking cur," the boy said cheerfully. "He's not a fighting man, Lessing. He's a bungler. You could count ten, almost, every time he made a move. He seemed to think that he might hurt me, and he let me know beforehand what he was going to do. He signaled with his eyes, or with his shoulders, or with his hands. You could read his mind half a second ahead."

He laughed again at the memory, and the rich sound of that mirth made the trapper blink. This was not the voice of the lad that had gone up there into the woods to fight for his life.

"Son," Lessing said, "suppose you tell me every blessed thing that happened between you and that Injun?"

The boy told him, not in haste, but slowly. He dwelt upon the incidents, often laughing, until he came to the point in which he described the throttling of the big red man.

The trapper, during that recital, stroked his throat once or twice. But then he shook his head.

"Tell me," said the boy curiously. "Don't you believe what I've said?"

Lessing shook his head again. "I believe you," he said.

"You don't," persisted Messenger. "Do you want me to show you the broken blade of his knife, where I stuck it into the tree? Do you want me to show you the place where he slid down the bank, tearing the brush out as he grabbed at it?"

"Son," said Lessing, "I believe every word that you've

told me. It's hard to believe, I grant you. But I believe. Like gospel. And now I'm gonna give you some good advice."

"I'm ready to hear anything you have to say, Lessing."

"Then listen to this . . . never tell this yarn to another man in the world."

"They wouldn't believe, you mean?"

"They'd never believe."

"Well, I'll have to jog along after that tribe, I suppose. I'm no trailer, but I suppose that they'll not be hard to follow . . . if there are enough of them."

"You can't do that. Meeting them down here by the fort is one thing. If Summer Day has anything that he fears about you . . . and, by your yarn he has aplenty . . . the minute you heave in sight, he'll pass a word to the young bucks, and they'll come out in a swarm and sting you to death!"

Messenger squinted his eyes, considered. Nothing disturbed him now. He was at ease. Nothing could excite him.

"That sounds like a good prophecy," he admitted. "I'll have to take my time about finishing him off. And it won't be hard. If ever I get close to him, he'll turn to pulp, Lessing. He ate some of his own sauce today." He laughed again, with that little purr in the voice that had troubled the trapper before this.

"What are you going to do, son?" he asked.

"They'll think that I'm a coward, if I go back to the fort?" said the boy.

"They'll think just that, and they'll think it hard."

"I might take them up here and show them the knife and the place where he fell down the bank."

"They'd say that you broke the knife after the fight, and that you just rolled the stone over the edge of the bank."

135

"Would they say that?" inquired the boy without heat.

"They'd certainly say that!"

"Tell me why?"

"Didn't you stay more'n an hour in the woods, after the fight was all over?"

"What of that?"

Lessing struck his hands together impatiently. "You beat all!" he exclaimed. "Would a gent that had just finished off a job like Summer Day idle around, or would he come out and take some applause and cheerin'? What would be likely?"

"Ah, I understand," said the boy, musing.

"And what did make you stay in there? You didn't have no wound to tie up. Was you lookin' at the trees and pettin' the grass?"

"Yes," said the boy. "How did you guess it?"

The scowl of the trapper blackened, for he thought, at first, that this was a poor jest. But then suddenly he understood that the boy meant what he had said.

"You stayed there to enjoy life, sort of?" he asked more gently.

"That's what I did."

"Well," said Lessing, "I'm tryin' to understand, but you're a mite harder for me than long division ever was when I was a kid in the winter school. You're a good mite harder for me, young son. Heaven gimme the good sense to be able to foller you along. That's what I pray for, but I could swear that there ain't another man in the fort or anywheres around here that ever would foller the trail that you think along. D'you believe that?"

Young Messenger looked gently on his friend. "Do you mean," he asked, "that I appear to be different from other people?"

136

Lessing cleared his throat. "What d'you think yourself?" he asked.

"I've had the very same idea," replied the boy. "A little different before, but, after today, I'm going to be the same."

"And what's your first step?"

"Oh, I'm going back to the fort."

"Are you?"

"Yes."

"There might be trouble."

"What sort of trouble?"

"We got a bad breed of men around there. Men ready with their hands as dogs are with their teeth. They think that you showed yaller to the Injun, and some of 'em are likely to make free with you."

"Let them take all that they can get," said the boy, and chuckled again. With that, he loosed the reins a little, and then turned the pony toward the fort.

But, whether it was that the horse did not like the way in which the white man sat the saddle, or because he scented the trail over which the Indian had galloped around the side of the hill, he refused to budge along the proposed route, and, when the boy urged him, the shaggy brute fought like mad. He seemed about to put off his rider, until the boy un-shipped his feet from the stirrups, and then he gave that wild bit of horseflesh a dressing down with whip and heel that made the eyes of the trapper start in his head. In two minutes the little affair was over.

Curiously Lessing looked at the boy, who sat erect in the saddle, the new laughter ever welling from his throat.

"A good, fat-footed, tricky dodger," said Messenger. "His old boss should have learned something from the tricks of this little rat."

Again he started on, the trapper following him in haste

until he could put his hand upon that of the boy.

"Messenger," he said, "don't go ahead."

"Where? To the fort?"

"Yes. That's what I mean. Don't you go to that fort."

"Where should I go, then?" Messenger was amazed.

"Any place but there."

"Because I'm to be afraid of the half-breeds . . . and the whites there . . . or is it the Indians, Lessing?"

"All of 'em, and something more. You think that you're like other folks now."

"Ah, but I am, Lessing."

"You're not. You're a whole wide mile from bein' like other men, and there ain't nothin' but fire gonna be knocked out of rock when you meet up with them."

"What sort of fire, man?"

"Why, cut-throats, and bullets through the brain, and that sort of thing."

"Ah, I'd never hurt anybody, man. There's no harm in me . . . if they leave me alone."

Suddenly Lessing was shouting, the veins swelling in his forehead. "Don't you see it?" he cried. "They'll think that you're just an ordinary dog, now, and that they're the wild wolves! Nothin' in the world could ever keep them from tryin' to put teeth into you. Nothin' in the world!"

"Ah, well," reflected the boy, "that'll soon be over. But I'll never strike back too hard, Lessing. I'll promise you that." He laid an affectionate hand upon the shoulder of the older man. "Ah, Lessing, Lessing," he said, "they're such great, helpless babies, these other men. They're so soft, so slow, so blundering, so clumsy. They're like calves just learning to walk. How do you think that I could find the heart to really injure any of them?"

Chapter Twenty-One

Having gone out to battle almost an assured hero, Messenger came back a presumptive coward. After his dealings with the two Indians in the fort, there was not a man within the palisade who would have matched himself against this young man of mystery. When he returned from the battle on the hill, there was hardly one who did not feel that, in some way, Messenger was beneath his contempt. He had been apparently guilty of the greatest sin, the one unforgivable failing. Nature had undoubtedly endowed him with great gifts that had been perfected by scientific training. All the more shame then, that he had failed in a crisis and begged his life from an Indian brave. For the story of the medicine man was everywhere believed.

Red men have their faults, but in one thing they are almost religiously believed—and that is when they recount the tale of their battles. They are apt to throw in a bit about the spirits who assist them, but the narrative of facts as they happened is rarely altered from the truth. Too much depends upon this truth. When the coup stick is passed around at the feast and the warriors are invited to enumerate their deeds, the man who tells a single real falsehood has damaged every other man in the tribe. If he claims six coups instead of five, which actually belong to him, all the true holders of six coups are injured by his rivalry, and the honest possessors of five are falsely eclipsed. Therefore, all ears attend to the warrior who talks. Embroidery is delighted in and appreciated. But a falsehood, once detected, makes the liar worse than a woman in the tribe from that time henceforward. His wives scorn to stay in the teepee of such a creature. His friends desert him. He is included in no war party. He dares not rise to speak in the council. The small boys laugh in his face when he walks through the lanes of the village.

For these reasons, an Indian's battle word could be trusted scrupulously and there was only one man in the fort who doubted the story of the medicine man, and that was Henry Lessing. Even he would hardly believe what the boy had told him. An instinct, merely, assured him that it would be harder for Messenger to lie than for an Indian.

But Messenger, coming back to the fort, found all eyes cold and hostile, and walked, surrounded by sneers. He paid no heed to them. The faces of other men had not been the books that he had read. His studies had been of another nature, and, therefore, he went serenely on his way. The mere neighborhood of other people was to him a pleasant thing. The new idea possessed him. It made little difference that he had failed to kill the red man. At least, he had demonstrated his measureless superiority, and the finishing of the work that must be done was not worth consideration. So, at all events, he felt.

He went up to the store with his friend, Lessing. The whiskey stall was always open. The rest of the store was only unlocked in the mornings, when the trafficking was done. But as for whiskey, that was another matter. Rare profits flowed into the coffers of the trader from the sale of the liquor at all times of day and the night. When the sun set, only the Indians were forced to leave the fort, the gate was locked, and only the whites and a few half-breeds remained. Money bought the liquid poison then, or fine furs, usually taken off the person. Desparr was scrupulously honest during the day, never cheating more than his good wits allowed him to do. But outside of office hours, as it were, at the whiskey counter he took in what he could. He traded whiskey for anything from beaded moccasins to good new rifles. His profits here ranged anywhere from a 100 to 1,000 percent above his daylight trafficking.

Beside the counter, over which the whiskey was ladled into small cups, there was a little room usually lighted with two lanterns that were fed with the oil of fat. The light they cast was dim, the smell of the burning was far from pleasant, and the air was always wreathed with the pale-blue drifts of smoke from long pipes. But there was enough illumination to show the spots on cards, and here the gambling went on. Sometimes a blanket was unfolded on top of a table or, better still, on the floor, and dice were rolled. But usually cards were the game. Men came in here with three years' value in furs and went out after a single morning with their pockets empty. It hardly mattered. Life lasted forever—unless a bullet stopped it—and hands that had been filled out of the treasures of the wilderness would very soon be replenished.

There was never a bigger crowd for whiskey than on the evening after the fight, for three boats and seven white men, all in a party, to say nothing of four or five half-breeds and a great, hulking Negro, had come up to the fort. The supplies that they brought fairly gorged the magazine of the place. And the heart of Louis Desparr waxed big and warm with hope.

Money was current, now. It was fairly in the air. Louis told his wife, who served the liquor across the counter, to make the drinks of whiskey big—the cups should fairly brim with the stuff. Sometimes he even thought that white traders should be given the whiskey free, because it made them adopt so liberal a policy that often what they had earned during a three or four months' journey returned to him, via the whiskey route, before the next morning. He hoped that the money would soon be in the air on this occasion. Louis was not an evil man, but his great sense of thrift amounted to greed. If he had lived forty years later, he would have been rich enough to build railroads.

When young Messenger saw the swirl of people going into the saloon, for that was what it really was, although not in name, he insisted that the trapper should go in with him. He wanted to buy a drink, and, at the same time, he wanted to pay Lessing for his horse that the Indian had stolen.

"I'll take that hoss he left with you, son," said the other.

"He's a ragged rat, you wouldn't want him," insisted Messenger.

The trapper merely laughed. "D'you know who the medicine man is?" he asked.

"I suppose I do."

"If a slick-lookin' hoss would've served him better, he would've had a slick one. But he knows what he's after. That rough rat will probably carry twice as much weight twice as far and twice as fast as my pinto. I won't lose by the trade, if you want to make it."

"But there's a rifle and other things in the saddlebags."

"Nothin' worth talkin' about. No, sir, if I get Summer Day's pet war hoss, I'll be satisfied, all right."

"Then come in and have a drink, anyway."

"Look here, son. How much of this trade whiskey have you drunk?"

"I've never drunk a drop of anything in all my days."

"Never a taste?"

142

"Never a taste. I've been training for today all my life, and now that today's over, I'm going to celebrate the way other people do."

The trapper merely chuckled. "You come and have that taste, then," he said. "I reckon that you won't want more'n one."

So young Messenger went into the whiskey shop with his friend.

They stood at the counter at the side of the game room, and the intent faces of the gamesters and the tang of the tobacco smoke seemed all foolish signs to the boy. However, he was intent upon learning. There were ways in which the rest of the world enjoyed itself, and he was going to try them out.

Mrs. Desparr ladled out the whiskey cups. She recognized her husband's friend with a broad grin. She greeted the boy with a still more patent scowl. But orders were orders, when they came from Louis Desparr, and, therefore, she filled the cups to brimming.

The drinkers faced one another.

"Here's to you, son," said the trapper, grinning over the edge of the cup.

"I say the same," the boy said, smiling in the new way that had come to him. "Here's to you, Lessing. You've been a friend to me. And I've never had a friend before."

"Hold on," said Lessing, lowering the cup. "Not even a playmate?"

"Playmate? I've never played a game in my life," said the other, shrugging his shoulders. "Except boxing. And it wasn't a game, the way I had to box."

Lessing stared. "Then . . . here she goes down," he said.

And they drank.

Lessing, slowly replacing his cup on the counter, began

to grin. For the boy had gripped the edge of the big board and hung there, making odd faces. First, fire had run down his throat and still was burning fiercely in the pit of his body. Then nausea struck his stomach and his brain with a double blow as he got the full, awful taste of the stuff. But, after that, as his mind spun into a thin, colorful mist, a hot feeling of careless joy followed.

He was amazed. He looked up from the counter and began to laugh. "Take another one. I want to buy it," said the boy.

"I'll take no more. You come outside with me and get some fresh air into you," advised the trapper.

"Go outside? I'm only beginning inside," answered the youngster.

"You might as well jump off a cliff as to drink any more of that stuff," stated Lessing. "Why, the hardest of them go down after a few shots of it. It takes getting used to. Honest whiskey ain't like this stuff. You come along with me, before you get sick."

"I'll stay here," Messenger said with a sudden and gloomy stubbornness. "I'm going to stay here and have another one."

"Don't do it," pleaded Lessing.

"I'm going to," insisted young Messenger. "Will you stay with me?"

Lessing hesitated. He knew what whiskey, such as was served at that post, will do to unaccustomed brain, but he decided that there might be a better way of meeting the problem, and that would be to persuade his friend Desparr to close up the counter for that evening, before trouble started. So he went off to find the trader, and young Messenger went back inside the shop.

He found a chair in a corner and sat down. The taste in

his mouth was horribly unpleasant, but a giddy sense of happiness had mounted to his brain. When he looked around upon the gamblers, a greater and a greater content possessed him. They were his people, and all these years he had not known them. Good fellowship shone in the their faces. Honesty and strength was theirs. Affection for them welled up in the heart of Messenger, and tears stung his eyes.

Chapter Twenty-Two

The young man had another drink, and the mighty slug of hard liquor and adulterants smote his brain like a hammer on an anvil. His head swayed a little; things began to waver before his eyes.

I'm weak, he said to himself. *I'm strong in other things, but in this, I'm weak. Practice is the only thing that will teach me.* And he took another.

He was barely back in his chair, after this potation, when another delegation of three came into the room. Two of them found stools. The third was left without one.

He was one of those big fellows all of whose muscles seem hardly enough to manipulate their great frame of bone. His name was Buck Chandler. He was hardly twenty-five, and already had left behind him, scattered in various parts of the mountains and the plains, three squaw wives and the beginnings of three families. He had traded, trapped, hunted buffalo, hunted men on the trail, and committed enough crimes to send a half a dozen men to the hangman's rope. Yet, out there on the rim of civilization, people were often glad to have Buck Chandler about. He united the cunning of an Indian with the patience of a white man. He was as strong as a mule and as enduring. If a battle came the way of the party that he had joined, they could count on him as upon four ordinary fighters. With his bared fist, it was said that he had killed a man in Kansas, cracking the other's skull as though it had been a nutshell. It was Buck Chandler who now found himself without a place to sit down, and he looked around the room with his bright little animal eye ready to make trouble. For trouble he loved. He enjoyed fighting as other men enjoy eating and drinking. He had a dog-like satisfaction in laying his hands on the weaker flesh of other men.

Resting his elbows on the edge of the counter and balancing his cup of whiskey in the palm of his hand, he faced the little crowd, staring from face to face through the smoke. Almost with the first glance, he spotted the tenderfoot in the gray woolen clothes and with the pale face that could not have been long upon the frontier. A muttered question over his shoulder brought from Mrs. Louis Desparr a rapid account of the recent battle between the white boy and the Indian medicine man—the account that the great Summer Day had himself spread.

Buck Chandler finished his drink, grunted, and strode straight across the room to the place where the boy was sitting, smiling vacantly into the smoky air.

"How come you sit when there's a man standing?" asked Chandler.

The boy started to answer, but his tongue was oddly thick, and the words came to his lips in a mere faltering stammer.

"Get up and get quick!" said Chandler, and he reached his hand for the collar of young Messenger.

The latter laughed, and gripped at the extended arm. He should have been able to seize it, just as it was in motion, at the wrist and at the elbow. A moment later, Mr. Chandler would have been upon his back on the floor—or nursing a broken arm! But the hands of Messenger refused to obey his will. He saw what he wanted to do. He knew exactly how to do it, but a singular lethargy possessed his nerves and his muscles. His hand should have jumped faster than the striking paw of a cat—which is faster, by a good deal, than the stroke of a snake. Instead, he made merely a feeble, pawing gesture.

Buck Chandler, the next instant, had him by the collar of his coat and flung him flat on the floor.

Fumes like the fumes of a green fire poured through the brain of Messenger. He lay sprawling for a moment, then picked himself up slowly to his hands and knees. He wanted to bound to his feet and whirl and dart in at this newly found enemy. Instead, he could only drag himself up slowly, and, when he turned, he found that Chandler was waiting, his feet spread, a brutal grin of pleasure upon his lips. Messenger struck straight out. That good left hand of his, carefully educated for so many years, should have found its mark on the edge of Chandler's jaw. But it was no longer a good hand. It was feeble, slow, and useless. Buck Chandler brushed it aside with contempt and smote Messenger fairly between the eyes. The force of the stroke knocked Messenger's head back as though his neck were a loose bit of rope, and he flopped heavily, inertly, upon the packed dirt floor of the shack.

"You've knocked him silly, Buck," said someone.

"Yeah, he's knocked silly. But he was silly before he was knocked," suggested another.

A hard-faced trapper broke in: "We'd oughta bring him around. We'd oughta give him some air. Maybe a coupla throws in a blanket would help him a pile to come to."

They jumped at the idea. Games were instantly abandoned. Someone produced a buffalo robe, and Messenger, just beginning to stir feebly, was dragged outside and thrown into the robe. Half a dozen strong pairs of hands grasped the edges of the blankets, and, as the men leaned back and the robe came suddenly taut with a popping sound, Messenger was flung high into the air. His loose body revolved there, head over heels, and he descended again on his head with a force that well nigh broke his neck. The blanket yielded under the impact, was instantly jerked tight again, and up went Messenger, higher still, spinning still more rapidly. He began to recover his wits, but, half stunned as he was, amazed, not knowing what was happening, a wild yell of fear, of distress, broke suddenly from his lips.

It was answered by a demoniac chorus from below. To torment a victim was a delight, but to wring from the unlucky man such a cry was more than could be hoped. Tugging and jerking at the blanket in unison, they kept Messenger helplessly in the air. Once he landed on his feet and managed to keep them long enough to make one step toward the edge of the blanket, but up he went in the air again, with a pop and a cheer from the others.

People gathered to watch, laughing and shouting, until old Henry Lessing came up. He laughed in his turn, until he made out who the victim was. There was not much light to see by—only the mountain rays that struggled out through the door of the saloon—but finally he distinguished the tenderfoot by the color and cut of his clothes. At once he interfered, and at the sharp sound of his commanding voice, two of the torturers suddenly dropped the edge they were holding and stepped back.

Messenger, landing headfirst in the robe again, slid down the sharp slant that this gave to the surface and rolled and tumbled head over heels upon the hard ground. There he lay still, utterly unconscious, while Buck Chandler approached Lessing with a snarl.

"Who are you?" he said. "Who made you the judge and the jury to tell us what we're gonna do to a sneakin', lyin', cowardly tenderfoot that we don't want around Fort Lippewan?"

Lessing was not perturbed by the youth or the strength or the well-known reputation of the bully. He looked steadily back into the eyes of the young giant and answered: "I'm Hank Lessing. I oughta have twenty-five, thirty years more experience and sense than you have, Chandler, and I reckon that I have."

Chandler laughed loudly. "You're an old loon," he said, "and I'm here to tell you about it."

"Words," said Lessing, "don't hurt me. No words that you can say will make a fool out of me, young man."

It looked, for a moment, as though Chandler would strike the trapper, but he changed his mind at the last moment. The difference in their size was too pronounced, and, besides, those dry, hardy old frontiersmen like Lessing were sometimes amazingly agile and fast with their pistol hands. So Chandler went back into the saloon, still snarling over his shoulder, but attempting no further violence.

The thing he had done to young Messenger was not criticized. It was merely applauded. There had been twenty pair of hands aching to put Messenger in his place, but certain memories of what he had done that morning to the two young Indian braves had held them back. Now he had been bludgeoned to the ground, and the onlookers were glad of it. By tomorrow, they would make the fort so hot for him that he would be sure to start back for the civilization that might possibly serve to hide him and his shame. That was the universal feeling.

Only Henry Lessing remained out there in the dewy coolness of the evening and watched over the boy until

Messenger opened his eyes and, groaning faintly, sat up. He raised a hand to his forehead. It was blurred and sticky with the red that had run down from the cracked skin.

Lessing, in the meantime, helped him to his feet and took him straight off to his own room in the fort. It was just beside the ones used by Desparr and his squaw, and Desparr himself came in for a moment to look at the half-conscious boy and the trapper's care of him.

"He's got only what's comin' to him," said Desparr. "A sneakin' young skunk and coward, we don't want him around here, and you're a fool to waste your time over him, I tell you, Hank."

Lessing looked sharply up over his shoulder—for at the moment he was kneeling beside the form he had stretched out on the bunk. "Louis," he said, "if I were you, I'd sashay right out of this room before the things you say might be understood by somebody."

"You think maybe that he'd throw a scare into me, Henry?" asked the trader.

"Louis," replied the trapper, "the fact is that he licked the hide off of that lyin' red Injun. You won't believe that he did, but I've told you the fact. Now, get out of here before he comes around and spots you in his mind. He's got a memory. Some of the boys here in the fort, they're gonna find out what he can do."

Louis Desparr came over beside the bunk, and, looking down at the still bleeding face of the boy, he grinned broadly. "He got enough," he said. "I heard him holler, clear up here. He had the wits pretty near scared out of him. A drunk, too. Yeah, you've picked up a fine, big, clean-hearted boy, all right."

But Lessing paid no heed to him, beyond giving him one more warning glance.

There was nothing in that glance that would have stirred Desparr, however. But Messenger groaning again in his torpor, made a flashing movement of his hand. Instantly a knife glittered in it. The fingers of the hand relaxed at once and the knife fell with a clatter to the floor, but the speed of the movement, the deadly nature of the weapon, and the fact that it had been drawn when the man was only half conscious, made Desparr gape.

He turned upon his heel and left the room at once.

Chapter Twenty-Three

It was a night that Lessing was never to forget.

Another half hour passed before he discovered that the eyes of the boy were open and that he was staring straight above him at the ceiling of the room.

"How does it come, my lad?" asked the trapper.

Slowly Messenger turned his head, and the look in his eyes made Lessing wince. In place of answering with words, the boy extended his hand, gave that of Lessing a long grip, and then returned to his staring at the ceiling.

The trapper did not speak for some time. But he could see the breathing of Messenger increase rapidly in speed. The face of the lad turned crimson, and then white. The last fumes of the whiskey were gone from his brain, but he was left in a mental torture that caused his nostrils to quiver and his hands to grip into fists.

"Lie easy," Lessing advised at last. "Lie easy and don't you worry none."

A slight, impatient movement of the hand answered him.

"Try to sleep," said Lessing.

The boy nodded. "Yes," he said. "I have to sleep. I must be fit in the morning. . . ." He raised himself upon one arm and looked about him. "This is the only bed you have, Lessing," he observed.

"I could make myself comfortable for a night on a chunk of rock," Lessing assured him, with truth enough.

But young Messenger stood up. "If you'll spare me one blanket. . . ."

"Aye, half a dozen, if you want 'em. But stay there on that bunk and get your sleep."

"I've slept on hard floors as long as I can remember," answered Messenger, and, coiling the blanket around him with a single flip of his hand, he lay down near the wall, opposite the bunk, and closed his eyes.

In ten seconds, while Lessing was still protesting, he could tell by the regular rise and fall of the youngster's breast that he was either sleeping or expertly shamming sleep. But he guessed the former to be the case, and this amazed him a great deal more than anything he had yet seen the boy do or heard of him performing. To have throttled that huge fellow, Summer Day, was really as nothing compared with this feat. One moment, Messenger had been lying on the bunk, writhing with a fiercely controlled shame and hate; the next, he had composed himself on the floor and was soundly asleep. With incredible power of will, he had banished all thought from his mind, composed his body, relaxed every nerve, and now he slept like a baby, with an unperturbed face!

He would not sleep long, Lessing could guess as he watched the inert figure. Anyone who could relax as perfectly as this was sure to get his completed repose in half the time that normal humans require. Lessing, walking up and down the floor and even stamping upon it, made sure that young Messenger was utterly unconscious. When he was confident of this, he went into the adjoining room to speak with his host, and found Louis Desparr sitting beside the fireplace. For the night had turned cold, and in the chinks of the wall was the whine of a rising wind.

Mrs. Louis Desparr, despising chairs, was squatted in a

corner of the room on a folded robe and doing beadwork on a deerskin shirt with incredibly rapid hands. Her fingers seemed far too big, but the little needle glanced and flashed like a machine, so rapidly she worked on the beads. The pattern grew quite sensibly, flowing slowly but steadily out from beneath her hands.

When she saw the white man enter, she rose at once. She placed a chair for him and stood behind it like a well-trained servant, looking from Lessing's face to that of her lord for instructions.

Lessing waved her away. "I'm not sitting there," he said. And to Desparr: "Louis, there's gonna be an explosion around this here fort, and the time of it will be somewhere about the middle of the morning, when there's a crowd to see the damage done."

Desparr looked steadily at him, his eyes glassy with weariness and with content. His thought only half followed the words of his trapper friend, for he was now looking rather dreamily into the future.

This had been a great day in his life. The arrival of the new stock, the presence of half a dozen well-known hunters and traders, and the fact that more than half the Blackfeet, including the famous War Lance, remained to trade in spite of the sudden departure of the medicine man of the tribe—all these things convinced Louis Desparr that the days of profit-taking had arrived. He was looking at the future and even around the corner of the future, for he was deciding that he would leave the wilderness in another half dozen years, put his business into trusty hands—like those of this very Henry Lessing—and, retiring to the settlements, he would pick up a wife and raise a family. It was late for such a career to open, but better late than never. An old husband makes a wise father, very often. Besides, he would live a long time. He felt in his very bones the sense of longevity, like a comfortable warmth. For these many reasons, he now paid little heed to the words of his friend, but sucked at the stem of his pipe and blew a long whiff toward the fire.

"We get our crowds pretty early, after the store opens," he observed.

"Then the explosion may come early," Lessing said, and pointed toward the next room.

"You still got that blasted kid on your mind?" demanded the trader in open anger.

"Oh, Louis," said the trapper, "you act like one that won't believe he's been blowed up till he falls out of the air, again, and gets his fool neck broke. I've warned you about three times. I ain't gonna waste no more words on you!"

At this, Desparr roused himself a little.

His wife, alarmed by the tone of Lessing, was looking anxiously from one man to the other, striving to make out the meaning of these words in the unknown white man's tongue.

"What d'you want me to do?" Desparr asked. "Throw him out of the fort and lock the gates on him?"

"It wouldn't do any good," said the trapper.

"What wouldn't do any good? Locking him outside the gates? Those gates would keep out the whole Blackfeet tribe, I wancha to know, Hank!"

"They'd keep out a tribe, but they won't keep out one Messenger. He'll either climb over or he'll burrow under. Or else he'll pull up the poles and walk in through a gate of his own makin'."

Desparr snorted, and his contempt was real. "Let him go and try it. But if you don't want us to throw him outside, what do you think we should do with this young hero of yours?"

Lessing shook his head. "You're gonna groan, when you remember how you talked this evenin'," he warned. "You're gonna fair wring your hands, poor old Desparr."

"Go on, go on," Desparr insisted impatiently. "Lemme hear what you can say about the thing, will you?"

"Yeah. I'll let you hear. If I was you, I'd throw young Buck Chandler out of Fort Lippewan, and I'd do it fast, and throw him far, and tell him that he wasn't never wanted back inside again."

"Would you?" gasped Desparr. "What you talkin' about, Hank? That Chandler is one of the toughest *hombres* north of the Río Grande. I never seen a harder man than that young feller is."

"Louis, you won't take my word, but, compared with young Messenger, he's softer'n new-fallen snow. He's softer than the down off the breast of a baby duck. That's how soft he is compared with Messenger."

"You've gone loony," Desparr responded, totally unconvinced. "That Chandler, he knocked the kid over like a ninepin, this same evening."

"The boy had had too much of your whiskey, if whiskey is what you call it. He won't be that sort of a thing when he sees Chandler again."

"What'll he do?"

"He'll kill Chandler, I think," said the trapper, lifting his head and looking at the wall and through it toward the future. "He'll pretty sure kill Chandler."

"Chandler's got half a dozen murderin' bad young fellers around him," remarked the trader.

"If they step in, he may kill them, as well. And every gent that was in your whiskey room, he's likely to remember them and polish them off, too."

At this, Louis Desparr leaned back in his chair and

laughed, long and loud. "If he kills off that whole bunch . . . why, if he does that, he oughta have a chance to get away with it. I won't interfere none."

Lessing drew in a great breath. "I've warned you the last time," he said.

"Why, Hank, you don't talk with no sense, when you talk about that boy. What's he done? Floored a coupla fool braves that was already half drunk, likely. And then he's taken water from a Blackfoot, and then he's got himself licked by Chandler, a fair and square stand-up fight. After that, he's got himself throwed in a blanket . . . and served him right. Then my partner, Lessing, he goes and takes this young skunk and lays him out in his own room, like a fool, I'd say. Henry, I sure respect your ideas usually, but not this idea at all!"

Lessing went back to the door. "I'll do my best," he said. "I'll try to keep close to him and keep track of him. I'll lock the door and put the key in my pocket . . . but I figger that tomorrow is gonna give you and all of us a terrible shock."

Desparr shrugged his shoulders. He began to feel that the mind of his old friend was a little upset. So he settled in his chair to finish off his good-night smoke, and Henry Lessing went back to his own room.

He looked at the sleeper, who apparently had not stirred, and then, locking the door and putting the key in his pocket and making sure that the window was too small to allow a man to squeeze through it, he lay down to sleep.

For a long time he could not close his eyes, for he kept remembering little details of this most wonderful day and, not least of all, how young Messenger had lain upon the bunk and watched the ceiling with a face as white as chalk.

Chapter Twenty-Four

When Lessing wakened in the morning, he instinctively reached into his pocket, and sighed with relief when he found that the key still was there. Then he looked toward the door that was closed—toward the window, through which the sun was pouring brightly, and showed that he had far overslept himself—toward the guest of his room, and found that he was not there.

This discovery, he would not believe for a time. He leaped at last to his feet and, turning in a rather staggering circle, he looked about the room wildly, as though he thought that he must find the boy stowed somewhere in a corner. But there was no sight of Messenger. He was gone like a whiff of wind.

Running to the door, the bewildered trapper found that it was locked, just as he had left it. He rushed next to the window, and there looked for some sign. Dust lay thick upon the lower part of the embrasure, and it was certain that no man could have gone through without disturbing that dust. At this discovery, Lessing clasped his head with both his hands, for he felt his brain whirling.

He unlocked the door, at last, and rushed out to find Desparr, but Desparr was long since gone from his room. The store had been opened and the trading of the day was going full blast. Down into the store passed Lessing, more excited than ever. He hunted up his friend, Desparr, at once.

159

The store was filled. For War Lance's Blackfeet had come in throngs. On the preceding day, they had adjusted prices and arranged all the necessary details of the business, and now they brought in squaw loads and horse loads of robes and beadwork, and all the articles of Indian manufacture for exchange with the goods in the fort.

War Lance himself was there, stepping through the crowd like a giant wading through a turbulent river. He went slowly, and the throng divided its tangles before his coming.

To him, however, Lessing gave not a glance. He leaned across the counter before the trader, actually elbowing two angry braves aside. "Have you seen young Messenger?" he asked.

The other grinned. "Not hide or hair of him," he said.

"He faded out of my room, last night. Without a key, he unlocked the door and locked it again, and got away," panted Lessing.

"He must've took wings and flown, then," said Desparr, "and I reckon that he'll keep right on flying till he gets pretty far away from Fort Lippewan. He ain't wanted here, and he knows it, I guess."

Lessing went out into the enclosure. Vainly he ran his glance over the faces of the swaying crowd. There was no glimpse of Messenger among them. Here came a squaw beating before her a stubborn mule that was piled to the staggering point with a ponderous load of robes. There was enough in that load to make the possessor rich for three seasons with all the luxuries of gun, knife, ammunition, beads, and trinkets. But probably the greater part or all of the treasure would be exchanged for whiskey.

No, this part of the Blackfeet tribe would not trade for alcohol. The great War Lance himself had forbidden it.

Lessing, still bewildered, drew a great breath. Another thought had come to him, that perhaps his apprehensions were entirely wrong and that the boy really had not been in an agony of shame and rage when he lay on the bunk the preceding evening, but was overcome by fear. Fear, also, might have made him flee from the fort before he had to encounter the rude hands of big Chandler again. In that case, Desparr was right. Lessing hoped that he was. He grew easier, after this.

A moment later, he had a view of Chandler, head and shoulders above the crowd, making his way through the hurly-burly by weight and elbowing. Many a black look went at him. Many a hand was laid upon the hilt of a knife. But the man was too well known, and no one cared actually to fight with him. The bravest of the Indians rather avoided him; the young men simply pocketed their wrongs.

In the wake of the ruffian, the trapper allowed himself to drift. If trouble came, almost undoubtedly it would come to Chandler. Lessing might, therefore, be in time to ward off violence, although he rather doubted even his own influence upon Messenger. It would take vast mental persuasion to turn that youth aside from the current of his determination.

To make the danger greater, Chandler was not alone. He was the point of the wedge that cut through the crowd. Behind him went three of his associates, characters as depraved as himself and proud of their association with this notorious gunman.

What would happen if their united weight fell upon slender young Messenger?

For half an hour, Henry Lessing wandered behind that quartet. Then suddenly it paused like a craft that has put its nose upon a rock. There was a rapid, excited muttering among the Indians, and these quickly gave back so that a small, open circle was left. By making this space, the crowd was compacted so thick upon the rim of the circle that Lessing could not break through it. He could only look helplessly on between heads and shoulders and see, facing Chandler, the form of Messenger himself. For there he was, a little paler than ever, but erect, easy, and meeting the eye of Buck Chandler with a steady gaze.

"Here's the tenderfoot again!" shouted Chandler, and laughed. "Get out of my way, rat, before you're stepped on." He struck out with the flat of his heavy hand.

He might better have struck at a dancing leaf in the wind. Only the air was cuffed aside, and the iron fist of Messenger went home with an audible *thud*. It put down Chandler as though he had been sandbagged.

"He clubbed me," said the dazed voice of Chandler. "Smash him, you fellows. . . ."

He hardly needed to ask. Straight past him charged his three adherents in a solid line. One of them was drawing a gun. The other two trusted to their fists, and, as a yell of excitement went up from the bystanders, Lessing saw the two forces meet.

He squinted his eyes, horrified. It looked certainly like death for the boy—and yet he had seemed capable of working miracles in the past and perhaps he could work one now. At first, it seemed to Lessing that the charge had knocked Messenger to the ground and was trampling upon him. He himself pressed forward, but he could not make ground through that barrier of tightly packed bodies.

He saw a revolver swung upward, grasped by the barrel, and the next instant saw the tawny head of the boy, for which the blow was aimed. But, that instant, the man of the clubbed revolver went down like a stack of cards struck by the wind, although Lessing could not see the punch that had dropped him. A knife flashed, and that instant its wielder was staggering backward, his face already blurred with crimson. The fourth of the number, seeing what had happened to his fellows, turned to run, but the solid human wall checked him, and he was struck down from behind.

Still, the battle was not ended. Buck Chandler, recovering his senses in that short respite, was lurching to his feet again. He had tried his bare hands and found them wanting. His three assistants had gone down before the magic of this tenderfoot, and now he would try what was in the force of powder and ball. The revolver was in his hand as he rose.

This was seen by Lessing, but then a shift in the shouting crowd threw several heads between him and his line of vision. Men were fighting and struggling to get back from the naked weapon. No bullet could miss. If it failed to strike the target aimed at, it was sure to drive on into the flesh of the human wall that stood around. But still there was not an explosion of a gun. Instead, Lessing saw a gun thrust upward high in the air. It was the hand of Buck Chandler that held it, and another hand, lean and narrow, was fastened upon it at the wrist. That imprisoning hand was seen to work suddenly to the right and left—and the gun dropped from the unnerved fingers of Chandler. Now Lessing could see the face of the bully. It was contorted with fear, with horror, with despair. His lips parted. He screamed terribly—the prolonged cry of a man in agony.

Every other sound in that crowd was hushed. Those, who had been fighting to get away from the bare guns, now turned back. They were shocked into that quiet. For such a man as Chandler would have been suspected of destroying himself before he would utter a sound of complaint.

What was happening to him, Lessing could not make out. He could only see the dreadful, contorted face of the big man, and then, horribly clear in the sudden silence as the scream ended, there was a dull, crackling sound unlike anything he had heard. It brought from Chandler another shriek, and then he disappeared, sinking to the ground.

No one spoke immediately. Lessing half expected a great outcry from among the warriors, for Chandler was famous and thoroughly hated by the Blackfeet for many reasons. But there was not a cheer. The warriors stood about with a stunned look. Presently Lessing could see the boy clearly. For the crowd was falling away to either side before him, as though all who he faced half expected that they might become the next victims.

There was only one whisper from nearby, in the tongue of the Blackfeet: "The iron hand! There is big medicine in his hand!"

But the boy walked slowly forward through the opening lane and, seeing Lessing, made straight toward him. There was now a faint color in his eyes, but Lessing paid little attention to that or to anything other than the eyes of the fighter. Again he was reminded of the gray sparkling of pure iron broken newly and the fracture sparkling in the sun.

Messenger came to Lessing and laid a hand on his arm. It was a friendly gesture, but enough excitement remained in the boy to make that grip bite into the arm of Lessing to the bone.

"We might go and have breakfast together," said the boy.

"Breakfast," Lessing repeated hoarsely. "Breakfast . . . with those fellows loose and plotting how they can murder you?"

"They?" said the boy with a careless shrug. "I don't think that they'll ever lift their hands again . . . not even from behind."

Chapter Twenty-Five

They went back, accordingly, away from the center of the crowd, and, when they were apart, Henry Lessing said: "What's happened to them, Messenger?"

The youngster looked at him with glimmering eyes. "Something will make them feel unlucky for a long time," he said.

"What did you do to Chandler? I thought I heard a noise . . . like bones breaking?"

Messenger shrugged again. "I thought," he said, "that there were no ruffians in the world. All at once, I thought that everything was all right, and that the world was full of my friends. I sat there and swilled whiskey like a beast. That's what it is like to be like other men. To be a beast is to be most like them. I see that now. I didn't see it then. I've met one man I could call a friend. He's a man who has spent a great deal of time by himself. He's a man who prefers the wildest mountains to life with other men. And you're right, Lessing. I see that now. You were right about the Indians, too. They are wild and they're savage. But they would not take advantage of a sick man. They might scalp him and kill him. But they would not disgrace and shame him as Chandler and the rest of his pack did to me last night. I want only one thing, and that's the names of the others who were with him."

"You'll never get them from me," said Lessing. He felt

exceedingly uneasy, because of the question that had been asked. Something, beyond a doubt, had happened in the nature of Messenger since the day before. He had come to the fort with the hardness of an automaton, a machine-made creature. He had passed from that into a reckless springtide of abandoned joy in living and affection for all his fellow creatures. All in a moment, in a single night, he had passed beyond this and grown into what could only be called a soured maturity. He had the grimness of one who knows through long experience, and the trapper feared him like an unnatural thing.

"I won't need to find out the names from you," the boy said after a moment. "They'll tell me their names themselves."

"What makes you think that they will, my lad?"

"Why, I have an idea that they'll be very shortly leaving the fort, Lessing. They won't stay around here until I find out from some other person."

"Nobody will tell you, Messenger."

"You're wrong," said the boy with a click of his teeth. "If I let it be known, for instance, that I'll pay a hundred dollars a name . . . or even fifty . . . or perhaps even ten . . . do you think that some cur won't come forward to tell me everything that he knows?"

His lips curled as he spoke, and the face of Lessing grew hot. In this condemnation of all mankind he felt a peculiar interest. He could see the truth that was in it. In any crowd, there is very apt to be some craven who will sell himself. Yet the judgment, on the whole, was wrong. There was the swift bitterness of a young man in it. He felt shame for the human species, and yet at that same time he could have smiled at the headlong boy who was so sure.

"If no one tells me," the boy went on, "still, I think those fellows will be uneasy. They've seen what's happened to Chandler and his crew. Any trapper, or trader, or half-breed who leaves the fort within the next day, without having finished his business thoroughly, will be a man for me to trail."

"What will you do when you catch them?" asked Lessing.

"Those four," answered Messenger. "I wanted to kill them . . . every one. The next that I come on . . . well, I don't know. It's a wild land, Lessing, and one has to adopt wild ways to suit it." His lips quivered as he spoke. Anger had seized him at the mere thought.

"Some of those fellows threw you up in a blanket," said Lessing. "And now you want to run a knife into every one of them. Is that reasonable, son?"

"It may not be that," replied the boy. "I don't know what I'll do until I see them."

Lessing fell into a brown study. When he looked up, he saw that people were passing them thickly, making a wide eddy as they came near to the boy. They were eying him with a profound curiosity. He had passed beyond the ranks of ordinary mortals in the opinions of those Indians. He had become a great medicine man, whose touch was sheer disaster to whoever was unlucky enough to feel it.

A thought had come to Lessing. "Will you tell me how you got out of my room this morning?" he asked.

"I unlocked the door and walked out."

"You had no key."

"There are ways of opening locks without keys," Messenger said, smiling a little. "I've been taught some of the ways. I'm no great expert, but experts are not needed for simple locks like that one."

"Then do one thing for me."

"Lessing," said Messenger with feeling, "I'd do anything that I could for you."

"Then go up and unlock that door and go into my room and sit there until I come up after you. Will you do that?"

The other hesitated only for a moment. "I go now," he said, and, turning on his heel, he made for the interior of the fort.

Lessing watched him go, and was still staring when a burly trader said at his shoulder: "Sleight-of-hand. That's what he's got! I never seen nothin' like it, and I was standin' as close as from me to you."

"What did he do?" asked Lessing.

"It is a hard kind of a thing to tell you about. His hands, they moved as fast as a cardsharp's. There's one heaves up a revolver over his head. I thought that the kid would have his brains bashed out. He reaches across as fast as a bird could flick a wing, and with the edge of his open hand . . . like this! . . . he chops Dan Vincent across the arm, close to the shoulder. You would've thought that Dan had been cut with an axe. He lets the gun drop and his arm falls to his side like it was paralyzed. And, while it's fallin', the kid shoves a fist into the pit of his stomach, and Dan drops onto the ground and begins kickin' and squirmin' to get back his wind. He was like a chicken with its head off. Casey Martin is takin' a free swing at the kid, and Messenger lets the punch fan over the top of his head and he steps in then and smashes Martin in the middle of the face. You could hear the slug of it goin' home. Then Martin starts walkin' backward on his heels, and trips and goes flat. It was 'Home, Sweet Home' for Martin, I tell you. He heard the birdies sing right *pronto*. Jip Oliver, he seen enough and got going, but the kid pops him behind the ear, and it's as though he'd had a bullet go through his brain, right there. Down he goes on his face, and gives one shudder, and lies still."

"And what happened to Buck Chandler?" asked Lessing.

The other made a wry face, and his voice lowered to confidential tones. "He had the gun wrung out of his hand," said the man, "and then his left arm was jerked around and twisted, slow, and sure, and easy, so's to linger out the pain for him . . . it was a sickenin' thing to see. You heard the arm pop, I reckon? I'll never get over the sound of it, if I live to be a hundred. I seen him where he dropped on the ground, kickin' and gaspin' like Dan Vincent, because the pain had got his wind. I seen his right hand throwed out. And around the wrist, where the kid had grabbed him, the skin was red and it was swellin' fast, and it looked like a wheel had run over it. I tell you, Messenger has a hand like iron."

"Aye," Lessing agreed, "he has a hand of iron."

"Davis and Toomey Johnson will be packin' out of the fort pretty *pronto*," said the other. "They was on the firin' line when the kid was tossed in the blanket last night. Think what a fellow he is. To let himself be throwed around like that, just to work up a good grudge, and all the time able to clean up that whole bunch like nothin' at all!"

Against this opinion of the superhuman prowess of the boy, Lessing did not argue. The fact that Messenger had had too much to drink would not have appeared reasonable to any man in the fort, accustomed as they were to the kicking powers of that so-called whiskey. He merely said: "I tell you what. Go say to Toomey and Davis that they'd better stay tight in the fort. The kid don't know the faces or the names of the gents that throwed him. It was too dark for that. But tell them that the kid is likely to foller the trail of any man that pulls out of the fort sudden. He knows that

169

he's throwed a scare into the boys, and he's likely to see which ones feels guilty."

The burly man started violently and clapped a hand over his mouth, Indian fashion. "Aye," he said. "I hadn't thought about that. I . . . I'll go tell the two of 'em." And he went off with haunted eyes, like one who knows more than he cares to tell.

Chapter Twenty-Six

For his part, Lessing went straight to War Lance. War Lance shook hands and gave the white man the smile that so perfectly softened his stern face.

"Come off here to a corner of the yard with me," said the trapper. "I have something to tell you, War Lance."

He walked beside the chief to the edge of the yard, near the palisade. Still, as he talked, War Lance kept his glance roving among the crowd of his braves and the women and children who filled up the interstices of the crowd. He knew how quickly a fight can start—a nudge, a word, a mere laugh might start knife play that only the thunder of his voice could stop. So he watched his people like children while he listened to the white man.

Lessing began with care. He took from his belt a little knife with a hilt inlaid with mother-of-pearl, in black and white, and at the butt of the hilt there was a big piece of red glass cut into facets so that it glittered. The steel of the knife was poor. The whole thing might have cost a dollar. But the eye of the chief flashed when he saw the color of it.

"When I came across this, some time back," said the trapper, "I thought about you, War Lance, and I've kept it ever since, carrying it around with me till I'd have a chance to give it to you myself."

The chief received it with a deep breath of satisfaction. His dignity was not entirely proof against such flattery as this. "All my nation," he said, "knows that you are a friend. And what is better than to have for a friend such a warrior as Two Buffalo?"

The trapper swallowed a smile of pleasure. Long ago, a chance shot from his rifle in running buffalo had clipped the spinal column of one and dropped it dead, and, ranging ahead, it had struck another cow to the heart. Two at one shot, and both of them young cows in the prime for meat—that was a thing that the Indians would not attribute to chance. Lessing's name had been given to him upon the spot.

Now he said: "Who is luckier than the hunter who has the Blackfeet for friends? But all of the Blackfeet are not my friends, War Lance."

"Who among them," the chief asked, "is an enemy of Two Buffalo?"

The trapper hesitated a moment, both to arrange the somewhat unfamiliar words of the language, and also to make the most diplomatic approach possible to a delicate question.

"Sometimes," he said, "the wisest men are not the kindest."

"That is true," said War Lance, and nodded.

"Sometimes the strongest hand is not the most gentle man."

"Yes."

"Sometimes the greatest medicine man is easily made angry . . . when the spirits have made him nervous?"

War Lance looked straight into his face and said nothing. The trapper saw that his diplomacy had been in vain. He began to grow hot in the face, and he came straight out with the next words, throwing all diplomacy aside.

"The great medicine man of the tribe, the great Summer Day, hates me, brother, and wants to take my hair and dry my scalp in his lodge."

War Lance, never stirring a feature of his face, continued to stare fixedly at the white man before him, and made no reply.

It was difficult to bear that glance. It was always hard to tell what the relations might be between the greatest chief of a nation and the greatest medicine man. Usually there was a trifling difference between them, because one worked with his hands and his brain, and the other used magic, a chicanery that the war chief was apt to see through to some extent, although he dared not divulge his disbelief to the rest of the tribe. Just what the relations between War Lance and Summer Day might be, Lessing could not tell, but the noble brow and the big, open eye of the brave gave him some reassurance.

"Summer Day hates me," went on Lessing carefully, but honestly. "And I hate him. We get back from people what we give them."

"That is true," War Lance agreed, and the trapper was glad of the words. Anything was better than the critical silence of the big red man.

"Now, then," said Lessing, "when I go out into the mountains alone, it is not a good thing to remember that the great Summer Day is my enemy. He may call on his spirits to keep the animals out of my traps. . . ." He looked, as he spoke, into the face of the chief, and, although there was no change of feature, yet the slightest glint of light appeared, he thought, in the eyes of the warrior. "And," said the trapper, "I never ride over a hilltop without looking to see the face of the medicine man grow up on the other side, his rifle leveled at my breast, for he is also the greatest

173

fighting chief among the Blackfeet, except one."

The cunning tribute did not stir the chief, who still waited impassively, listening.

"When the great Summer Day was here," said the trapper, "I wanted very much to make him my friend again. I am a humble man, brother. I am not one to keep up a hatred if I can buy my enemy off with words or with gifts. I would have given many horses and good rifles to Summer Day, if he would have become my friend again, as he was before."

"Was he once your friend?" the chief asked.

"He was. There was a summer of trading between us, and the rifle he got from me burst in his hands . . . because he overcharged it. But he always felt that I had bewitched the gun."

The other nodded.

"And then," said the trapper, "there came the battle between Summer Day and my young white friend. . . ." He paused. There was no Indian name for the boy as yet. The word Messenger would hardly make any meaning in the Blackfeet tongue.

"The young brave with the iron hand . . . the Iron Hand is your friend!" said the chief. Thereby, Messenger had his name given to him, and by no small authority.

"That's it." The trapper nodded. "The Iron Hand goes out to fight with Summer Day, and comes back, and Summer Day says that he has won the fight, and, at the same time, the spirits tell him to move camp and go seven days to the west." He stopped. War Lance, with unfailing presence, met the inquiring eye of the white man, and Lessing repeated the idea, more slowly: "It was a strange battle. Many things about it were strange . . . to be told and hardly believed. We know, now, what a great warrior the

Iron Hand is. We have seen him take men and break them like twigs."

"I, also, saw it," the chief said calmly.

"The touch of his hand," said the trapper, "is like the touch of a bullet, and men fall down as if the stroke had passed through the brain."

"It is true." The chief nodded. "I have seen it with my own eyes." He said no more, but the muscles about his shoulders swelled visibly. The sight of such prowess must have made the heart of the great warrior stir in him, and the memory of it made his muscles taut.

"I will tell you other strange things," said the trapper. "Summer Day conquered this great fighter, but he did not take his scalp. Although without mercy, yet he showed mercy to the white man. Although Summer Day is a great . . . singer . . . yet after the battle he made no song. He did not stop to dance about the fire. He did not stop to tell the coup. He had too many spirits talking in his ears and telling him to go west as fast as he could go. Is it true?"

The war chief frowned. He looked up at the sky, almost as though to consult it, but then he nodded. "It is true," he said doubtfully.

"Summer Day won the great fight, there in the woods. The white man, however, had a strange dream. He dreamed that he won the fight, and that he almost throttled Summer Day, and that Summer Day, to get away from the Iron Hand, threw himself over the edge of the cliff, and slid down, and the Iron Hand thought the Blackfoot had fallen into the river and been torn to pieces among the rocks. Then he dreamed that he sat down to rest, and finally he went to get the horse of Summer Day, and ride it around to pick up his own horse . . . but he found that it was all a dream, and Summer Day had galloped away on my horse and gone home shouting about a great victory . . . and about voices of the spirits that ordered the whole tribe to go west, seven days."

War Lance looked earnestly into the face of the other. "If the Iron Hand ever was on the throat of the medicine man, then there are marks of the fingertips," he said.

"There are," said the trapper. "Of course, there are! And big marks, I'd take it. Yes, sir, big marks, War Lance, and you'll find that Summer Day has taken to wearing something or other around his neck to keep it warm, or to make the spirits happy."

War Lance frowned. He said rather tersely: "What made you tell me . . . about this dream, my friend?"

The trapper threw his last card upon the table, face up. "Because you hate Summer Day," he said, "and because you know that he is a cheat and a sayer of that which is not true."

The blow was so sudden and so unexpected that War Lance wavered backward a little. He recovered himself at once, and drew himself up to his full height.

"Think a minute," said the white man soberly. "If I am not wrong, you are going to get a treasure from me, War Lance."

Suddenly the war chief broke out, although struggling with his voice: "Summer Day is a great chief among the Blackfeet. I have not said that he is my friend."

"Very well," said the trapper. "If he's a liar and a cheat, you don't want that sort of a man making false medicine among the Blackfeet and giving them wrong medicine to take with them on the warpath. What has he done for you? Has he ever gone with a great war party and had a great victory? No, he hunts like a buzzard. He prefers dead things. But War Lance goes out and wins great battles, and comes home covered with scars! Now, then, my friend, listen to me. The Iron Hand has not forgotten the medicine man. He wishes to see him again. He wishes to stand in a Blackfoot teepee, where there are many chiefs standing around, and he wishes to say . . . 'This medicine man, this great and famous Summer Day, he is no more than a liar and a thief. He told a lie and counted a coup that he had no right to count. Therefore, he is no more a medicine man than a barking dog. Let him admit that this is true, or else let him fight with me again, not in the woods, but in the open plain, where every man can see and judge the truth!' That is what the Iron Hand wants to do. Will you, War Lance, take him with you?"

The breast of the chief expanded in a great breath. He looked almost fiercely to the right, and then to the left. "If he comes with me," said War Lance, "it may be said that I have taken the enemies of the Blackfeet into my lodge and given them comfort, like a friend."

"He is no enemy to any man," said the trapper, "except the ones who injure him . . . but to every man that lays the weight of a finger on him, he'll not hesitate to lay the weight of iron on his heart in return."

The chief smiled suddenly. "It is a good fault," he said. "May my own sons have such a fault, Two Buffalo."

"Let him go with you, then. Take him as soon as the trading is finished. Take him away, and let him have a chance, as soon as the time comes, to stand face to face with Summer Day. It will do you no harm. It is a good thing for every tribe to know where the liars sit and to throw them out of the circle of the brave men."

War Lance suddenly gripped his hand with all his might.

The force made the fingers of the trapper crumble together and rolled the joints one on the other, giving great pain, but he smiled and gave no token.

"Send the young man to me," said the chief.

"I go to find him," Lessing responded, and went off with a sudden joy in his heart and lightness in his step, for he knew that he had crossed a very long bridge, indeed—if only he could persuade the boy to go with him.

Chapter Twenty-Seven

For two days young Messenger hesitated. It was true that there seemed no other logical way of coming at Summer Day, if he should fail to join the band of War Lance. If he went out by himself on a solitary trail, he would be passing alone into a country swarming with hundreds of wild red men, and, although he might outmatch almost any three of them in single combat, there was hardly a brave in the entire tribe who was not capable of outmaneuvering him and lifting his scalp with expedition and ease. On the third day, he agreed with the trapper that there was nothing else for it. Together, they rode out in the evening to the camp of the war chief.

The trading of the latter's party had by this time been completed. They had given in their robes and other articles of commercial value, and they had received in exchange the ammunition, guns, knives, and trinkets of the fort. An ordinary party would have lounged around the fort for some time, drinking up their profits, trading back most of their gain for whiskey, but, since this was impossible under the strict leadership of War Lance, they had to prepare to depart at once.

In the dusk of the evening, they came to the camp when the western sky was bordered with crimson, pale green above, and verging into the deeper blue of the upper heavens. As they came closer, two braves appeared, as it

179

were, from nowhere, and rode toward them.

"Don't be worried by 'em," explained the trapper. "You take most Injun camps, and they don't bother about sentinels and mounting guard. They trust to luck mostly, and take their chances. They've got eyes as sharp as the eyes of lynxes, of course. But a lynx can catch a lynx, and War Lance knows it. You'd think that he was a white soldier, the way that he works everything out. Nobody's ever surprised one of his camps. He's never lost so much as a single hoss by the stealin' of Crows, or Sioux, or any of the rest of 'em. These two gents, they'll ask a few questions, and take us into the camp."

That was exactly what happened. When the horses came near, they called out to know who was there, and, when they heard the names, they immediately formed up beside the white men and accompanied them into the center of the camp. They seemed sufficiently proud of their mission, at that. When children and dogs scampered across the lane down which they were riding, one or the other of them would call out, saying: "Out of our way! Are you going to make the horses of chiefs and warriors fall over you? Is there no politeness in the Blackfeet children? Out of the way, and let two white braves come into our camp . . . Two Buffalo and the Iron Hand!"

It was clear that the second name was to the youngsters like an explosion of gunpowder. They yipped like young coyotes when they heard it, and while some swarmed close alongside the younger of the white men, others scampered ahead and roused the lodges along the way.

Then the flaps of teepees were thrown aside; squaws and old men stepped into the entrances; and young Messenger, as he went past, had glimpses of fires twinkling and smoking in the interiors of the lodges, and he saw the glitter of beadwork and weapons, the colorful patterns on the backrests, or the gaudy, childish paintings on the walls of the teepees. A pungent odor breathed from the whole camp. There was the taint of wood smoke and the smell of unfamiliar foods cooking. By the sense of smell more than anything else he recognized that he had passed into quite another world.

It seemed as if all the life in the camp was rushing to view him. Warriors dignified under their robes, women, old men, youths with the step of antelopes, children, and myriad of scooting, howling, snarling dogs. An uproar began like the noise of a sea.

As they came to the center of the camp, the guides took them at once toward the largest teepee in the last circle of lodges. Before it stood a lofty form that the boy recognized easily, even through the dusk, as the great War Lance himself.

They came up to him and dismounted, the trapper holding up his right hand as he said: "How!"

This example the boy imitated, and the chief returned the greeting, his deep voice vibrating in the ear of young Messenger.

"I've brought him in as I promised," said the trapper. "It's for you to hold him if you can, War Lance."

The latter replied: "Come into my lodge. There we can talk. There are so many eyes watching us out here, that it is enough to make any man a mute."

He threw aside the flap of the lodge, and into it they passed. A low fire burned in the center, with the usual big iron pot hanging above it. The steam of the boiling meat within passed out with the odd fragrance that he had noted before in riding through the camp. On her knees at one side of the teepee, a woman was busily sharpening a knife with a very long blade, and near her a baby of two years rolled with a toy. It got up on its chubby legs, and the mother rose, also. She still had some of the light grace of body that distinguishes Indian girls, but her hands were big from labor and her face was not beautiful. She had big, intelligent eyes, but certainly War Lance was not above the ordinary taste of his nation when it came to picking out a wife for himself.

The two white men were seated on either hand of the host just opposite the entrance to the lodge, which was the place of honor. Reclining there against very comfortable backrests, they were offered food, which they barely tasted, and which the boy found perfectly flat and tasteless because of the lack of salt in the cookery. Next they accepted the pipe, which was filled and lighted by the chief, who blew smoke to the spirits of the air and to the underground people.

After these preliminaries, it was possible to talk seriously. The trapper was the go-between.

"The Iron Hand," he stated, "because I see that name has been given to my friend by your people, will come to you, War Lance, and be one of your men. He only asks that, while he fights for you in your battles, he shall be allowed to live his own life as it pleases him. And when he finds the man you know of, his hands shall be free."

"The Iron Hand," said the chief, addressing the trapper, "is a great brave, as all the Blackfeet know. It may be that the medicine man put a spell on him and made him dream a strange dream. But the affairs of Summer Day are not my affairs. He has the Sky People to talk with him and to advise him from time to time. They can protect him from all dangers, as he often has said. All that I wish to know is that the Iron Hand will be a warrior in this tribe, and that he will swear not to leave it for one great sun."

"A year!" exclaimed the trapper. "You want him to promise to live with you for a whole year?"

"Yes. Unless something happens in the meantime that forces him to flee for his life from the revenge of the Blackfeet!"

The boy nodded. "I understand," he said.

"And if ever you lift a hand against a member of the Blackfoot tribe," went on War Lance sternly, "it must be because you have seen good proofs that the man is a criminal, and that you will be able to show those proofs to all the nation."

"Hold on," said Messenger to the trapper. "He wants me to promise what I'll probably not be able to do."

"If you challenged the medicine man to a fair fight and he was beaten by you, they'd take that as a pretty good proof that his medicine was no good and that he was a great liar and had lied about the first fight that he had with you."

Young Messenger nodded. "That seems better," he said.

"Will you make the promise?"

"Why does he want me for a whole year?"

"Because," said War Lance, "if you stay with us a month, you would then leave us forever. If you stay with us a year, you may never wish to change."

Messenger looked quickly around at the bare, earthen floor of the teepee, the steaming meat pot, the awkward paintings on the wall, and, although he did not smile, he could not help shrugging a little.

But the trapper took the thing more seriously. "He may be right. Will you do it, Messenger? You'll get the taste of this life before long, just as you'll learn to like that sort of boiled meat a lot better than anything that the French chefs can serve up to you with their sauces and what not."

"I go with him," Messenger said softly to himself, "or else I never reach Summer Day. So go with him I must." Then louder: "War Lance, I will stay with you a year, and injure no Blackfoot except to protect myself, or because I have proof that he is a guilty man in the eyes of your people. Is that enough?"

"No," said the chief. "It is not enough." He went to a corner of the lodge and took down a bridle from a whole cluster of them that hung from a peg. "I have eight friends," he said, "who ride with me. Sometimes they ride hunting by themselves, and then they use their own bridles and their own horses. But when they ride with me, they use my horses, and they ride with these bridles. Will the Iron Hand do as they do? Will he be one of the companions?"

The trapper started. "Did you see it?" he said aside to the boy. "He's asking you to join up with that sacred band of his. He's making you the ninth man in the lot, and that's enough to set the whole tribe by the ears and make them buzz, because there never have been more than eight of them before."

The eyes of Messenger glittered. He had not forgotten those eight splendid warriors who had ridden past him at the gate of the fort.

"Yes," he said.

The chief reached one side of the bridle toward him and retained the other in his own grasp. Then he raised his right hand above his head and looked upward. "Iron Hand," he said, "from this moment my lodge is your lodge, my food is your food, my weapons are your weapons, my horse is your horse, and my life is your life, brother!"

He spoke with a solemn emotion, and the boy looked at him as though hearing the voice of a ghost. His eyes widened. Suddenly he repeated in a tone that was uncertain at first, but that rose and rang toward the end:

"War Lance, from this moment my lodge is your lodge, my food is your food, my weapons are your weapons, my horse is your horse, and my life is your life, brother!"

The trapper looked on agape. He could not tell exactly what had happened, but he guessed that a spirit miraculously strong had touched the soul of Messenger, and strange things might be the spiritual fruit of it.

Chapter Twenty-Eight

Now that the trading was ended and the tribe was to start on the following morning, Lessing decided that he would accompany them. All trails were the same to him, so long as they plunged deeply enough into the wilderness, and, since War Lance was leading the tribe to the west and north—in the same general direction that the party of the medicine man had taken, as a matter of fact—Lessing was willing to follow them, although his chief reason, as he admitted to himself, was that he wished to be in touch with the further adventures of young Messenger. Messenger himself he left in the camp of the Blackfeet, where hospitality was offered him in the lodge of the chief.

Lessing went back to wind up his affairs at the fort, prepare his pack, and start off, early the following morning, to join the Blackfeet in their march. He was busied until well into the night in arranging his pack of traps and other essentials. He had bought a small but strong mule to carry most of the pack, and the Indian pony that had once belonged to Summer Day would carry the rest of the pack and the trapper himself.

He was in bed late, but he was up when the dawn was still a pale pink and life had hardly begun to stir in the fort. It was high time, however, to set out after the Blackfeet, for they would be early on the march. Perhaps already they were streaming away through the woods and over the hills.

Two things delayed and infuriated Lessing. First, the Indian pony bucked off saddle, pack, Lessing, and all. When he had been re-saddled, and a precious half hour or so had been wasted, the mule, tired of the chill of the morning, refused to budge. He balked in spite of the ingenious tricks that the half-breeds at the fort played upon him, and nothing would urge him out of his tracks until the sun was well up and beginning to warm the air.

By that time, Lessing knew that he was a long distance behind the Indians, and that it would be most difficult for him to overtake them during this day's march, unless he made it a long one. Then, just as he was about to make a belated start, a third interruption made him grit his teeth.

For up to the fort came a new party. There was a half-breed guide, and two sturdy frontiersmen who had been manning paddles or pull ropes all the way up the river, and, in addition to these, there was a man with as strange a personality as ever had come to Fort Lippewan—or to any other place where the trapper had been.

No sooner had this stranger arrived than he asked questions that caused a messenger to run over to Lessing. He was wanted, it appeared, because the stranger was inquiring eagerly for a young man of the exact description of Messenger.

Lessing was on the verge of refusing. He had halted far too long already, but curiosity checked him for a little while. He remained there while the stranger came up to him with his two big canoe men flanking him on either side and a little behind. Lessing well knew what that attitude meant. They were getting wages so high that they were willing to play the subservient rôle of domestic servants, even. They watched over their employer like two faithful and formidable dogs.

As for the man himself, the trip up the river had blown and burned raw the end of his nose—which usually makes men appear ridiculous—but the rest of his face was as white as a stone, and very like a stone was it in its rigid chiseling. He was a man of, perhaps, forty-five or fifty. It seemed apparent that he had just recovered from an illness, and that he was about to sink again—it was hard to make any other explanation of the hollowness of his chest and the extreme emaciation of his face. His cheeks were so hollow that one grew conscious of the teeth behind them, and his mouth was puckered, as if by famine. This leanness was exaggerated by the hawk-like cast of his features, but there was one thing about him that most attracted the attention of the trapper, and that was his eye. For it was the color and brilliance of iron, newly broken, and glittering in the sunlight. Lessing knew that he had seen that eye before.

"You're the man who knows the young fellow?" asked the stranger.

"Messenger, you mean?"

"Messenger?" said the stranger. "Yes, that's the name." But he gave the trapper a strong suggestion of hearing the name for the first time at that moment. "I mean," said the stranger, continuing, "a tall, rather slender young fellow, with gray eyes, and the general appearance. . . ." He paused, not as one in doubt, but rather as one anxious to pick out the most accurate word.

"General appearance of a cat?" suggested the trapper.

The stranger did not smile. Yet he seemed to accept the description as identifying Messenger once for all. "They tell me that you know where he has gone?"

"I do."

"Where is he, then?"

"Stranger," said Lessing, "I know Messenger pretty well,

188

but I never seen you before, and I dunno why you're on his trail."

This bluntness did not either offend or discourage the other. He merely said: "My name is Thomas Vance. I've come a good part of two thousand miles to see that young man. You'll help me to find him, I hope?"

"He's gone off with the Blackfeet," said the trapper.

"With the Blackfeet?" said the other. "He's gone off *with* the Blackfeet, did you say?" His eyes literally shot fire as he spoke.

"He's gone off with them. He's made friends with War Lance."

"War Lance? Who is he?"

"The biggest chief among the tribe, and the biggest power, next to Summer Day, the medicine man."

"Where have they gone?" snapped Thomas Vance.

"West, I reckon."

Vance struck his lean, white hands together and took two or three excited steps up and down. Then he caught a quick breath and turned again to Lessing. "Your name is what?"

"Lessing."

"Lessing, I see you're about to travel. Are you going in his direction, by any chance?"

"I might be," said the trapper noncommittally.

"If you will, I'll pay you well for it. I would go myself, but I'm worn out. I want you to take a letter to young Messenger. One of these men of mine will go along with you and bring back his answer."

"Hold on," said one of the canoe men. "I know them Blackfeet, and they know me, and the only use that they'd have for me would be to toast me on one of their fires. I'll keep clean of them, thanks. I don't want none of them in my part of the game, Mister Vance. They'd be wearin' my hair five minutes after I got into their camp."

"How about you, Bray?" snapped Vance, looking at the other big frontiersman.

The latter was the younger and the bigger of the two. "Waal, I dunno," he remarked. "They've gone and got themselves the scalps of my pa and Uncle Henry Wales, and my cousins, the two Wales boys. But we've kind of evened up on our side. I've lifted the hair of three, four of them myself, and there've been others in the family that's been kind of free with Blackfoot hair, too. All in all, I might say that we've broke about even. I dunno why I should give 'em a chance to play the game with a cold pack, at my expense."

The traveler said dryly, coldly: "I'll give you a hundred dollars if you take this message, and from Messenger back to the fort."

The canoe man shook his head. "It's a pile of money," he admitted. "It's a hundred beaver pelts all in a heap . . . but a hundred dollars don't do no good to a dead man, so far as I ever have heard!"

"Bray," said Vance, without the slightest emotion, "I'll give you a hundred and fifty dollars!"

"Hold on!" said a bystander. "I'll go for that. I'll go for the hundred, for that matter."

Vance hardly looked at the profferer. "I know this man, and not you," he answered in his crisp way.

Bray took off the hat and ran his fingers through his hair. It was as long and almost as black as an Indian's.

"A hundred and fifty is a hundred and fifty," he announced wisely. "I reckon that I'll have to die someday, no matter what turns out. Hey, Lessing, you're a good friend of the Blackfeet, and you might help me out with 'em."

"I think that I can," said the trapper, "but no man is

ever sure of a red Injun, unless he's a sworn blood brother to one of 'em."

"Aye," said the canoe man, "and that's true, but I reckon that I'll take this job. Where's the letter, Mister Vance?"

"I've got it . . . and here's the money."

"Leave the money with Louis Desparr. If they get me, it'll be a comfort to think that they didn't get the coin, too. I'll need that letter?"

Vance took out a wallet made of pigskin, rubbed smooth as glass almost, and brown with time and fingering. This he opened, and from an inner fold he took out an envelope that carried, as the close eye of the trapper saw, a foreign stamp—two of them, in fact. The face of the envelope was soiled and covered with much writing and rewriting of addresses. This Vance wrapped with much caution in a piece of oiled silk that went several times around it. He tied the package with a string, and gave it to Bray, saying: "I'll do better than I said, Bray. On second thought, I'll give you two hundred and fifty dollars . . . gold. And I'll add two hundred and fifty more if you'll bring back his answer safely to this fort."

Money was not easily come by in those days and along that frontier. Exchange was usually by barter of articles of trade or personal use. $500 in gold was a sum that made the eyes of Bray pop from his head.

"For five hundred dollars," he said, "they never could get me. For five hundred dollars, I can dodge bullets and jump through mountains. I'm gonna bring back that letter to you, all right!"

Vance, pleased for the first time, smiled. It was only a shadow of a smile, cold as the light in his eyes, and both reminded the trapper forcibly of the smile and the cold eye of young Messenger.

Now there was still another delay while Bray secured a horse, for which the inexhaustible purse of Vance paid without question, but, inside of an hour, Bray's small pack was lashed firmly behind the saddle, and off he went in company with Lessing.

Chapter Twenty-Nine

For half the day the conversation of Lessing and his companion was limited to the following remarks:

"Kind of strong, the Lippewan is running," said the trapper, after they had been two hours on the way.

"Kind of dang' strong," said big, young Mr. Bray.

At about noon, as they were trudging along a narrow pass between hills whose sides were strewn with boulders, big and small:

"Hot," said young Mr. Bray.

"Hot," agreed the trapper.

Although they spoke seldom, they were not unaware of one another. Each examined covertly, but with a religious interest, the way the other's pack had been built and bound on, and how the saddle was placed on the horse's back, and the horse itself, and the clothes, and the weapons of the stranger.

Well on in the early part of the afternoon, they came to a place of shade under some big trees beside a sparkle of running water, and there they halted, without asking the other's opinion. This unanimity of silent opinion pleased them both, more than they cared to say.

Finally, as being the older of the two, the trapper took it upon him to break the ice.

"You've been in the mountains before," he suggested.

"I reckon you was *born* in the mountains," answered Bray.

Suddenly a wall fell down between them. It was invisible, and its fall made no sound, but both of them knew that it had stood there stronger than steel and higher than the moon. Now they knew that it was gone.

They did not divide tasks in preparing for that noon meal.

As the older man, Lessing simply rigged up an improvised fishing line and went out on the edge of the rocks, where he sat with a humped back and fished. The younger man, without a word of doubt or of challenge, did all the serious labor of removing the packs and saddles from the backs of the animals, and hobbling them in a good grassy meadow nearby. Then he, with a small hand axe, cut up a quantity of brush and laid and kindled a fire.

By the time it was going, old Lessing came casually back with half a dozen good-size fish, speckled with the brilliance of the rainbow and glittering with silver scales. These he cleaned with the expedition of one who knows how to work with a fast knife for a hungry stomach. He wrapped the fish first in some herbs that grew nearby and then in broader leaves, and, putting the fish in a pile covered with dust and ashes in the center of the fire, he piled the brush around it and made it burn fiercely.

Young Bray had been expecting a quick meal of fish toasted on the end of a stick, but he controlled his appetite and went calmly ahead with the boiling of water for tea—a luxury, but one that they could enjoy when they were so close to the fort.

In a few moments, however, the heat of the fire had done the trick. The fish were drawn out of it, with the leaves burned away completely, and the herbs a mere powder, the essence of them having entered the flesh. So thoroughly had the cooking been done that the skin flaked away at a touch, and the flesh came away from the bones. Bray ate ravenously, and, when he had finished his share, he took without a word the extra fish that the trapper did not want to complete his portion.

By this time, when the meal was done, they lighted their pipes and laid back against the big roots of a tree that offered support like Indian backrests. Up to this point, neither of them had spoken during the meal or the preparation of it, but each had been aware that the other was working scientifically and performing an adequate share of the labor.

Then Lessing allowed himself to speak of the thing that was eating his very heart for curiosity. "That Thomas Vance . . . ," he slowly began.

"Yeah, that Vance," said the younger man. "Yeah!"

"You wouldn't see many. . . ."

"No, you bet you wouldn't see many." Then Bray added eloquently: "He's made of money just about!"

"Five hundred dollars?"

"Yeah, for a letter."

"Well," said Lessing, "I'd sure like to know. . . ." Again his voice trailed away. He seemed to be fighting against his hunger for gossip.

"So would I," said Bray. "I'd sure like to know."

"You picked him up a piece back?"

"Yeah. Eight hundred mile back was where we picked him up. He never done a hand's turn all the way."

"No. He wouldn't do a hand's turn. He wouldn't know how."

"No. He wouldn't know how."

"Kind of a snaky look."

"Yeah. He sure made the creeps go up my back. They never stopped, all the way."

Then Bray, as though feeling at last that he could talk to

this man, said: "One night I woke up, the middle of the night, and there's a moon. I see Vance settin' up in his blankets and smilin' at the moon. I watch him an hour. He still is settin' there and smilin' at the moon. And that's the only smile that I ever seen on his face."

"Yeah, he wouldn't be smilin' much. He wouldn't be wastin' his face."

"No, he wouldn't be wastin' his face. That's right," agreed Bray. "Never smiled and never cursed, all the way up. He was a great one for stumblin' in the trail, though."

"He'd be lookin' at his own ideas, maybe, instead of the trail."

"Yeah, he'd be lookin' at his own ideas."

"Not much of a comfort around a camp, that kind of a gent."

"Not much more comfort'n a sandstorm or a blizzard. I would've paid money to hear him swear a coupla time."

"I reckon you would." The trapper was silent, but he kept nodding his head to show that his mind was still upon the same subject.

The boy, after watching him for a time, almost wistfully broke out: "He ain't out here for no good!"

"I'd lay my money that he ain't," said the other.

"Not with his face."

"And his eye!"

Said the trapper: "He never said nothin'?"

"No, not a word about nothin', except Blackfeet. He's pretty curious about 'em. He wants to pick up about their ways. Maybe he's gonna write one of them fool books."

The trapper shook his head. "Whatever he does, it won't be foolish."

"Well, he's deep," said Bray.

"Yeah, he's deep."

The pipes being finished, they re-saddled the horses and the mule, and mounted. But, when they resumed their way, instead of riding one behind the other, they rode abreast, where the windings of the narrow wall permitted. Before them, they had innumerable signs of the Indians who had preceded them, not only in the long, snaky marks of the travois poles, but also other sign—a worn-out moccasin, for instance, in one place. They could tell that the band was not very far ahead, and, therefore, they did not urge their animals strictly. If there was any likelihood of trouble between Bray and the Blackfeet, it would be far wiser to come upon the band at night, when the tired warriors, after the day's ride, would have less mischief than weariness in their minds.

"This fellow, Messenger," Bray said at one time. "Tell me, just what's he like?"

"I dunno," said the trapper. "He's a friend of mine. I've known him one day," he added with a soft chuckle, "but I've seen a great deal of him. A couple days is all that I've known him."

"He ain't like nothin'?" asked the other, point-blank.

"Wouldn't say that he's like nothin'. Except a sort of a cat."

"Why, that's what old Vance is like, too," Bray said, surprised.

"Yeah. They're something alike. You'll see. They got some of the same blood in them, I reckon." As he said it, surety came upon the trapper. Who Messenger was, from what place he had come, why he had been sent out to the West on an errand of blood revenge, who had trained him to the present physical perfection and adroitness that he possessed—those all seemed questions which might be answered before long by something that was to come to pass between Vance and the boy.

They had bad luck, later on in the afternoon, for they came to a strong young river that rushed and roared through a narrow valley. At the place where it was narrowest, the Indians had felled all of the trees near the bank, and over this natural bridge they had taken their way. Then, once across on the farther side, they had tumbled the logs into the stream and gone on their way. For Indians like to leave a broken trail behind them even in the most peaceful times.

This was a great stroke of bad fortune for the two who pursued that trail. They would have had to spend half a day felling logs and rolling them from a distance to the same point, and, therefore, they worked up the stream several miles before they came to a place where it divided and the separate channels could be crossed, although with some danger and difficulty.

Night was close on them when they reached the farther side. So they camped, and the next day had to return downstream to the point where they had lost the trail the night before. This was a serious loss.

For five days longer they pushed on behind the party of Blackfeet, for, on the third day, their march had been again interrupted in an exactly similar manner. But, on the fifth day, they came at evenfall upon sight of a small hollow, spotted with the white-glowing teepees of the Indians, and down toward them they went, glad that their long pursuit was over.

Bray, with the calm of a brave man and a philosopher, showed not the slightest nervousness, but he allowed the trapper to do the talking when they came into the camp and were encountered by the mounted scouts on the rim of the lodge circle.

They, at the name of Two Buffalo, showed every sign of pleasure. As for Bray, he was not regarded, because his face could not be seen in the dark of the evening. So the pair were conducted straight to the teepee of the chief.

War Lance was not there. The squaw was busy weaving a willow bed with great care and skill; the child was asleep on a robe; in a corner, stretched against a slanted backrest, his hands behind his head, and his eyes turned up to watch the flight of the smoke through the vent at the top of the lodge, was Messenger at last.

Chapter Thirty

When the boy saw his friend, he leaped to his feet and seized his hand. No matter how indifferent he might be to the rest of the world, he had opened the door of his heart to the old trapper, and the face of the latter glowed when he recognized the joy in the eyes of the boy. There had been such a long delay in overtaking the tribe on the part of Lessing that Messenger had almost given him up.

They must sit down. They must eat, and they must smoke. Gladly they did so, and the squaw served them from the meat pot, where there was fresh meat stewing, for the hunt had been very successful this day. They ate gluttonously, and then, as they sat back to smoke, the letter was given to the boy.

He unwrapped it with a frown, but, at the sight of the postmark upon the outside of it, he started. Then, scrutinizing the handwriting carefully, they saw him bound to his feet. He turned white. Standing with a hand pressed against his forehead, he remained immobile for a moment, his lips stirring but no sound coming. He could not open the letter until he had slipped down to a seat again. The squaw, watching him like a hawk, darted across the lodge and leaned over him, but he waved her away.

Then, opening the letter, old Lessing marveled to see the iron hand was shaking. Once or twice the boy lowered the letter and leaned his head back, with the sick look of one almost overcome. But he read on, and, when the letter was finished, he went patiently through it, again and again.

A sudden fury made him crush the paper and hurl it in the fire. But a reaction sent him leaping after it faster than the stroke of a snake. He had it out of the flames, unscorched, and examined it with a shaky attention to make sure that nothing about it was harmed.

After this, he remained for a long moment holding the missive in both his hands, his face weary, his head far back and a little to one side, with the look of a man who is finishing a long-distance race.

Finally recovering himself a little, he rewrapped the letter in the oiled silk with the same care that Thomas Vance had shown for it, and placed it carefully in his wallet, and the wallet in an inside pocket of his coat, for he was still wearing the same gray clothes that he had had on when he came to Fort Lippewan. Never had they seemed so out of place as here, in the Indian teepee.

Lessing was more amazed than if the ground had opened at his feet. He would have ventured his life that there was nothing in the world that could so shake the nerve of that young creature of steel and rock. Bray, in the meantime, was curling his lips a little and looking askance at those exhibitions of emotion. Well, Bray would have to learn his own lesson, if he wanted to make a fool of himself about the boy. He, Lessing, would give no more warnings to the uninitiated.

Once the letter was put away, the boy recalled himself. He began to show more attention to his guests, asking them about their journey, and Bray put the matter bluntly, as an honest man should.

"I didn't come out here to do you a favor, man. I come here to earn five hundred dollars that Vance offered, and I want to get out of here with your answer to him as fast as I can get, before these red men get a chance to recognize me. There's bad blood between the tribe and me, Messenger."

"My answer back to him!" exclaimed the youngster, turning as crimson as he had been white before. "Go back and tell him . . . tell him. . . ." He checked himself, and they saw his hands working. "He'll have to wait for his answer," Messenger stated at last, almost sullenly. "He knew that. You'll have to stay with us for a while if you want to get the message back to him. Didn't he tell you that you would?"

"No, he told me nothin' about it. Only, I was to take back your answer to him. Messenger, whatever the answer is, I gotta have it now. I can't wait. I ain't scary. But I got a little common sense."

"You're afraid of these fellows?" Messenger asked, waving his hand. "They won't hurt you. Not a man of them would dare to touch you, Bray. You're in the lodge of War Lance. That's enough. If it weren't, you're my friend. You came here to see me. That's enough to keep their hands off you."

Bray, in spite of himself, eyed the slender body of the boy and sneered faintly.

"I dunno how thick of a shield of bull's hide you're holdin' over me, Messenger," he said, "but I know how straight Blackfoot bullets can fly and what they'll cut through!"

The suggested doubt did not trouble Messenger. He replied quietly that everything would be well with Bray. He would pledge his honor for that. War Lance, at that moment, came in. He greeted the trapper gravely, but kindly. On Bray he turned a cold and still eye.

Said Messenger: "This man, War Lance, came to me as

a friend. He traveled for a week to bring me a message. Is he safe here with you and the rest of the braves?"

War Lance paused a moment before he replied: "This man has been an enemy, but he has been a brave enemy. We are willing to have him with us, and every man in the tribe will be his friend so long as he cares to stay. When he leaves us, every man will try again to count coup on him. For there is more honor," said the chief, "in counting one coup on a brave man than counting fifty on cowards."

After his speech, which Bray followed fairly well although he was not an expert in the language of the Blackfeet, the canoe man was much relieved, and he said to young Messenger: "Once they've passed their word, no man will be harmed by 'em. I'll trust to luck. You can't tell me how long I'll be waiting here for your answer, Messenger?"

The latter shook his head.

Preparations were next made for the sleeping quarters of the two white men who had just arrived, and they were given beds in the lodge of War Lance himself, because, as he said, the young men of the tribe were a turbulent lot, and it was better to have Bray under his own protection. As for Two Buffalo, he was an old and trusted friend.

So they turned in for the night, with the fire flickering low in the center of the lodge, and the shadows leaping and falling upon the hide walls. For an Indian night, it was comparatively quiet. Only now and again a small child would wail for a moment, and sometimes a wave of wolfish howling and snarling swept from one side of the encampment to the other as a tangle of dogs started fighting and spread pandemonium.

But to men tired out by a long march, such disturbances were hardly enough to make them open their eyes. The sounds that began with the dawn were of an entirely different nature.

For then one could hear the young men shouting as they ran down in groups for the early morning plunge that, winter and summer, marked the beginning of the day for them. The dogs started yipping in a higher key. Horses neighed and answered one another, and, when Bray and the trapper went to the entrance, they saw a strong-armed brave in an adjoining lodge giving his young son of ten a tremendous thrashing with a fir branch. It was not punishment, but discipline, they observed. The lad endured with his face swelling and his eyes popping out with the pain. Finally, as the blows grew heavier and heavier, he drew a short, gasping breath, and the flogging ceased. The youngster showed no pleasure because of this cessation. Instead, he dropped his head in a sort of despair, but the father said gruffly and briefly: "The top of the mountain is a slow climb, and patience takes you there."

At this, the boy gave him a flashing glance, and then off he scooted for the river.

"Buildin' up endurance." Bray nodded. "No wonder the redskins can last so long in the fire . . . or on the warpath, for that matter. They got their skins toughened all the way through their lives."

"Where's our friend, Messenger?" queried the trapper.

Down the lane, as though in answer, a wild voice broke out in a war chant, and they could see a young brave prancing in a circle in front of the lodge.

"That one's had a lucky dream," the trapper said, grinning. "He's seen his medicine animal, or something like that, and he's gotta publish the news. But where's Messenger?"

They wandered out to the edge of the camp, and there

they could see the flashing curve of the little stream, rosy in the morning light. Sounds of shouting and laughter came up from it, and presently, over the edge of the bank that hid the place where the swimmers were bathing, there flashed a line of twenty young warriors, naked except for breech-clouts and racing desperately for the camp. They carried their clothes under their arms; their half-dried bodies, from which the water had merely been whipped with the edge of the hand, glistened brightly as they flew over the ground. But on one figure of that racing line the two watchers fastened their eyes.

This was one who was made slenderly, except about the shoulders, and his body flashed a pure, dazzling white. From his head, too, there blew no dark banner of long hair, such as streamed behind all the others.

"Messenger!" exclaimed the watchers, with one voice.

"Somebody else watching," Bray stated, and gestured aside. "And white, too, by jumping Jimmy!"

The trapper glanced in the indicated direction and saw a picture that startled him. It was a girl who was perfect Indian in her clothes, and with a face sun-browned almost to the coppery darkness of the Indian skin. But the hair that was drawn forward over her shoulders and dropped in two heavy braids well below her waist was shining gold.

She, with clasped hands and glistening eyes of pleasure, watched the race sweep toward the village. Others came running from lodges—women, older warriors, children. They set up a shout, for now the line grew ragged. It bowed out in the center, and here, side-by-side, appeared a pair of racers who were evenly matched. One was a lofty Blackfoot, straining every nerve and his face ugly even in the distance with effort. The other was the slender, gleaming body of the white boy. Although he matched the Indian stride for stride, he seemed to be running without a great effort.

Fifty yards from the camp they were shoulder to shoulder, those two rivals, with the others dropping rapidly to the rear, but here it seemed as though Messenger leaned forward a little. His stride increased. He leaped away like a greyhound unleashed and shot into the camp by himself.

A tremendous and cordial shout went up from all who watched the contest. But the trapper, regardless of the victor, regardless of all the others who were whooping, kept his eyes fixed fast upon the white girl—or was she a half-breed?

She had not turned to stare after the victor. Neither did she regard the other runners, but, with her hands clasped together, she was looking toward the brightness of the eastern sky.

"Trouble," growled Lessing to himself. "Trouble ahead for her, poor girl."

Chapter Thirty-One

They found out about the girl easily. She was Yellow Antelope, the daughter of Rolling Thunder, a good brave now
considerably past his prime. She was as white as her skin,
it appeared, for she had been taken from white people, not
on a raid, but from the stricken camp of a poor emigrant
whose wife already had died of the terrible spotted disease,
and who himself was on the point of death. They had with
them this one child, and because the teepee of Rolling
Thunder was totally without children, his heart had been
touched by the little one. So he had taken her, apparently
untainted by the disease. He had purified her with the
smoke of sweet grass, given her a name suggested by her
young grace and the color of her hair, and adopted her
into his family. The war party that was with him, dreading
the mortal sickness, had refused to allow him to ride with
it. So he had gone alone across a considerable distance,
caring for the little one, holding it in the saddle on his war
pony, while he walked beside and led the horse. From that
time on he had doted on her. This adoption, this whole
achievement of the long march through enemy's country,
was looked upon by the tribe as the most honorable exploit
of the brave.

An old woman gave this information to Lessing.

"There is a girl of eighteen or nineteen," said the
trapper, "and that is four or five years past the time when

most of your girls are taken as wives. Will none of the warriors have her?"

"Friend," said the woman, "in these last years, twenty of our best warriors have tied their finest horses outside of the lodge of Rolling Thunder. There was Two Eagles, who brought not only horses, but robes and deerskin beaded suits, and two saddles with guns and lances. Of horses, he brought his whole herd, except one. He kept one horse and he brought more than two-tenths of the rest to tie outside of the lodge of Rolling Thunder. The same day they were sent back, and, ever since that time, we have known that she is not to be sold until she finds a man who pleases both her and her father. Well, that is a foolish thing. If matters had been handled in a better way, she might now be a mother with two or three children about her, and some chief would be made happy to have her. But a man with one daughter is like a hunter with one bullet. He is never ready to spend it."

Lessing discovered that it was not the first time that the boy had distinguished himself in a minor way since he started with the tribe toward the west on the long six-day march. Each day he had ridden out with the hunters, and the finest marksmen in the band, even the chosen companions of War Lance, although they had over the other braves the advantage of an endless amount of ammunition to spend for practice, were not able to match the skill of the young white man. He rode, too, with a wonderful disregard of the perils of rock and fallen log and sudden trench. In all things, he was as the Blackfeet nation would have had him—except that his hair was short and that he had taken no scalps and counted no coups. For that matter, there were others in the tribe of his age who lacked similar distinctions. He was, in short, the perfect picture of a rising brave, and War Lance was considered to have done well by himself and all his people in adding such a champion to the list of his chosen fighters.

Lessing had a chance to talk to the boy later on in the day. He had gone down to fish, and he found that the boy was already there, by the bank of the stream, not fishing, but musing over the sun and shadow that rippled upon the bottom of the shallow creek. For there was no march this day—War Lance intended to make a halt here to extend over a considerable period. Lessing made ready his fishing gear slowly. Silently the boy helped him to untangle the line.

"You're getting sunburned, Messenger," said the trapper.

The boy nodded.

"And you've got a few of the wrinkles out of your forehead, too."

Messenger lifted his head and touched the fingertips across his forehead. Still he did not speak.

"You came out expecting to find it hell," suggested the trapper, "and, at least, it ain't been that."

At this, Messenger smiled faintly. "No," he answered quietly. "It's been almost the reverse." He added, with the look of one fumbling in his mind: "There's nothing shadowy about these Indians, Lessing."

"What do you mean by shadowy?"

"I mean that white men . . . they're always showing only half a face to me. Policy, forethought, afterthought, that sort of thing. They're more slippery than fish. But the Indian . . . you know how to take hold on him."

"You've been wrestling with some of the braves, then, I reckon?" said the trapper.

"A little." The boy nodded. "They're strong, but they haven't been trained. But they don't bear any malice. There was one fellow . . . his name is Bear-That-Wakened–In–The-Middle-Of-The-Night, or some such thing. He was proud of his wrestling. I put him down softly, three times, but he came dancing back for more, and finally I had to throw him hard. It whacked the wind out of him. He got up and grinned at me. What do you think he said?"

"That he'd wear your scalp someday?"

"He said . . . 'Fire burns four times for a child, once for a wise man.' And ever since that time, we've been great friends."

"I thought that you'd be kind of lost out here in the wilds," suggested the trapper.

"Not when I have men like that along with me. I've never been lonely. You can get hold of these people," the youth repeated. "They're real. They're so real that the rest of my life seems smoky and half lost already."

"What's going to happen about the medicine man, Messenger?"

"The medicine man? Oh, War Lance sent a message to him three days ago, by a fast-riding young brave who went ahead and ought to be back with a reply today."

"What was the message?"

"War Lance sent it himself. He said that he had a new warrior who had joined his party . . . they call me the Iron Hand, do you see?"

"I know that. He said that the Iron Hand was with him. What then?"

"He said that I swear the account that Summer Day gave of the fight was a thing not true . . . they don't seem to have a word for lie."

"No, they haven't."

"The result is that I am supposed to say that Summer Day has weak medicine, says a thing that is not so, and has counted a coup that is not a fact. I am willing to support what I say by a fight in the open, or in the woods, or anywhere that Summer Day says, but I prefer to have it in front of the braves of both the parties, if possible."

"That why War Lance camped here . . . to get the answer?"

"No. There's been a whisper in the air, it seems, that there's a big band of Crows trailing up through the mountains and ready to eat us up. War Lance has a couple of men scouting to the east, and he's waiting here to get more definite news. If they're behind us, I dare say that he'll try to do some of the eating himself."

"Well," Lessing said gravely, "I never expected it, but it looks like you're pretty fond of the Blackfeet. Lemme warn you about one thing. Would you listen?"

"Certainly," said the boy.

"It's this. A lot of the whites think that the Injuns are plain beasts, which they ain't. And when they find out, all of a sudden, that the red men are about as straight as the whites and in their own way just as honorable, then sometimes they go to the other extreme, and the first thing they know, they wake up one day and find out that they've gone and got married to some Injun girl."

Messenger raised his head a little, but he said nothing. His bright, hard, gray eyes looked fixedly at the trapper.

"But the time comes," Lessing continued, "when every man is a lot better off with his own kind. And if there ain't anything else ag'in' it, it's the half-breed children that count ag'in' the thing. And though sometimes you find a white girl living with the Injuns, it don't matter. The color of the skin don't count, if she's been raised in the Injun ways of things."

"Why d'you say that to me?" asked the boy.

"Because," said the trapper, "when you was runnin' that race this morning, I noticed that Yellow Antelope sure was lookin' at you, and I reckon that you've looked at her, too."

Messenger half rose, but, by an apparent effort of will, he forced himself to sit down again. "You think that she has noticed me?" he asked. His eyes were shining very brightly.

Lessing bit his lip. "Maybe I've talked like a fool. But remember what I've warned you, son. This here wild free life, it can go to the head of a man quicker and stronger than whiskey."

"I hope not," Messenger said more gravely than before.

They remained silent for a moment, but there was a speculative and contented light in the eye of young Messenger that made the trapper curse his clumsiness of speech. It occurred to him that in attempting to prevent the growth of an idea, he actually had planted the first seed of it. The line, in the meantime, had been dropped into the water, appearing by refraction to be slanting away at a sharp angle with the surface.

Just then another man joined them, a stalwart brave well upward of six feet in height and with the look of a hero.

"Brother," he said to the boy, "War Lance wishes to speak with you."

Lessing, watching, saw the head of Messenger lift, and the first thoroughly gentle smile he ever had seen appeared on the mouth of the boy. Patently he and this big warrior were sworn friends.

"It is Walking Bear, as we call him for short," explained Messenger. "I come at once."

"It is a message from Summer Day," said the warrior.

This made the trapper snatch up his line. "I'll go with you, Messenger," he said, and he hurried up the slope with them, envying the long and smooth elasticity of their steps.

They came to the chief, and found him like an angry statue in front of his lodge.

"Summer Day," he said, "returns word to me that the Iron Hand has dreamed, and that he deserves not that a warrior should fight him to prove that he is wrong, but that he should be whipped like a child until he realizes that he speaks the thing which is not true. He says that the Iron Hand is a boy who has done nothing, taken no scalps, counted no coups, killed no enemies. Why should he be answered by a warrior and a wise man?"

Chapter Thirty-Two

They walked back through the camp together, Lessing and the boy. People looked at them with round eyes, for the tidings of the message had run like quicksilver through the camp.

"What will you do now, son?" asked Lessing.

"What I've known all along that I should have to do. I'll go to Summer Day's camp and find him, and fight him man to man."

"Why, Messenger, you've gone crazy. You got a touch of sun. He'd simply have you clubbed to death by his young braves that are always wild to be the first to do what their medicine man wants!"

"Nevertheless," said the boy, "there is nothing else left for me to do. And I must be quick . . . I must be quick!" He stopped short, stung by some idea, and then went on again, slowly, stepping softly as though he feared to break in upon his own ideas.

He did not see the girl coming toward them, carrying water to the lodge of her adopted father, but the trapper saw her, and the flash of her braided hair. Lessing saw her falter, almost stop, and then come on with her eyes strictly lowered to the ground. She had been walking like a young goddess before; she approached them now like a humble dairymaid. She was hurrying, and it seemed to the trapper that she had a shudder of satisfaction as she reached the lodge of her father and turned in hastily toward the entrance.

Young Messenger saw her at the same time, and Lessing heard the intake of his breath. He had stopped again, and this time not by his own thought. Fixed in mid-stride, the boy paused there, with his face flushed and his eye bright, and at the entrance flap the girl turned, as Lessing somehow knew that she must do. She turned, and her eyes widened with something more than surprise as she looked back to Messenger. More clearly than words or deeds, something happened between them in that instant before she stooped and passed quickly into the teepee. Then Messenger went on his way down the lane of the village, saying nothing, but his head was still high and his eyes were still brilliant.

In that moment, Lessing decided that he would make more than a short stay among the Blackfeet, for he saw that he might be needed by this youngster to keep him from taking some irremediable step. Squawmen were Lessing's idea of an abomination. The thought haunted him all that day.

In the evening, Bray came back, walking on air. He found that he had been accepted everywhere in the village with a perfect courtesy. Warriors had stopped and talked with him. Children had smiled at him. He had been made thoroughly welcome.

"It's Messenger!" said Bray. "They all ask me questions about him. I ain't got enough Blackfoot lingo to answer . . . I ain't got enough information, neither. But I was popular everywhere, because they all wanted to talk about how he killed the deer at six hundred yards, and how he shot the head off the squirrel . . . and I guess you've heard the rest of the stories?"

"I've got something else to think about," Lessing stated honestly. And he had. It kept him awake that evening in his bed in the lodge of War Lance, and it was late before he closed his eyes. There was trouble ahead, as he saw it, for young Messenger, and, if he escaped from the infinite wiles of the medicine man, still there were other dangers that he might worry about.

At last Lessing slept, but it seemed to him that he had hardly closed his eyes when a whisper ran through the camp, like a gust of wind, and then the *clang* of a rifle shot jerked him to his feet.

A hundred voices were shouting one thing: "The Crows! The Crows!"

That babble was overcome by the roar of a lion's voice. It was War Lance, shouting his orders, even while he flung the saddle on the back of his favorite horse. Like eight arrows whirring to the mark, came the eight of his bodyguard for their mounts. They snatched their bridles from the hands of the squaw of War Lance. Almost instantly they were mounted.

Both the trapper and young Messenger were much behind them, and it seemed that every available man in the village already had flowed out to the south, where the attack was being delivered, when at last they got on their horses and galloped down the central lane that led in that direction.

The squaws and children were out, as a matter of course, but they made way for the riders and screeched encouragement as the white men went past, with Bray thundering at their heels, the last of all. But three good rifles, in expert hands, would be no slight reinforcement to the Blackfeet in the time of need.

Out they galloped past the fringe of the lodges, only to

find that the need for them already had vanished. The Crows, attacking in much force, had nevertheless expected easier going than they found, and the sentinel system of War Lance had detected them while they still were at a little distance. A flurry of rifle shots had checked and turned them, and now they were retreating to wait for a better day.

All up the valley through which the little stream flowed, the whoops and the screeches of the fighters echoed and rang. The explosions of the rifles showed like the flare of great fireflies, suddenly gleaming in dark brush and instantly fading again. The lines of lights, however, showed that as the Blackfeet skirmished forward into the ravine, the Crows were retreating, not rapidly, but slowly, as people not afraid, but unwilling to press a fight in which they gained no advantage. Victories in Indian warfare are not counted glorious so much because of the number of the enemy slain as because of the impunity with which the damage is inflicted. Every step of their retreat made the Crows strong, because the walls of the ravine drew together like a funnel and gathered them in a more solid line.

The trapper and Bray, looking on, rode on more slowly toward the fight, leaving the screaming voices of the village behind them, advancing closer to the shouting warriors. Once fairly committed to the ravine, they found that the roar of the guns and the human voices was deafening. The Blackfeet were coming to a standstill or advancing very slowly, feeling their way among the brush and the boulders.

"Where's Messenger?" shouted Bray in the ear of the trapper.

Lessing looked back. There was no sign of Messenger! Either some accident to his horse, or the loosening of a girth, had caused him to fall back, or else. . . . Might it not be that the story of Summer Day was the perfect truth, and that, fearless as young Messenger was in hand-to-hand fighting, he did not care for the sound of guns and the wasp-like humming of the bullets?

He shook his head, but the thought would not leave him. Then, with a shrug of his strong shoulders, he went on with Bray to join the fighting Indians.

Chapter Thirty-Three

But Messenger, as he galloped out with his two white companions toward the fight, had had a new idea the instant that he saw the battlefield, and, when the thought struck him, he drew in his horse to a stand. Yonder, the valley drew together to a point. There was merely, at the head of it, a narrow bridle path that wound along close to the cliff, between the water and the mountain. On the other side of the stream, there was no path at all, but the sheer rock went straight up from the border of the swiftly flowing water. He had gone so far the day before and seen the lay of the land.

Now, as his idea came to him, it made his heart leap with joy. For the ravine was a bottle. The Blackfeet closed the bottom of it solidly. The ravine walls, impenetrable as they were and unclimbable, were the sides, and there was only the narrow mouth of the valley that needed corking.

He wondered that such a chief as War Lance had not seen the thing. Perhaps he would, later on. In the first place, he simply had galloped out to be in the midst of his men as they attacked the enemy.

Loudly the boy now shouted for Lessing and Bray, but the two had swept forward, well out of hearing. The noise of the women, as they left the village and straggled toward the scene where their husbands, fathers, brothers, and sons were taking the chance of life and death, drowned the calling of Messenger.

He could not venture on mere starlight to help him find them. Besides, whatever was done must be done quickly, for in a few minutes, no doubt, the rearward of the retreating Crows would be through the narrow gap and spreading out over the safer tableland behind it. Perhaps, from that point, they might swing about and attempt to deliver another attack upon the unguarded side of the town. At any rate, he determined on acting alone, since it must be so. He pulled his horse to the side, and started on a dead run for the hills.

Two or three women spotted him at once. He was recognizable by the shortness of his hair, if from no other reason, and instantly their throats were straining on his name. They hurled insults. They called him woman, coward, and traitor. He went on, heedless of their opinion of this apparent flight from the battlefield.

The next moment, the pony was galloping up the slope, and he had enough work and thought to keep himself in the saddle safely. For the noise and the touch of the spurs had driven the pony half frantic with excitement. It galloped furiously, blindly, forward, carrying the rider up and up almost like a bird among the dark heights. Once the branches of a small tree flogged him violently across the face and breast and knocked him back almost to the tail of his mount. But he regained his seat.

Over the first rise, he turned the pony to the left, and shot down a dizzy bank, thirty yards long, to the bottom of a depression. At the foot of it, the pony turned a complete somersault, and, taken unawares, young Messenger was hurled a rod ahead. The wind was knocked out of his body. But when he regained his feet, he found that the horse was gone. With it was gone his chance of quick retreat, in case he got to the vital spot and found the Crows already there.

He hesitated only for an instant. The roaring of the battle just beyond the shallow range of the hills called him more than the roar of the sea ever called a sailor. He ran on, leaning well forward for the slope, straining himself to the utmost. There was, at least, not far to go now. He came to a last upward pitch; beyond it the ground sloped down almost precipitously sharp, and there beneath him was the neck of the valley. To his right extended the tableland, with the star-lighted waters of the little creek flowing in a meandering line across it. To the left, the battle was rolling and thundering up the pass, crowding closer and closer to the exit. But still the rearmost warriors were not there!

He took a breath, freshening his grip on the rifle, and began the descent. Halfway down, he lost both foot and handhold. The rifle flew down before him and landed with a *clang* in the rocky, narrow floor of the trail. He himself followed after and well nigh broke a shoulder as he struck. But he was up at once. He dared not rub bruises or wait for a staggered brain to clear. The rifle was the first care. He passed his hands swiftly over it, and told himself that all was well with the mechanism. Then, staring down the pass, he made out distinctly the dark loom of a mounted man, coming toward him at a little distance.

They were there—they were ready to pour over him and blot him out. On foot as he was, he had no retreat. He was like one who stops the thrust of a bottle of nitroglycerine with his thumb. There was enough power of man and beast there to dash him to atoms, unless he held the pass.

A boulder, a ponderous mass, lay at the verge of the trail, and, getting his hand under the back rim of it, he managed to give it one half turn. He would have been glad to budge it a little farther, but the weight of it was well beyond his power now. He only had succeeded in toppling it, because it lay in a state of balance. However, it almost entirely blocked the path now, and it afforded to him a perfectly safe breastwork.

Behind it he kneeled down and leveled his rifle over the top of it when an oncoming Indian was a scant ten yards away. To the boy, the starlight was as clear as the sun now that he was looking down the familiar, faintly gleaming barrel of the rifle, with the stock tucked comfortably against his shoulder. All except his head was shielded by the rock. A sudden compunction came over him as he saw the loftily nodding feather crest of the man before him. It was some notable warrior, some chief, perhaps, a man who had done great things among his people. Should he lie there in safety and clip away the life of this brave as securely as a woman clips a flower in her garden? He hesitated, panting with doubt, as he had done on that other day when he had faced the medicine man in the wood. Then he set his teeth.

This was no fair, open daylight fighter. He and his lot would gladly have rushed into the Blackfeet camp and slaughtered all who they found there, old and young. No compunctions would have stopped those worthies, not soft babies at the breast or shrieking women. So setting his teeth, he shouted a ringing warning and pulled the trigger. The hammer fell with a *click,* and a little jangling sound of broken metal. There the weapon had broken—at the very point of the lock. There was still the revolver. It jumped into his hand like a living thing.

The Indian had answered that warning shout with a frantic yell of fear, surprise, rage. But he seemed to know the meaning of that telltale *click*. Now he spurred his charger suddenly forward, still whooping at the top of his lungs.

There was no time for a careful bead. It was plainly the

plan of the red man to vault his horse over the boulder and spear the enemy as he flew across. So young Messenger pressed back as close as he could against the stone wall of the ravine and fired across his body with the revolver.

The feathered brave swayed from his saddle and pitched down, the pony vaulted the rock and fled on up the table-land, whinnying. Straight behind him came another, and another.

The first man, Messenger stopped with a bullet through the head of the horse. The rider, plunging down, was stunned by the fall. The third of the procession, seeing what had happened to his two predecessors, wheeled his horse about and fled. He would have made an easy target, but Messenger was not there to slaughter. He was there to stop the mouth of the pass. The fugitive, meanwhile, had fled back, yelling the alarm at the top of his lungs, and the retreat of the rearmost ranks was patently stopped.

They would rally again, of course. There was plenty of courage among the Crows. No Indians ever fought more bravely, unless it were the frantic Cheyennes, who despised death. But Messenger felt that he could rely upon a short interval. Red men love to talk before they act. There might be a short moment during which they would hold council, and that he could use to fortify his position.

To the feathered brave, the youth went first and by a leg dragged him from the water. He was rewarded by a feeble groan, and Messenger gritted his teeth. Dead men were better company for him, just then, than living prisoners, even if in bonds. But he drew the wounded man from the stream, and tied his hands and lashed him with the bridle reins of the dead horse, back to back, with the stunned warrior who had fallen face down. He, too, was living.

But most valuable of all was a repeating Winchester rifle

that the second Crow had dropped in his fall. Nine shots
had been fired from it. From the pouch of the warrior, Messenger reloaded the gun and stood on guard, straining his
eyes down the hollow.

The turmoil at the neck of the cañon had not been overlooked by the Blackfeet, it appeared. For now a great
screeching and whooping arose from the farther end of the
valley, and the line of twinkling fireflies stood still. The
Crows, between two millstones, were silent as a tomb. Not
for long. Perfectly well Messenger comprehended that the
silence came before a storm, and that the storm would
break in his direction. But, at the best, they would only be
able to attack him two abreast—and in his hands was apparently an excellent rifle.

He tried it, half hating to waste the bullet, and heard the
shot *click* against the rocks far down the ravine. It was as
though he had fired a signal shot.

Suddenly, out of the very ground before him, as it
seemed, men arose and leaped in at him. He was lying behind the horse, now, a shallower and less perfect breastwork, but it gave him some protection and a perfect rest for
the rifle, as he lay flat.

Right into the faces of the oncoming braves he drove his
bullets. He upon the right of the foremost two swerved far
out and, falling into the rapid waters of the stream, was
tumbled down the bed by it. He upon the left bounded into
the air with a death yell that ceased, half uttered, as though
a hand had been clapped over the agonized lips. Two more
were behind. One of these stumbled forward upon his face.
Then the rifle jammed as Messenger curled his finger to
take the life of the fourth of that attack. He dropped the
useless weapon. With the revolver—he could bless now the
hours of practice in making a swift and perfect draw—he

shot upward, and the brave, staggering, turned and went uncertainly back down the trail, trying to run, but with his feet dragging.

Yonder, in the back of the pass, Messenger could see only very indistinctly, but enough to make out that there was a general movement in retrogression, and he heard loud, wailing voices of lament, great shoutings, groans of despair. Yet they could not face that catastrophe, it seemed. Back they rolled.

The pass was empty, just before him, and suddenly the boy was aware, for the first time, that waspish sounds had been humming about his head, and that his left shoulder was stinging badly. He felt it, and found that his sleeve was soaking wet with blood. However, it appeared to be no more than a surface scratch, for his left arm was still perfectly at his command. He turned to his prisoners, then. The groaning of the feathered brave had ceased; he might be dead by now. So young Messenger kneeled beside him and placed a hand over the man's heart. It was beating steadily. He tried him in the Blackfeet tongue.

"My friend," said the boy, "where did the bullet hit you? Are you badly hurt?" He had aimed for the head, he remembered, in that first attack.

The voice of the brave answered him with a perfect calm, and in the only Indian dialect with which Messenger was familiar: "The bullet struck my head, but it must have glanced along the skull. It struck me like a club, but I thought that I fell into the water."

"I drew you out," said Messenger. "Are you hurt in any other place?"

"My left shoulder was broken by the fall. Otherwise, I am not hurt."

"If your shoulder is hurt, then the rein of the bridle is

torturing you," said Messenger.

"That is nothing," answered the other.

"What is your name?" asked Messenger.

"It is known among my people," said the warrior. "The Blackfeet also know me, if they have memories. You will hear me sing it in the fire."

"Fire?" cried out the boy.

"He is Red Feather," said the other captive. "You know that you will kill me in the fire with not very much pleasure, but the women will taste the death of Red Feather for a long time."

"They will come again," Red Feather said slowly. "They will not remain there below. They will come again surely. They know that I am here. My sworn blood brothers, they will not keep their lives while I lie here."

"Four men have come, and four men are dead," said the boy. "I don't think they'll try the pass again." He stared down into the darkness. Then cautiously he loosened the bridle strap and shifted it under the injured shoulder of the chief. The latter, in spite of his resolution, could not help uttering a faint groan of relief.

"There will be no fire for you, Red Feather," said the boy.

"It is the new warrior of War Lance. It is the white man," said the companion of the chief, interrupting again.

"Is it so?" said Red Feather.

"Yes."

"The Iron Hand . . . ," the chief uttered slowly. "The Iron Hand and the gentle heart. If you take your knife now and drive it into my heart, the spirits of the Crows who have gone before me will praise you in the sky, brother."

"There will be no fire," repeated the boy. "Not unless they hang me, also. Lie quietly, and trust to me for your life, if the Blackfeet come to you. I must keep watch. I think your friends are coming, as you promised. Heaven help them, poor fellows," he said, and could not help adding: "The odds are horribly against them here!"

Chapter Thirty-Four

Straining his sight into the dark of the hollow, Messenger thought again and again that he saw shadowy forms before him. But his eyes deceived him.

At the bottom of the ravine, the Blackfeet, still slowly advancing, made the place ring with pandemonium; in between, the Crows were still as silent as death. And death, perhaps, already had come to some of them.

Messenger made sure that all was as well as could be, and, returning to the Crows, he separated them and bound them by their hands to jagged projections of the boulder that he had overturned in the trail. In this manner, they were able to sit up and look over the scene. Messenger crouched beside them. He had taken up a third rifle, one that had fallen from the hand of the second warrior to die under his bullets.

"Why did you leave the pass unguarded, Red Feather," he said, "if you are the leader of this band?"

"Because I was a child," Red Feather answered. "All the blood . . . all the blood that has been spilled here, it flows out of my folly. All the scalps that are taken are torn from my head. All the shame of the Crows is my shame. I should have put a guard here. Two warriors would have held it against a thousand . . . one warrior, such as the Iron Hand, if there is another like him. But I was a child. It was hard to hold back my men. They were hungry to rush through the village, and every one of my young men already saw the red scalp of War Lance hanging at his bridle. So we charged, and were turned. They are all owls, the men who ride with War Lance. But when we had to retreat, then I looked up the pass and recognized the trap. I hurried on with Straight Arrow, who sits here beside me in sorrow, and two others, to get to the trap and hold it. But it closed on me. It set its teeth in me, and here I sit and wait for the end. But all the blood is my blood, and all the dead are my dead. I have been a fool!" His head bowed, and the crest of bedraggled feathers nodded above it.

The boy was silent, out of a great respect. There was a nobility about this war chief, no matter how he had come skulking through the night to win scalps and count coups on his enemies. He remembered what Lessing had said. The ways of the red man are not our ways, but their honor is just as great. Their taboos are as strong, but merely different.

Still they looked together down the valley, when a fresh sound of shouting beat up to them, and there was a sudden roar of many hoofs of horses, galloping together.

"They charge! They charge!" shouted Straight Arrow, in a voice like thunder.

"Go home, good lance!" Red Feather yelled. "Knife, find the heart and the throat! Bullets, drive true! Axes strike and clubs shatter skulls! Kill the Blackfeet dogs! Count coups . . . rip away scalps! Take glory, glory, back to the Crows!"

As he shouted this war cry in a vast, whooping voice and ended with a yell that fairly curdled the blood of Messenger, the firing in the valley redoubled. The noise of shouting grew beyond belief. Then the almost straight line of the fireflies, whose gleaming had marked the position of the Blackfeet, grew irregular. In some places it swayed forward. In others it sagged back.

"Kill, kill!" shrieked Straight Arrow. "Now for honor! Now for the scalp dance! The old men will honor you. The children will honor you. Oh, my brothers, strike hard and with great hearts!"

He and the chief, Red Feather, whooped frightfully in unison.

The flashing of the guns in the valley formed a great, irregular pattern, out of which appeared a long, streaming point of those deadly, gleaming fireflies, and behind them glowed a more thickly clustered group. Far down the ravine they sped.

"The Crows have not driven the Blackfeet before them!" cried out Red Feather. "They have only broken through, and now they flee for their lives, and the Blackfeet follow on these swift horses, striking down the laggards, spearing them, counting many coups. Do you hear their battle yell rising, Straight Arrow? It is the Blackfeet, the howling of dogs!"

The fighting scattered far and wide across the increasing width of the plain, and the uproar settled with wonderful suddenness to a few almost dissociated sounds, the aftermath of the great fighting. Still, in the distance a spark of gunfire winked and was gone, but this was rapidly ending, and the voices of the triumphant Blackfeet flowed back toward the site of the victory.

Out of that hollow now, there went up, here and there, wild whoopings and yells of victory. And, amidst other sounds, a long and mournful chanting.

"Listen, then," said Red Feather. "It is a Blackfoot. One of the dogs now is howling his death song."

"It is good," Straight Arrow stated in a voice of infinite satisfaction.

"Oh, Crows," the chief declared, in a voice of desire, "have you struck your wings in their faces, and your claws in their hearts? What scalps have you taken? What coups have you counted? No, no," he added gloomily. "You were fleeing. You were fighting for your lives, not for the lives of others. Your chief put you in a trap, and the trap has closed, and the women of our nation will howl and cut off their hair and curse the day that Red Feather led the warriors out to the battle."

"They will trade you back to your people," the boy said, "for something that they wish . . . for a long peace, perhaps, or for horses. Well, you will live to see men following you on the warpath again, Red Feather."

Straight Arrow struck in: "It is true that no Blackfoot closed the pass behind you."

"True," the chief affirmed, pondering the thought.

"Who could have known that with War Lance there was a man of such a medicine as this? Their prophet was not with them. Summer Day was not there. But the Iron Hand was there . . . he looked through the dark. His eye, like the eye of a night-flying owl, flew through the night and saw the place where he should stand. He went there with his iron hand. With it he closed the pass. It is true, Straight Arrow, that a great medicine was against me in this fight. Will the Crows remember?"

"The Crows will remember, in time," suggested Straight Arrow. "They will remember all the better after other enemies of the Blackfeet have learned to know the Iron Hand. The Assiniboines and the Cheyennes and the Pawnees will feel his hand."

The hoofs of the horses rang now, up the trail that led toward the pass, and a voice shouted loudly toward them in the Blackfeet tongue. The boy did not answer at once, and

231

the voice called again.

"Who are here? What heroes of the Blackfeet are here who closed the pass? Or if you are spirits who used thunder and lightning, give us some sign?"

"I am here," the voice of Messenger said in answer. His intonation of the tongue, slightly untrue, seemed familiar to them.

A sudden shout answered him. "It is the Iron Hand! He has closed the pass."

The hoof beats came closer.

"Stop!" called Messenger.

Instantly he was obeyed.

"What chief is there?" called the boy.

"Strong Bow is here. Strong Bow, come closer and speak to him. He is stopping us for some reason."

"I am here!" called a deep, rather husky voice, as of a man whose vocal chords have been frayed by much violent usage. "What is it that you wish, brother?"

"There are with me," said the boy, "two brave Crows."

"Dead men?" broke out the impatient voice of the chief.

"One dead man fell in the stream and was carried down among the rocks. Two dead men lie in the path before you. Be careful with your horses. Two living men are here with me."

"Living men!" shouted many voices together.

Messenger, who was close to Red Feather, felt the shudder of his muscular body.

"Let us have them! Let us have the prisoners!"

"They are his own until the scalp dance!" answered the commanding voice of the chief. "Iron Hand, you have done great deeds. The old men will sing songs about you. Come with your prisoners, or, if they cannot walk, we will put them on our horses."

232

"Wait where you are!" commanded Messenger. "These are my prisoners. I want them to be safely kept."

"They must die!" answered the chief instantly.

"They must die! The women will take them!" rejoined the braves behind the chief.

"They must live," Messenger replied firmly, "and they must be traded back to their people for whatever you wish . . . horses or other captives, or whatever you will."

"Brother," said Strong Bow, "you are like one who puts food into the mouths of the starving, and then snatches it away again. Have they names, the two men with you, or are they young braves, fighting their first fight?"

"Whatever their names may be," replied the boy, "I make this bargain with you, Strong Bow. They must live. I must have your word, or else send for War Lance, and he will give his word, instead."

Very audibly, he heard the groan of the chief.

"What other men are with you, Iron Hand?" he said. "If you led them to that place and fought as their leader, the chief glory is yours . . . but they have a right to lift their voices and say what shall be done with the prisoners they have helped to capture."

"Yes!" shouted the other Blackfeet. "They have their right. They have their battle right. Let us hear their voices. What other brave men have been counting coups with you, Iron Hand?"

A slight tingling passed up the back of Messenger. He took a breath, and then he answered quietly for he was swelling with instinctive pride: "There are no others. There is only one voice to speak about these men, my friends."

Silence lasted for two heartbeats, and then Strong Bow replied, or started to reply, when a yell of wonder and of delight stopped him. It was a moment or so before Strong

Bow could make himself heard, and then he cried out: "If you have such a strong medicine that you alone could stand in front of all the warriors and turn them back like sheep before a wolf . . . if you alone could do that, brother, the men are yours! Do with them what you will. No Blackfoot will touch them. But the old women will gnash their teeth when they see the murdering Crows in safety."

"Now," Messenger said, "I give you their names. You have given me your word in exchange, Strong Bow?"

"I have given you my word."

"As if they were your blood brothers, you will protect them?"

"I have given my word," said the chief. "Now, tell us their names?"

"First, there is a warrior and a strong man called Straight Arrow."

There was a terrible groan from among the Blackfeet.

"We know him!" they said in unison, and a single voice added: "I have a token of him in my side. Why do I ride bent over, except because of Straight Arrow? Must he be left free and safe?"

"I have given my word," said Strong Bow. "I must protect him like a brother, though I had rather be handling his heart. What is the other name, Iron Hand?"

"A name you know, Strong Bow. The other is a great chief, and his name is Red Feather." The youth stepped back a little as he spoke, like one braced against a strong wind, and he had reason, for the screech of rage and hate that rose from those warriors was enough to drive needle points of apprehension through his brain. They raved like madmen. They swept closer up the path, so that he could see the gleaming of their faces, and their angry gestures.

"We are dead men," Red Feather stated. "Let us stand

234

up, Iron Hand, and die on our feet, like warriors and men."

"Strong Bow!" shouted the boy, "I have your promise! The honor of a chief is pledged to me. Red Feather is now like a blood brother to you, while he is in our party."

Strong Bow himself pushed to the front. His shout forced the others to be obediently silent, although their silence was rather a deep growling in their throats. "It is true," he said. "I have given my word. It is stronger than my hand to break my promise. Now give them to us freely, and each of them is as safe as though he were my father's son."

Chapter Thirty-Five

It was, on the whole, very sad business for the Crows. They had left many—and many a one of their best warriors—dead on the bottom of that ravine. They streamed away through a close rifle fire that could not help but tell on them, no matter how hard they flogged their ponies or how they lay along the sides of the horses.

Lessing and Bray had done their business for the Blackfeet in the coolest and most logical manner. When they saw what was likely to happen, they simply had dismounted and taken a good position on a slight, rough rise of ground. Each of them faced toward opposite sides, and, when the charge of the Crows came, their horsemen naturally split around that slight eminence, like water flowing around a boat. Bray and Lessing, lying in perfect comfort and safety, emptied their rifles at close range, never troubling about hitting warriors, so long as they could shoot down horses, for dismounted men would have not a chance in a hundred of escaping from the swarming Blackfeet in the pursuit.

So the charge swept through, and, as the Blackfeet went off like a cloud of hornets behind their foes, the trapper and his companion sat up and stared up the valley.

"That War Lance," said the younger man, "he's got a brain. I never would've thought of corkin' up that ravine that way."

"That War Lance is a wise man," admitted the trapper, "but that ain't any reason that we should overlook some of the things that are laid out right here at our feet."

So they went down, of one mind, to plunder fallen horse and fallen man. There was plenty that was worth taking. Lessing got a steel battle-axe with a richly decorated handle, three curiously mounted medicine bags that were to their former owners as so many souls, two excellent Indian saddles, no fewer than four knives, a beaded suit in perfectly good condition, a long, feather headdress, a beautifully made and tapered lance, a good, new, repeating rifle, and over twenty pounds of ammunition.

His horse had run away during the charge, while its master was lying prone among the rocks, but Lessing more than recouped himself by catching two wandering ponies that he found riderless in the ravine. On these he carefully loaded his spoils.

Bray had been similarly occupied and had gained even greater spoils. He had gained something more than spoils. He had won peace of mind, for it was not likely that the Blackfeet would foolishly hold old grudges against a man who had just showed his feeling by fighting for them in defense of their village.

Meanwhile, the warriors returned from the pursuit. They had cut down those who were mounted on slow horses, or those who lagged because of wounds. They came back like ravens to the battlefield, and into the ravine, also, the women came with torches, shrieking in their exultation as they found the plunder of the fallen.

Scalps had been taken and coups counted. Some of the young men could not hold in their exultation, but were starting their scalp dances in the very middle of the night, out there with none to see them. Their voices sounded like the clamoring of enormous roosters, ringing through the ravine.

A rumor swept the ravine. A single man had dared to go to the head of the valley and close it against the retreat of the Crows.

Old Lessing shook his head. "There's the start and the makin's of a grand lie," Lessing said. "If any one man did do such a job, he's gonna be more famous than War Lance himself, and all in one stroke. But no one man would ever've dared to try such a thing."

"No," agreed Bray. "Nobody in the world. Besides, I seen the winkin' of the rifle fire, and it must've been three or four men up there, shootin' side-by-side. We'll get the truth, pretty quick. We'll find out what it's all about. But where's your friend, Messenger, that you thought so much of?"

"Aw, he'll turn up," answered the trapper, embarrassed.

"Yeah," replied the other. "It'll be about the right time for him to turn up, maybe . . . after the shootin' is over!"

Lessing, for some reason, found no word to say against this, at the time being. He started with Bray across the ravine, leading their captured war ponies, and on the way they came to a woman carrying a torch and hunting wildly for the dead, and plunder.

Of her, Lessing asked after the Iron Hand, his friend. The answer was a furious exclamation of disgust. "I saw him, with my own eyes, running on his horse like a coward toward the hills behind the camp," she replied.

This quite took the wind out of the trapper's sails. He and Bray were headed back for the encampment, by this time, but they checked themselves to watch a procession that was coming down the side of the ravine. It was made bright by the burning of several torches that the first women from the town were carrying. They bounded like mad creatures, high into the air, and whirled the torches, and screeched with their joy.

Other sounds of a different nature were ringing through the ravine: the isolated whoops of the rejoicing warriors, the laughter of the women, and, here and there, a sudden outburst of lamenting as one of the torch carriers who hunted among the fallen came upon a husband or a relative lying dead. For the Blackfeet had not escaped without loss.

But Bray and old Lessing paid no heed to anything except the procession.

"They're bringing down the heroes that stopped up the end of the ravine . . . and heroes they are," said Lessing. "I'd like to see their ugly faces myself, Bray. Let's get over there and watch 'em go by."

So they pressed to the side of the ravine in time to see, first of all, the bodyguard of the great War Lance coming down the slope. They were intact, but they showed that they had been through the hottest kind of water. No lances were carried. These must have been broken in hand-to-hand fighting. A bullet had ripped open the face of one of the youngest of these distinguished braves, but he rode on, and carelessly allowed the blood to dry and blacken. Others had been struck, as the dark patches on their clothing showed, but none was incapacitated, and they looked wilder and more formidable now than they had when riding into the gate of Fort Lippewan. Behind them came the chief himself. He had headed the pursuit of the enemy, and then, rapidly returning, he had gone up the valley after Strong Bow to find the heroes.

Just to the rear of the great war chief himself came Strong Bow. He was on foot, and he led a horse in each hand. Upon one was mounted a badly wounded Crow;

upon the other sat a Crow whose face was a mass of ugly wounds, but who sat straight enough.

The eyes of the two frontiersmen, accustomed as they were to the different regalia of the tribes, easily distinguished the two as captive Crows.

"That's Red Feather, or I miss my guess," said Lessing. "If they've got him, they've got the Crows in their pocket, I tell you. They've got them eating out of their hands."

"Hush," cautioned Bray. "Here come the heroes. Listen to the women . . . how they're goin' wild. Listen to 'em, Lessing. They're gonna bust their throats. My ears'll ring for a week."

At this particular point, just behind the two captives, there must have been a score of torchbearers, at least, and they were frantic with excitement, yipping, yelling, literally screaming out a jargon that had no meaning other than "victory" many times repeated, mixed with a few frightful insults for the enemies who had been beaten.

As they came nearer, the flaring, shaken light of their torches shone brilliantly upon the object of their admiration, and Bray grasped the shoulder of his companion. "By glory," he breathed, "it's that boy . . . it's that Messenger!"

It was Messenger, in fact. He was mounted on a pony not selected at hazard from the spoils, but given by the hands of War Lance himself. At the first glance, it was seen that the war chief of the Blackfeet had bestowed his own best charger upon the white man. A steel-dust gray, glancing and brilliant with sweat, it fairly danced down the ravine with young Messenger sitting almost gloomily in the saddle. That compliment was not foolishly paid by War Lance. It was like a crown on the head of Messenger, however. At the sight of the horse and the man, realizing what the thing meant, the squaws went half insane with joy. They rushed in before the proud horse, brandishing their torches. They whooped and screamed and lifted their strong hands toward the boy. Messenger rode on with his eyes straight before him. Behind him closed the same shouting mob of women.

"That's him, and there's only one of him," Lessing said with an infinite satisfaction. "Look at him, boy, and look at him ag'in! He stopped up the ravine like a cork in the bottle. He's gone and got himself more famous in one evening's work than most big chiefs do in a whole life."

"It's him," Bray said hoarsely. "Let's get on to the camp. There's gonna be a lot of feastin' and whoopin' and dancin', tonight."

They turned together, and made rapidly toward the camp.

Chapter Thirty-Six

Just as the dogs of a village clamor and clatter with their barking, and two or three big timber wolves come down to the edges of the cultivated fields to howl a dismal answer, so the people of the Blackfeet village clattered and whooped and shouted in their joy. Here and there, a few voices went up to the sky more dolefully than the crying of wolves. There were the women lamenting for their dead.

There were few killed. Plenty of wounds, from slight to serious, had been distributed through the tribe, but, for that great victory, they had paid with only three lives, all lost when the Crow charge broke through the defending line of the Blackfeet. Three lives were a very slight payment for such an overwhelming triumph, but the mourners must be heard.

It reminded young Messenger of the sounds in a nursery, where laughter comes from one corner, and sad wailing out of the next. But the high-pitched tremor of the keening never ended during all that followed. It wavered in the background like a conscience. It oppressed the heart suddenly in the midst of all the shouting and the dancing.

He passed by one melancholy group. They were bearing into the camp one of the dead men, and before the horse, on which the body was bound, walked the widow. She made a frightful picture. She had slashed her hair short, and so gashed her scalp in doing so that the blood ran down all around her shoulders. Her very face she had deliberately hacked more horribly, and cut her arms and her legs, for she was crimson nearly from head to foot. The knife with which she had performed these self-mutilations, she still brandished in her hand and held it up to the sky, while she demanded of the ruling spirits of the air why they had envied her happiness so much that they had to take her spouse from her? She asked them if there were too few heroic ghosts in the blue fields of the happy hunting grounds, that they had to rob her and the Blackfeet of the greatest of the warriors on earth? These things she howled out, sometimes at the top of her lungs and sometimes she sobbed it in a heartbroken gibberish that distressed Messenger to hear and see.

But the mourners paused to let the triumphal procession pass by, and, when it did so, the sound of the wailing became dim in the rear. Yet it never passed entirely out of the mind of Messenger. It hung there like a dark cloud of thought.

The rather deliberate and slow approach of the procession of victory had been preceded by a rush of most of the women and warriors into the village, and there the preparations for the scalp dance were made at once. It was rare for a tribe to have such a chance of rejoicing. Usually their warriors came back lean and dusty from the warpath, and the hint of what they had done had long come in before them, but this was another matter. Here the smell of the smoke of battle was fresh in all nostrils. And with eager hands they set about building the great pile for the fire. They heaped it high, and by the time it was lofty enough, the braves already were taking their places, their faces twitching with a suppressed emotion in spite of their self-control.

They had freshened their paint for the festival. Their

ugly faces were hideous with deliberate intent. If they had seemed terrible to the enemy, their purpose was now to exemplify the terror that they had caused. Several of them, however, who were favored with surface wounds that were not dangerous, disdained pain and allowed the dried or still oozing blood to speak by itself, and, on the whole, they were the most hideous of the lot. Instead of good, new weapons, many of the warriors preferred to appear with axes, bows, and lances that had been broken in the battle and, therefore, were honorable for the ceremonial. A number carried fresh scalps, some of them clotted with gore, and the sight was almost too horrible for Messenger to watch. For he could not help feeling that practically every death that had occurred among the Crows was due to his action in blocking the pass.

Moreover, he detested this publicity and would gladly have left the scene, but he could not do so with any grace. For the attentions of the bodyguard of War Lance had been, by his order, transferred to the white lad, and they were grouped closely around him. He could not stir unattended by them. When he rose from the place where he had been asked to take his seat on the ground near the fire, the eight rose in turn, and looked at him with expectant faces. He was forced to take his seat again.

All around the fire they were gathered in a great circle, those fighters of the Blackfeet, and behind them stood the youths on the verge of manhood, those almost ready to pass the final test of torture before being acclaimed as brave. Yet behind these, and mingled among them, were the women and smaller children, and some of the squaws held up little infants with shining faces, in order to look on at the wild ceremony.

The fire, in the meantime, had mounted to the top of the

pyre and threw vast red and golden arms into the sky, where the stars seemed to be set in a whirling, dancing motion by the heads of flame. So great was the heat that the face of Messenger almost blistered, but the Indians seemed untroubled by it. Drums began to beat in furious cadences, and horns blew, and whistles shrilled and trilled through the confusion of sound.

Every now and then, excitement, or memory of the battle, forced some brave to spring to his feet with an echoing war cry, and perhaps twenty men would leap up and rival him at once.

The very force of the fire soon burned out the main portion of the wood. A great mass of glowing embers and glimmering flames stood then in the center of the circle, and now the great war chief strode out before his people. Utter silence fell all around him. He was seen to fill his pipe, holding it in a peculiar fashion, with the bowl to one side, and the stem pointing downward at a slant to the left. After it had been filled, he took from the verge of the fire a living coal that sparkled like a jewel with its power, and transferred it with a lightning dexterity to the surface of the tobacco in the pipe bowl. A few whiffs started the pipe, and then he blew smoke to the deities of the upper air, to the underground spirits, and north, east, south, and west, very solemnly.

These proceedings were watched with awe and in deepest silence. Afterward, he said: "Oh, my people, today we have had good fortune. The Sky People have been kind to us. And now is the time for us to count our coups and show the scalps that we have taken, according to the custom of our fathers. Let every man tell the truth. Let every man search his heart before he speaks. First of all, there is one who must talk to us and tell us what he did. He must tell us what spirits inspired him, and how they helped him to fight. Otherwise, what man could have done what he has done? His medicine is very strong. That I knew when I first saw him, and I was happy when he came riding with me to visit my people. He is going to stay a year among us. . . ."

Here, in spite of their respect for their chief, a wild whoop of jubilance rose from a hundred throats. It died out slowly, and, when he could be heard again, War Lance continued.

"If we can prove to him that we are his brothers, perhaps he will become one of us, always. . . ."

Another loud yell of approval went up at this.

Said War Lance: "We wait for you, brother. Let the Iron Hand stand up and speak to us and tell us how he acted when the Crows came down like wolves and hoped to eat us like so many sheep." He paused.

There was a stir, a whisper, and then a murmur of disappointment. Two or three of the bodyguard leaned close to the boy and tried to persuade him, but what was ceremonial to the Blackfeet was mere boasting to him.

The pause grew and grew.

Suddenly an old warrior uttered a shout, and, rising from the ground, he threw off his robe and stood in the flashing light of the fire. He must have been at least sixty years old, but his lean body retained a youthful activity. Only his long, straggling hair had turned white, but his legs and arms were burnished with long, hard strips of muscle undisguised by an ounce of fat. Old though he was, he was as erect as a youth, and every eye noted instantly that a scalp dangled from the truncheon of his spear. It was plain that he had been in the thick of the fight. Now that his robe was thrown off, he appeared flashing with paint—bright streaks of red, yellow, green, and blue covered his body and his face, and contrasted with the silvery shower of his long hair that became, when he moved violently, like a mist blowing about his shoulders.

"It is Striking Eagle," whispered one of the bodyguard to Messenger, "and the spirits have most surely spoken to him."

He appeared, at least, like one who sees a light dimly and follows it with an outstretched hand. So, like a sleep-walker, his head thrown far back, he advanced toward the fire. There he paused, holding the same attitude.

The eyes of the Blackfeet, all around Messenger, were fairly bulging and glittering with awe. Looking across the circle of the firelight, he saw on the farthest side, opposite him, the double gleam of golden hair, and the face of Yellow Antelope, transformed with excitement, her hands clasped as she prepared to hear miracles and to believe them.

"I have seen it!" said the old brave. "The spirits show me the truth. The eye of a hawk is in me, looking out and seeing all the things that the Iron Hand did tonight."

War Lance, without a word, stepped back to the edge of the circle and waited with folded arms. Everyone seemed quite willing to accept the word of this apparently inspired man.

"First," said the warrior, "I see him roused from the lodge of the great chief. The others leap out. But the Iron Hand goes more slowly. Where there is strength, there is also patience. He goes more slowly. Their galloping horses leave him. He comes out upon the valley where the fighting is. You have seen the valley, oh, Blackfeet!"

There was a brief, low shout of agreement and excitement from the warriors.

"The Iron Hand looks over the battle. He sees that the

Crows retreat. He sees the narrow head of the valley. He holds up his hands to the Sky People. He calls out to them and he says . . . 'My Fathers, shall I call upon the warriors of the Blackfeet to go with me to stop the Crows as they draw back, sure of themselves, and proud of their safety?' So he calls out to them, and the Sky People, who love him, come down close above his head, so that he can hear the swishing of their bodies in the air, and they answer him . . . 'There is no time to call for others, and your own strength is sufficient.' When he hears this, he doubts no more, neither does he linger. Who of you has seen the hare fleeing? Who has seen the mule deer bounding over rough ground, up and down? Who has seen the antelope racing over the plains? Who has seen the forest fire jumping from mountain to mountain in a great wind? That is how the Iron Hand rushed toward the danger. He did not turn his back. He had no fear. He laughed as he went, and the Sky People, flying above him, laughed, also, and exulted in the warrior. His horse fell and then ran away, with its reins flying in the wind, but the Iron Hand laughed, and went on. He was swifter than his horse. He was swifter than the wind. He came to the high place above the pass. You know the place, oh, Blackfeet!"

There was the same deep-throated, rumbling response as before.

"He looked down. He could see the fighting in the ravine, and he could hear the guns and the shouting. Below him, the pass was dark, like the throat of a well. It was a great distance. We all have seen the cliff. But the Iron Hand was not afraid. He laughed, and leaped out into the thin, dark air. Behold! It lowered him gently to the trail below. Then he saw beside the trail a great rock. Eight strong men could hardly lift it. . . ."

There was an involuntary shout of testimony on this point, and a murmur of admiration following it.

"But he seized it with his hands of iron," said the brave. "He took it lightly, as a child lifts a play bow or a warrior picks up the saddle to throw on the back of his horse. He picks it up, and drops it down in the middle of the trail. The enemy rushed on him. You know, oh, Crows, how you rushed upon him."

He whirled about suddenly, and pointed across the circle, and there for the first time, young Messenger saw the two braves whom he had taken captive.

Strong Bow, at least, had been true to his promise to treat them as brothers. For the arm and shoulder of the injured Red Feather had been bandaged, and the wound in his head had been tended. The two of them, with only their hands bound together to make escape impossible, were seated side-by-side, to watch the painful spectacle of the triumph of their enemies.

Red Feather's loud voice answered: "What can men do against spirits such as those who help the Iron Hand? We rushed up against him, it is true, with spears and guns. But he turned aside our bullets and changed our spears into straws. We could not harm him. He struck us from our horses. We fell senseless on the rock, and he bound us and made us captives. But the spirits, who helped him, made him save our lives. That is why we are here. Our friends, my blood brothers, came hurrying then to rescue me. But he threw them back, as a rock throws back drops of water."

As he ended, the Blackfeet shouted like one man. This was something more than mere compliment, this testimony from a beaten enemy and a great and proved fighter. If Messenger had but known it, he was receiving more than a crown of gold in the eyes of the friendly Indians who sat around that circle. But he only looked straight across the fire toward the place where the girl stood and saw, with a jump of his heart, that she was laughing with sheer joy, and that her eyes were shining toward him.

Striking Eagle went on with his speech, but it became less speech than pantomime. He fell into a frenzy. He shook the broken truncheon of his war spear. He began to dance and bound about the fire, illustrating his inspired picture of how the Iron Hand had met the enemy and thrust them back. He counted coups, he made shouting speeches of defiance, and, when he had ended, he was so exhausted by his efforts that he was barely able to retire to a place at the edge of the circle of watchers.

His place was taken by another, a formidable warrior of mature years, with a face like a weather-scarred rock. He told how, in the charge of the Crows for freedom, two braves had borne down upon him just as he fired his last bullet, and how he flung his shield edgewise at one of them and dodged the battle-axe of the second, then stabbed him in the side with a knife as the victim went past him.

He was followed by another and by another.

The enthusiasm of the warriors could not now be restrained. Half a dozen of the braves would be in the circle at the same time, frantically gesticulating, shouting, dancing, yelping out their own praises, and the drums began throbbing. In the whooping and roaring of the crowd, it was impossible for any man to make himself heard except by the spectators immediately in front of him, and, therefore, each man would make the circle about the fire, pausing here and there to reënact his feat.

There were solemn moments, as when one brave deliberately sacrificed a scalp for the recovery of his young son from a deadly illness. There was a wounded brave who insisted on dancing his war dance and shouting his story until he fell in a faint.

But young Messenger, watching the crowd, began to see and hear them no longer as individuals, but rather as units lost in one great picture. An absurd or a hideous picture it might have seemed to men dwelling securely in Eastern cities, but, out there between the mountains and under the stars, it was a different matter. Nothing had happened in his life like this. Certainly nothing had given him such a thrilling sense of pride and power. For these people worshipped strength and courage, and, at that moment, he was by far the most admired man in the tribe.

Chapter Thirty-Seven

There were two days of noisy feasting for the tribe after this glorious victory, for such it appeared to them. The object of warfare being to circumvent the enemy as cheaply as possible, the part that chance and the work of one man had played in their success over warriors every whit as brave as themselves did not matter. They could now look upon themselves as matchless men of valor. The stories of the old men became popular. The youngsters were more easily able now to hear about the prodigious deeds of the old time, since they had had a close taste of actuality just a day or two before. And, to make all well in the camp, a herd of elk was found close by and exterminated in a slaughter that supplied plenty of meat for all the possible feasts.

These, young Messenger did not attend. He spent his time very largely by himself, and, as Bray said to old Lessing, the boy seemed to be moving in a dream.

"He oughta be in a dream," said Lessing. "He's had half the girls in the tribe offered to him for wives, free of charge. He's been offered about a hundred hosses, guns, new lodges . . . everything that a man could want to set up in Injun life. He oughta be in a dream."

"He's thinking about old Summer Day," answered Bray.

"Maybe he is, and maybe not," said the trapper. "Likely we ain't gonna hear from Summer Day."

It was the main subject of conversation throughout the

camp. The great medicine man had declined the first challenge on what appeared to the tribesmen sufficient grounds.
He was a chief of established power, and the young white
lad had accomplished nothing in war. This was now all
changed. Whether he wanted them or not, at least five
coups won in a single fight were tenfold more glorious than
if they had been picked up in the course of a long career.
They were, moreover, first coups, all of them.

That very night of the battle, without delaying, War
Lance had dispatched one of the lightest of his young men
with three horses and orders to ride like mad to the camp of
the medicine man and return in haste with the answer of
Summer Day. For that answer the braves were now waiting.
Messenger waited with them.

But, as had been suggested, there was something more
than the medicine man in the mind of the boy. He had not
passed into a dream, as Bray thought. In fact, it seemed to
him that he was stepping out of a dream into reality. One of
those realities was as poignant as the odor of spring flowers.

He lounged, one morning, in the lodge of War Lance,
who had just reached a momentous decision. His hatred of
the Crows was as strong as that of any of his men, but in the
presence of the two great warriors as captives, he saw a
means to a great end. If they were sent home without
reason, without exchange asked, to their tribe, safe and
sound, the Crows, whose spirits must have been a little
daunted by their late defeat, would hardly fail to come to
terms of peace with such strong and magnanimous foemen.
Therefore, he had decided to dismiss them, and even to
send them with presents, as became a great war chief. With
this decision, the village was buzzing, and War Lance himself was at a feast where he would explain his policy to the
wise old men of the tribe. Bray and Lessing were off

hunting, and there remained in the lodge only the white boy and the squaw of the chief.

Messenger said to her, suddenly sitting up from the backrest, and idly fingering the smooth, straight shaft of a buffalo arrow: "When young men wish to marry, what do they do among the Blackfeet?"

She bent her head a little lower over the quillwork that engaged her. "They take horses and tie them to the lodge entrance of the father of the girl they wish to have for a wife," she said.

"I have no horses," he said bluntly. "But I suppose I could buy them."

"You have a name," she answered. "Leave that at the door of the lodge. Go speak to the father, and, if he is a wise man, he will take his daughter's hand and put it in yours."

"You are a kind woman," said the boy. Suddenly he sighed. "I must not go like a beggar," he said.

At this, she looked up with a jerk of her head. "There is no chief among the Blackfeet and no rich man who would not give you twenty horses to buy a wife," she declared.

"There, again, it is giving, giving, giving, and all on the part of your tribe. I have been here these days, sitting and eating and taking your good things . . . and giving nothing!"

"Except your blood for us," she said softly.

He waved this suggestion away. "But first a man must have the consent of the girl," he said.

"Yes. That is true. I remember when Crazy Elk offered thirty horses even, for the hand of Green Willow, and her father took the horses, but afterward he had to give them back, because the girl laughed in the face of that man."

"She laughed at him?"

"Yes, and made him a fool before all the tribe."

"What should I do first?" asked the boy. "I see that the young men do not stop and talk to the girls of the Blackfeet."

"In the early evening," said the squaw, "when the heat of the middle day is over and the sun is low down toward the mountain heads, then the young women go down to the edge of the river. They go down to bring up water."

"Yes," said the boy, "I think that I've seen them go. What of that? Shall I go and offer to carry up the water for her?"

The squaw laughed. "No woman would let a warrior carry a burden for her," she answered. "She would be shamed through her whole life, if she did such a thing. But if you watch, you will see that the girls do not go down when the young men swim, nor above where the horses are driven to water, nor above that, where the washing is done, nor above that . . . but still at a greater distance there is an easy bank down to the edge of the stream, and the girls go down there and get the water, where it runs pure and without anything foul in it. As they come back, sometimes, here and there, stands a brave with a blanket wrapped around him. When he sees the one he wishes to speak to, he steps to her quickly and throws the blanket about her so that it covers them both and no eye can see them. You must do the same thing. If she will stand still and listen to you, you may be happy. If she speaks and says no, then there is no further hope for you. If she speaks and at once says yes, then you are sure to marry her, if you can find enough horses or enough fame to please the heart of her father. Go to the bank, therefore, wrapped in a blanket. Otherwise, the small boys will see you and know you and mock even the Iron Hand. Small boys fear nothing in the world, not even the strongest man."

Messenger laughed, very faintly. His face was cold, and his heart beat uneasily.

"Go down to the river, therefore," went on the squaw, "and, when you see the shine of her yellow hair as she comes up to the top of the bank. . . ."

He started. He found that she was smiling very broadly at him.

"What do you know?" he asked.

"Oh," she said, "I am very busy, but between times I look up from my work and see a little sunlight through the edges of the lodge entrance. Sometimes I even hear a little more than the whistle in the wind."

The youth sat very still. "What will she say?" he burst out suddenly.

The squaw dropped her needle and made a gesture with both hands. "If she were two years younger, she would fall on her knees and thank the Sky People who sent her such great fortune. If she were two years older, only her father's will would matter to her. But as it is, she is come to a hard age. She is between girl and woman, and even the Maker of the world is not wise enough to know what such creatures will do or think. When the blanket is around her, ask, and then you will be the first to know."

That was late in the morning, but it seemed to Messenger that the day lasted a long year before the sun began to slide down the western arch of the sky, and another long year before he saw the girls of the village go out to draw the water. At last he took from the lodge of War Lance a great buffalo robe, and felt the smile of the squaw following him as he walked through the village and out over the sweet, fresh grass toward the river.

He was nervous. The uneasiness that he felt then was unlike anything he had ever known before. Twice he actually stopped and was about to turn back, but he mastered himself, and went on. He rehearsed in his mind everything that the squaw had told him, but suddenly he was disturbed by a loud pealing of boyish laughter. He turned, and there were a half a dozen bronzed urchins with their hands on their hips, rocking with mirth. Mirth directed toward him! Why? They pointed. They were designating his shoes and trousers that the robe did not cover. Of course, no other man in the tribe would be wearing such apparel as this.

He ground his teeth. He was between two minds, either to return in haste to the camp and the security of the lodge of War Lance, or else to chase the little boys in a fury. Wisely he did neither. His retreat could only have been interpreted in one way, and he saw that his feet were on the path that had been dimly worn by the feet of the water carriers in even this brief halt at the camp. So, drawing a great breath, he went on.

There had been nothing in his complicated education to teach him what to do in such an emergency. No one ever had prescribed for him the right course of action. He had to cling to the words of the squaw. At least, he would not wear a mask that was no mask at all. And, throwing the robe across his shoulder, like a useless cloak, he strode on his way.

The boys followed him, dancing. Doubtless they were in a great flurry to find out to whom he was about to make his proposal. So he turned, but, instead of berating them, a foolish joy fluttered like the bright wings of a bird in his spirit, and he found himself laughing at them. They laughed back, but in a different key. One of them, the oldest of the lot, sang out in a voice like the crowing of a rooster:

"May the golden color be real gold to you, oh, Iron Hand!"

Chapter Thirty-Eight

They left him, scampering back toward the swimming pool, doubtless to spread the news. But how had they known so much? He had no more than looked at the girl twice, and once when there was no one to mock him except Lessing, who was not a betrayer of secrets. Yet the squaw of War Lance had known, and so did these children.

It was a mystery. It was most mysterious of all that they laughed, no matter what they knew, even if the squaw had warned him beforehand. Since the evening of the battle, to be sure, he had not been able to stir abroad without being followed by troops, but these troops were stricken with the silence of awful adoration. If he passed a lodge, little boys and girls leaped out, breathless with excitement and haste, to see him walking by. Usually they joined the troop that followed. Some of the older dared to speak to him, their eyes big with the fear of reverence. He used to answer them gently and pleasantly, and they had run off with his words as if with treasures.

But now they danced behind him and laughed! No, they were gone now, but the tingle of their mirth still disturbed him. Yet he went on. He felt that he was doing a frightful thing. For how would the civilized women of the East treat this child of nature, no matter how white her skin might be? How would they sneer at clumsy table manners and lack of social poise? Yet he could not leave her behind him. She fitted into all that he desired. There was the medicine man to be disposed of, but, after that, she was the final consummation of life. As the boy said, the gold of her hair would be gold, indeed.

With the robe still hanging idly over his shoulder, Messenger reached, at last, the edge of the bank overlooking the stream. The sun was nearly down, and, puffing his cheeks, he blew through a mist a golden color that stained the trees, and the grass, and made the swift little river flow with metal and rose.

On the verge of the water he could see the Indian girls stooping to fill their vessels. The sound of their laughter went up above the chanting and the humming of the water, and fell most musically upon his ear. Their grace and their merry voices filled his heart to overflowing. With a sense of singular fellowship, almost of kinship, he looked at certain other forms that stood on the verge where the bank began to slope and where the path wound up. They were muffled to the head feathers with their robes. They looked like mummies, or like wind-carved forms of stone such as one sees in the upper mountains where the gales blow the hardest. But they were not mummies. Their hearts, at this moment, must be beating as his beat, and the same hope must make them giddy.

Was the girl there? Was she among those who leaned above the water and then stood there a moment, chattering so pleasantly?

A gleam beside him, along the path, made him turn. There she was! She was going down toward the water, but, when she saw his face, she started aside as a deer might start when there is a strange noise in the brush, and he thought that she suddenly grew pale and certainly her eyes widened as she looked at him. It was not joy that opened them, he could tell himself. It was not the same look that he had felt upon him as she looked across the fire toward him, during the scalp dance. But there was recognition and knowledge in it.

Did she know, also, for what woman he had come? How was it that the entire camp understood so well? What had he done? Had he spoken in his sleep? He grew angry as he grew mystified, and his face was stern as he stood there, watching the girls come up, bearing their burdens. They who had gone by him, during these days, like ghosts, stepping softly, their eyes upon the ground, they showed no fear and no consciousness now. They came up staring at him, smiling, even laughing, as though they well understood that he was not there for them.

I'm being a fool, Messenger thought. *How am I a fool? Because I haven't shrouded myself in the robe? But the boys laughed at me even when I was covered by it. This is a mystery. Someone has been talking, and certainly it has not been I.* So he spoke to himself, and he retreated so far into his gloomy reflections that Yellow Antelope was almost upon him, walking swiftly and lightly under her burden.

He stared at her with a sort of hopeless hunger, like a beggar child looking through the glass window of a bakery shop on a winter day, when rich cakes, and raisin-studded buns, and coffee rolls crusted with brown glaze of sugar, and well-baked loaves of bread are shown. So he looked at the girl, and she looked at him with the dread of something hunted that wishes to flee and cannot, being led forward by a hypnotic power.

Other girls were coming up the path, but they halted far away, as though they saw her approaching the Iron Hand and wished to observe, at casual leisure, what happened.

He, like a matador, flung the robe over his extended arm

and stepped forward. He would rather have been up there in the shadowy throat of the pass, when the Crows were charging home, than to stand there with the girl coming. She made a few paces toward him, and then she paused. She grew whiter than ever. Her eyes closed. By the eternal heavens, she knew what was about to happen. She knew that it was for her that he stood there. Surely she knew it, as though he had opened his heart to her already.

She stood with her head thrown back a little and one hand at her breast, and the other bare arm drawn down close to her side by the weight she was carrying. Like one about to die, he saw all things clearly, and swore that no other arm in the world was like this one, so slenderly shaped and so strong. What were those other women who had gone by him in the old life, that was a dream? What were they in their stiff corsetings, their frills, and their flounces? They were imitation creatures, and here alone stood true beauty.

He stepped to her and flung the robe around her. They were covered completely by it. Under the robe, the evening light made a deep, golden gloom through which he was looking down at her face, and at the hand that she moved from her own breast and laid against his. Her eyes were closed. The arm that held the robe around her felt her body trembling. Her head was raised, also, with the pain, and the white fear showing in her face.

He spoke, and the Blackfeet tongue made his voice deeper than usual, and graver. "Yellow Antelope," he said, "I have come here to ask you to be my squaw, and live with me the rest of your life."

She opened her eyes suddenly, and looked at him.

It seemed to him that she was not troubled by his near-ness, but that she was searching into his eyes in the effort to find there some hidden secret. Her head moved a little, from side to side, while she stared, but said nothing.

He, too, was almost glad of this silence. It gave him a chance to search her features with intimate care, to find there some trace of grossness, some savage wildness of expression. But all was pure and clearly cut as marble.

Then she spoke, and the sound of her voice so moved him that at first he hardly understood her meaning, but at last he knew that she was saying no, and three times over that she had repeated it.

"No!"

Why should he be so surprised? Why should he feel that the thing that he heard was unreal, and that it could not be that he had heard aright. Then, stunned and terrified as he found himself losing her, he cried out loudly: "Is there some other man?" They flashed before his face, those braves among the Blackfeet in their feathers and in their war paint. "There is some warrior among the Blackfeet, Yellow Antelope!"

She shook her head. Her hand pushed feebly against his breast. "Let me go," she said.

He stepped back slowly, and the robe fell back over his arm while the girl went on hurriedly, with a bowed, shining head. The brightness seemed, at a stroke, to have been taken from the day. Through the purple quiet of the evening, he saw the other girls coming up from the water. One after another they went past him, and they gave him no regard but stared straight ahead, as though they had seen some great catastrophe.

One of the young warriors moved forward. He was warned away with a raised hand. And the procession went on.

Messenger waited until they were all past him. Then slowly he went back toward the village.

Chapter Thirty-Nine

Very slowly he went on back to the camp, and, when he reached it, he made out that the news had gone there before him, and that it had an odd effect upon the Blackfeet. The little boys stared at him, but they no longer laughed. They acted as though they were looking straight into the face of calamity and expected to find trouble waiting for them behind their backs. The young braves, whom he passed, kept their heads downcast and pretended not to see him go by; the only person who spoke to him was an old woman who lifted both her hands to the sky and bade him be aware that all girls are fools. It was amazing that they should have heard the news of his repulse so quickly, and that they took it so seriously.

Then, going by the lodge in which Yellow Antelope lived, he heard a faint pulse of sobbing coming from within. He wanted very much to open the flap and stand there in the entrance and say to her: "Yellow Antelope, why are you crying? Are you sorry because you have made me unhappy? Have I insulted you in some mysterious manner by asking you to marry me? Let me stay here and talk to you until we understand one another." He wanted to say that, because he felt sure that something most unusual had happened in her mind regarding him. Certainly she had not looked across the fire of the scalp dance with the eyes of one who is indifferent.

But he knew that Indian etiquette forbade his entrance

into that lodge, and, therefore, he went straight on to the teepee of War Lance. The squaw was still at her work, and, when he entered, she lifted her head and gave him a long, fixed look.

"She said no at once, and that was the end of it," said the boy.

The squaw nodded. "She is young," she said. "She is very, very young, my friend. But a man who walks a long trail is sure to come to a turning, is he not?"

"What do you mean by that?" asked the boy curiously.

"Why should she say no?" asked the woman.

"Because I don't please her, of course."

"Three things displease an Indian girl," said the squaw. "Cowardice, poverty, and a foolish brain. Are you a coward, or poor, or a fool?"

This simple enumeration made the boy blink. "It's not as simple as that," he argued. "Besides, she's not an Indian. Her skin is as white as mine."

"What is the color of the skin? The color of the heart is what matters, Iron Hand, and she has lived almost all her life among the Blackfeet. What they are, she is."

"You make riddles for me," he said. "I don't understand them at all."

"Do you want a wife to take with you, or a wife to leave here among her people?"

"Why, a wife to take with me," said the boy. "That, of course."

"And married in the white man's way, forever?"

"Yes, forever."

At this, the squaw shook her head decidedly. "Then she is not such a fool. It makes an Indian sad to give up her country. If you like her here, you may not like her when she is in the house of the whites."

"How can that be?" he asked. "She will be herself, no matter where she is."

"She will not," answered the squaw firmly. "What would a prairie dog do in a forest, and what would a tree squirrel do in the prairie? What would a wolf do in the water, or a beaver in the desert?"

Young Messenger sighed. "Do you think that I could live all my life here?"

At this, she gave him the same fixed sort of look with which she had received him when he first returned to the teepee. "Were you happier among the whites?" she asked him, point-blank.

"Happy?" exclaimed Messenger. He drew in a long breath and closed his eyes. But he did not answer, for the question made his brain whirl into confusion.

A moment later, their talk was interrupted by a noisy shouting of many voices on the edge of the camp, a sound that rolled rapidly up until it reached the lodge of War Lance. Into the dwelling came Bray and old Lessing, in high excitement.

"Here's War Lance coming," said Bray, "and he has the answer from that sneakin' crook, Summer Day."

"What is it?" exclaimed the squaw. "What will he do now? Does he still say that the Iron Hand is a young boy without a name?"

"You'll hear it in a minute," said Lessing. "Messenger, it's a crooked business. Mark you that! Crooked business as sure as my name is Hank Lessing."

War Lance in person entered the lodge a moment later. He did not hurry to give his message, but first greeted his guests and then sat down with his usual dignity and lighted a pipe, ceremonially. It was only after a long moment that he said in his deep voice: "This is the way in which Summer

Day speaks. He says . . . 'The young white boy is driven to his death by a wicked spirit. I have tried to keep him from harm, but he will not listen to me. The evil spirit is stronger in him than good sense. If he wishes to meet me, let us meet alone. I hear a name ringing in my mind. It is the cañon of the Mighty Voice. Let us both ride into the cañon on the next day. Let us go into it in the afternoon, just after the sun has started toward the west. There we shall meet, and, while the Water People are singing, we shall fight. If the Iron Hand is afraid to do this, let the Blackfeet know that he is a woman, and send him away from their lodges. If he will meet with me there, let him come alone. Let them take an oath that no Blackfeet will ride with him, and I shall take an oath that no Blackfeet will ride with me. Let him make a vow that he will not permit a Blackfoot warrior to be with him, or near him to help, and I shall take the same oath before the chiefs and the old men of the tribe. Then I shall ride into the cañon of the Mighty Voice, and the Sky People help the young man, for help he will need!' "

When War Lance had finished repeating this long message, word by word, he resumed the smoking of his pipe, puckering his brow above it, in deep thought.

"You ain't gonna go," said Lessing to the boy. "You listen to me, lad. You ain't gonna go. Not till I've gone and scouted that cañon and seen that it's safe. Because Summer Day wouldn't take a risk with you. Not after what you done in the neck of the pass lately. No Indian would take a chance with you, man to man, unless he was a fool, and nobody could ever accuse Summer Day of bein' that."

Messenger listened, but he did not answer. Instead, he turned to the thoughtful chief and asked: "What would you do, War Lance?"

The other shook his head. "Summer Day has a very

strong medicine, but so has my brother with the iron hand. If there is to be a fight, why will he not fight where many warriors may stand by and look on? What harm do eyes do him? He has done his magic a great many times before the eyes of all the people. We have seen him call the rain, and it fell. We have heard him ask the thunder to speak, and it has spoken. Now, then, why should we not be allowed to see his battle magic, also? If he is going to call up spirits from underground, or bring them down from the sky, let us all watch him do it. But if there is something else in his mind, then that is a bad thing."

"What else could be in his mind?" asked the boy.

"A jack rabbit runs faster than a coyote, but coyotes eat many rabbits," declared the chief. "And that is because they use their wits, for their wits are sharper than their teeth, by a great deal. How will Summer Day use his wits, which are still sharper than the coyote's?"

"What would you do, then?" asked the boy.

"I would send back an answer and say that you are very glad to ride into the cañon of the Mighty Voice to meet him, or into any other cañon, for that matter, and that you do not want any Blackfoot warriors to help you. But you want to take in ten famous braves, so that they may see the great enchantments of Summer Day, because, in spite of those enchantments, you intend to kill him, as hungry people kill a fat dog!"

His voice rang and rang as he spoke. Everyone in the teepee nodded in assent.

"There'll be a trick! There'll be a trick!" exclaimed the trapper. "Oh, you can lay your money on that! He ain't a coyote. He's a fox, that Summer Day. He's killed more men by craft than War Lance has ever killed by open fighting."

"What can he do?" asked the boy. "He takes an oath before the old man not to bring in helpers. Isn't that enough of a surety for me? Will he break the oath?"

"Not in a million years," answered the trapper. "But he might find some way of slippin' around it. Take my advice, and Bray's advice, and the advice of War Lance, and don't you go near to that cañon of the Mighty Voice!"

"Aye," said Bray. "you keep away from that, if you've really got a head on your shoulders. I don't want to go back to Fort Lippewan and tell that gent that you've gone and disappeared in the cañon of the Mighty Voice."

"Do you think that it would trouble him?" asked young Messenger bitterly. He took from his pocket the wallet, and from the wallet he took the letter that he had been cherishing so carefully. This letter, to the utter amazement of Lessing, he tore twice in two, and threw it in the fire. Then he turned to War Lance. But those torn fragments were light, and the upward draft of the heated air just above the fire caused the papers to shelve off to the side and fall to the ground at Lessing's feet. He picked them up, and, freshening the fire with some of the wood that was piled near it, he made a gesture as if throwing the papers into the rising smoke and the flames. Instead, he conveyed them quietly into his pocket.

In the meantime, he heard the boy saying to the war chief: "My good friend, War Lance, everything that you say is true. It shows me that you are my friend. I think that Summer Day is full of tricks, also, and, as you say, his wits may be sharper than a coyote's. But if he can use them to eat me, he is welcome. He is the end of my trail. Whether I win or lose now, I hardly care. But I am tired of waiting. If you have a fast horse, give him to the messenger, and send him back with news to Summer Day that I will meet him in that cañon."

Chapter Forty

No one argued against this decision, because it was spoken in such a way that argument was not possible. Lessing left the lodge almost immediately after, and strolled from the camp into the woods, where the evening was coming down, moist and dark. He heard a footstep behind him, and, turning, he made out the face and the burly shoulders of Bray, through the dusk. He halted and confronted him.

"It's all right," said Bray. "I ain't here to make any trouble about it, but I hanker after seein' that letter as much as you do, partner."

Lessing nodded. "I seen that you was watchin'," he admitted. "We'll get a light here, and have a look."

They went a hundred yards into the heart of the woods. There they kindled a small flame, and by this light they set to work patching the fragments of the torn letter together. It was not a hard thing to do because the edges were irregular, and, by fitting the jags into corresponding depressions, they quickly managed to have the thing whole. Lessing, then, began to read aloud, stumbling a good deal, for he was not very familiar with print, to say nothing of swiftly running handwriting like this one.

The letter began:

My Dear Boy:
This ought to come to you through the hand of your

uncle, Thomas Vance. He has undertaken to bring it out along the same Western trail that you were to follow, though you need not be particularly grateful to him for the effort, as will be explained later on.

It may be that he will not reach you until you have found the Blackfoot beast of an Indian. If the fellow is still alive, I'm convinced that his ugly face will not be very hard to find, and my real hope is that you will have executed your mission before this letter is handed to you. Because, the moment you read this, all the obligation which you have felt ceases. From the moment you read it, you owe nothing to me, and nothing to the dead man.

This quiet air of Seville has not put my conscience to sleep, as one might have expected. Instead, it has wakened me to a sense of crimes that I knew before, but did not realize.

My dear lad, you are the one who has been chiefly injured by me. I have done various evil things in my time, but no one have I injured as I have injured you. I have injured you so much that, at a single stroke, I can destroy your nearest relative, as you think. You have thought of me as your father. I now remove your thought. I am not he.

Who is your father, then, and what is he?

That I cannot tell you.

What friend prevailed upon me to raise you as my son?

That I shall explain simply. When I saw poor Vance lying dead in the little camp, where the brute of a Blackfoot had left him, the dreadful look of his mutilated face made me swear that I would, in some way, take a revenge upon the red monster who had done the thing.

And that purpose was boiling in my mind when I left the place. I had buried Vance as well as I was able and put up a headstone, with his name chipped into it. Then I went off, carrying with me the chip of wood with the likeness of the Blackfoot cut upon it.

I traveled two days—or was it three?—and then I came out on a river and went down the bank of it for a number of miles until I reached a little cabin, the ashes of which were still smoking. In the ruins, I could see two dead bodies. While I stood there, I heard a sound like that of a small, helpless animal, and ran into the brush and found there a two- or three-year-old boy.

Now, then, my lad, inspirations of good or of evil will sometimes leap out of a man's mind fully grown. The instant that I looked down on you and thought of your murdered father and mother, that instant I decided that you should become my instrument in exacting vengeance from the Indians.

Why should I not have taken vengeance with my own hand?

You know the answer very well. I am not a brave man. I never have been. The frightful truth is that I crouched in the brush and saw the last of the torments of poor Vance, without daring to show myself to the monster of a Blackfoot!

Now, my boy, you know the worst of it, and, instead of regretting, you'll be glad that you are not the son of such a man as I.

However, I took you back East with me, and there I raised you, for all that you know, as though you were my own son. I took a peculiar pleasure in that education. I had a right, I felt, to make you a cutting instrument. Your own mother and father had been killed by the In-

271

dians. To what better purpose could you devote your life than to a complete revenge. Therefore, I determined that I would make you a white Indian and send you to tower like a hawk over small birds.

The Indians were enduring, indifferent to pain. I had you trained in daily torments, until you could smile while your flesh was being torn, or a candle singed you. I trained you to endure cold, heat, hunger, miserable weariness of body and soul. I had experts give you every manual dexterity with weapons. I refused to allow your time to be wasted in amusement. Even the horses that you rode were the hardest-mouthed, cruelest-spirited creatures that I could find. Your boxing teacher enjoyed knocking you down—until you were able to turn the tables on him. Your instructor in firearms never knew how to speak a good word to you.

In short, you went through torture. "In that hot fire," I used to say to myself, "he will have every bit of a weaker metal burned out of him, and he will become the purest steel."

Well, you became steel, my boy. When you grew older, I finally explained what my purpose had been in making you what I was trying to have you be. I convinced you that there was a holy necessity. I swore that you were the son of my bone and blood, and that all my property would go to you eventually.

Well, my lad, your so-called uncle, Thomas Vance, finally found out about this odd private school that I was maintaining for a single pupil, and, when he learned about it, he made inquiries. He could not find out everything, but he could find out enough to hold a gun to my head. That gun was the danger of a public scandal if he made clear two things. First, that I had acted a long, living lie to you. Second, that I had raised you like a fighting animal, with torments.

Thomas Vance showed me, incidentally, that he did not expect me to live very long, and that he expected a reasonable part of my fortune. His arguments, in short, were convincing, and, since I never have been a very bold man, I decided that he was right, and that, therefore, I would have to be wrong.

There was only one way in which I could recompense you, to a slight degree, for the harms that I have worked upon you, and that was to tell you the truth. Now you are free to detest and to despise me. But, at least, you are free also from the dangerous necessity of hunting down the Blackfoot fiend, whoever he may be.

I must close this letter.

You no longer are a Messenger. What your true name may be, I cannot tell you. That obscure little cabin in the woods—I don't think that I ever could find it again. I merely remember the white glimmer of the trunks of the birch trees along the stream that ran near it, and a pair of black-headed mountains that showed to the south of it. But, otherwise, I never could locate or identify the place.

You have lost me as a father. You have nothing to use in replacing the idea that you have lost except, of course, your own fiction, which will create an honest and strong pioneer for a father and a beautiful and good woman for a mother. No doubt, your imaginings will be right.

At any rate, at this point I pass out of your life.

What will become of you, I wonder, and in a rather melancholy sense. But Thomas Vance will have you separated from me. He will not see a penny of the Messenger fortune diverted to false blood. And I cannot fight back or argue against him. Being the strongest, he must be right.

Good bye, my lad. At least, if I cannot send you money, I can give you to the world as a sword with a cutting edge and a needle point that will stab through a foot of cold steel, without breaking or marring. There never was another like you before. There never will be another like you; hereafter, you are unique.

The best of good fortune come to you. Forgive me if you can, though you will find that hard.

Always with kind thoughts of you.

Charles Messenger

The trapper, having finished this letter, first crushed it between his hands, and then he dropped it into the dwindling little fire.

"Why, Lessing," said Bray, "maybe the poor kid, he sort of wants to die, after that."

Chapter Forty-One

That night, young Messenger, if he still had the right even to think of himself under that name, lay down in the roll of buffalo robe that War Lance furnished him and looked steadily up toward the smoke vent at the top of the lodge. It seemed to him that his life had reached the edge of a precipice, and that from it he was about to topple into nothingness. He had lost his name. He had lost his total identity. He discovered that he had given the precious years of a young life to a false goal and to a false ideal. And finally the woman he had found among the savages had thrust him away from her in fear and in disgust.

He turned these facts slowly through his mind, and closed his determination.

On the morrow, no doubt that the medicine man planned some subtle trickery in the ravine of the Mighty Voice. Once before he had met the white lad with gun, knife, and hand. He would surely not be fool enough to attempt the battle again. There was some resource of cunning upon which he would rely, and with which he hoped to seal the breath out of the boy's nostrils. Well, he should have his chance.

Young Messenger closed his eyes, and, by an easy effort of his powerful will, he excluded all thoughts of pain, all thoughts of regret or of remorse from his brain. In another instant, he was asleep.

When he wakened in the morning, he went down to the river and plunged into the snow water with the others, and with them he raced up the slope for the village, apparently as light-hearted as ever before. He rode out on a borrowed pony and hunted through the morning with a dozen young braves, letting them show him their secrets in the art with which they were most familiar. How delighted they were to be allowed to teach that peerless warrior, that incarnate hero of the fight, the Iron Hand. They would have poured forth their souls, their lifeblood for the hero.

So they came to noon in the day, and then, back at the village, Messenger took another of the ponies of War Lance, who refused all recompense, whether of weapons or hard cash.

"Suppose I had three times a hundred horses," he said, "how would they pay, if I gave them to you, for the glory you have won for me and for all my friends and fellows among the Blackfeet?" He took the hand of the boy, after the white man's fashion, and pressed it with a fervent grip.

Then Messenger went out into the open air and sun, rather glad of the keenness of it against his face and the bite of it upon his shoulders. He was dressed all as an Indian this day. His other clothes, worn to tatters by the hot work in the neck of the pass, that night of the battle, had had to be discarded, and the squaw of War Lance had managed to find a beautifully cut, but simple, suit of deerskins that fitted him very well, indeed, although perhaps the shirt was molded a little closely about his shoulders. In this outfit, all that looked strange about him, for the garb, was the shortness of his hair and the paleness of his skin, but even in this respect he was altering to the Indian color.

Every man, every woman, every child in that village knew very well why he was riding out and where he was going. He rode the finest pony that the chief could supply, a glorious bay stallion with an eye of fire, and a muzzle that could have fitted into a pint pot. Its legs were of hammered steel, and it went like flowing water.

Behind the boy rode War Lance himself, at a little distance, plainly dressed without a feather in his long hair, and with a look of sadness in his face.

The women, when they saw this attitude of mourning, set up a wailing cry that they ceased when the Iron Hand came to the place where the two Crow captives were, in turn, seated upon their horses. In spite of the hurt shoulder of Red Feather, on this day they intended to start out on the long journey toward their own people, going doubtless by the easiest sort of stages. Before them Messenger paused and gave them a cheerful wish for their journey.

Said Red Feather: "Oh, my son, I have remained with open eyes by the fire all night long to see your future in the flames. I have made medicine twenty times, but it fails, and everything remains dark. The will of the Sky People is to be accomplished. And what one man or what two men can stand before the Iron Hand?"

Messenger went on, and the women put up their doleful cry again. When he came to the edge of the village, there he found the eight lifeguards and companions of War Lance ranged in a double file, through which he passed. They were dressed very splendidly, equipped for the warpath, but their faces were blackened in token of mourning.

Of them, the oldest alone spoke to him, saying: "Brother, how gladly would we ride with you. Every breast here would be a shield to you. Now may the spirits help you and give you eyes like a hawk to see through the medicine and the enchantments of Summer Day."

Messenger raised his hand to them silently, and, with it

raised, he passed through that double file and went on over the open, grassy land, and into the woods. He came to a clearing, and there, in the dappling shadows of the leaves, he saw someone on horseback, sitting as still as the trees around. It was Yellow Antelope. There was in her face something that strove to speak to him, and that failed. She made a gesture with both her hands, palm up, but Messenger went past her with his eyes fixed sternly ahead.

He had a perfect foreboding that this was to be his last day on earth, and he rode on to meet the end of his life without weakness and without regret.

He had had the way to the cañon of the Mighty Voice described to him so clearly that he did not have to ponder over it, and his mind was free for other reflections. It seemed to him, as he went along, reining the horse gently over rough and smooth, that all had been ideally prepared to bring him to this humor. First, all his conception of himself and his place in life had been stripped utterly away from him. Then, when he had found another reason for clinging to life, he had been repulsed by the girl. There remained to him only the naked purpose for which he had come so far into the West—to meet Summer Day and fight out the battle with him.

He had no enthusiasm for the fight. He had no excitement or fear, either. If ever he had his chance to meet the medicine man at close range or at long range, he had not the least doubt that he could conquer, as he had conquered before. But he could guess that Summer Day would not venture on a battle unless he were sure, beforehand, of winning it. There was some contrivance, some stratagem on the way that the famous Blackfoot must have contrived before he asked for the meeting. The only real hope of the white boy was that the end might come to him with a merciful suddenness.

So he came, at the last, to the mouth of the cañon of the Mighty Voice. Its name was well given. For it was a great gorge, running north and south, with huge stone walls on either side, and at the base of these walls a thick apron of soil on which grew enormous trees. All over the central portion of the ravine's floor were scattered boulders as great in size as small houses—or even big ones. Winding and plunging among these, ran the currents of a powerful stream.

Sometimes the water leaped over a cascade; sometimes it fell with shattering force and a roar into a sheer descent; sometimes it was merely breaking the strength of its body against the boulder faces. But in doing these things, it set up a continual song that was composed of many parts. Thunders and bellowings and loud shouting rolled and reëchoed up and down the cañon of the Mighty Voice. It was like coming into the presence of a vast chorus that surrounded the listener, and yet obviously the one singer was the white water that flashed through the center of the valley.

The entrance itself was imposing, like the rudiments of a vast natural gate. A dark cliff went up on the left, a light-colored one upon the right, and it seemed as though immense panels must at one time have been fitted into these on hinges of adamant.

The boy looked up the pillars on either side with a quiet and contented eye. There could hardly have been a more solemn entrance to a nobler graveyard. Then he passed through, and, once fairly inside the cañon, he felt dwarfed and insignificant, and all his life seemed to shrink to a mere pinpoint without a meaning.

So he went forward, perfectly indifferent to the result

and, only instinctively, as he passed along the trail near the edge of the water, looking about him among the shrubs and among the boulders.

Then a sudden, thin, small screech reached his ears through the uproar of the water, and he turned suddenly in the saddle.

Chapter Forty-Two

It was merely the gray streak of a rabbit that leaped from the covert of a little bush and bolted in vain, for over it slid a long shadow that launched out from the rock above, and took shape as a wildcat with flattened ears and a gaping mouth. It scooped up the little fugitive, biting through its life and its death screech with strong jaws. Then, bounding back onto the top of the rock, it looked fiercely over its shoulder toward the boy, while it lashed its sides with its long tail.

The next moment it had sunk from sight, but young Messenger remained there for a moment, troubled and ill at ease. After all, it is well enough to philosophize about death. In the distance the thing seems not at all overpowering, but, at close hand, it is quite another matter. The yellow glare of the eyes of the cat, and the sinuous grace of the destroying leap, and the last poor cry of the little rabbit remained a picture for the eye and the ear of the boy. He could not help freshening his grip upon the rifle that balanced across his saddlebows.

Then he went on, but in quite another manner, for now he constantly probed everything about him with the keenest of eyes. Once he saw a movement at which he almost fired, point-blank—but then he saw that it was merely the reflected light from the face of the stream, shivering and struggling upon the face of a polished rock. It had given him a start, however. It was enough, in itself, to tell him that his calm had been an affectation, and that life was as sweet to him, at least, as it had been to the poor morsel of flesh and fur that had been the rabbit not long before.

There was beauty and splendor in this world. No, a nameless life in the tawny, smoke-stained cities of the East—that was not worth any great effort to retain—but here was a different matter. The cliffs were so lofty that now, although the sun was still high, the slanting shadows from the western wall had more than covered the floor of the ravine and were climbing gradually up the eastern cliff. As the floor of the valley darkened, a thin blue mist seemed to rise from the stream and fill the hollow, and soften the rocks, and tangle among the trees. The voice of the water was not—it seemed to him now—singing a death chant, but a glorious song of abounding life. The valley floor trembled with the music, and the air filled with it, and Messenger found himself drawing down deep, quick breaths.

He went on much more slowly now, probing at every suspicious thing with careful eyes. And suddenly he felt danger behind him! He whirled, throwing himself along the side of his horse as he did so, and swinging the rifle with one hand, so that it rested across the withers of the horse. He saw nothing. But something crossed the tail of his eye, he felt, gliding between two big rocks to the rear. He held his difficult position for another moment. But nothing stirred, and there was no sound to the rear.

Was it a dream? Although there had been nothing actual for his eye to fall upon, yet there was a breathless reality in the sensation that he had felt. It was that peculiar gripping at the small of one's back that means that an eye, a human eye, had been regarding one fixedly.

He shook his head, and made himself erect at the saddle

again. Say that he was being followed, say that someone was yonder among rocks that overlooked him, then certainly he would have been fired upon before this, and from such a distance the bullet could not have failed to strike home in its mark. No enemy could be behind him, unless it were a foe that confidently counted upon taking him alive—for future tortures and a slow death, say? He shuddered at that thought. But such confidence would hardly be found in the medicine man. No, he had tasted the danger of Messenger well enough once before, and he was sure to use any safe advantage as soon as it was his.

He must have dreamed, then. Messenger's imagination was too strong for him, and, with a wave of self-contempt, he banished all care for the moment of what might be happening behind him, and attended to what was ahead.

Now he came out into a small hollow. It was a steep-sided dip both before him and upon the farther side. The bottom was flat and bare except for a little nest of boulders in the midst. Moving ice sheets, perhaps, had gouged out this depression. To the left ran the water in a white, straight rush of foam and of spray, but making less noise here although the same river was bellowing above him, and below.

He considered crossing the hollow. It was dangerously open, but to turn to the side and work around through the boulders, although safer, would be delicate and wearisome work. But he was young. He was very young, and, therefore, very careless. He gave the problem a single moment of thought, and then pushed his stallion forward. On the verge, the good horse lowered its head and sniffed at the descent, not in fear, as it appeared, but to study the best way down. Then it started and, in a moment, was skidding through a few small stones and gravel, but keeping its balance perfectly.

So they came to the bottom and saw that, on the farther side, the ascent was far less steep. Messenger would be across and up it in a moment. So he gave the good stallion the rein and went on until the hard rocks began to slope up once more. In the meantime, he had been scanning the boulders that crowned like battlements the rim of the hollow, and nothing suspicious was seen. Yet, straight before him, there was the sudden *clang* of a rifle.

He had been leaning, that instant, to arrange the stirrup, and, at the sound of the shot, the stallion bounded violently to the side. Of what use, then, were all the long lessons in horsemanship that he had taken? He was flipped from the saddle like a stone, and instantly he heard a triumphant war whoop before him.

He lay flat, half stunned, and, looking up, he saw above a nest of rocks a feathered head rising, and the dark face of an Indian, then the whole body to the waist and the hands holding a rifle. But, miracles of miracles, it was not the medicine man—it was not Summer Day. Instead, if the arrangement of that feathered headdress meant anything, or the excessive length of the hair, this was a Crow tribe warrior.

He snatched up his rifle, and still lying flat, put in a snap shot. There was a *yip* of alarm and surprise from the other. Apparently he had thought that his shot had driven straight through the body of the white man, and that this was what had sent him to the ground. Now, starting back, the Crow tumbled out of sight, his voice still babbling out excited words.

The next instant, something that was not water hit the rock three inches from the face of Messenger, and stung his cheek with the molten rays that splashed from it. The report of a rifle directly behind him immediately followed, and he whirled to his feet. As he did so, another bullet cut the air with the sound of a wasp blowing down a strong wind, and he heard the report of a rifle from the eastern rim of the hollow. Then he understood.

How simple, like the explanation of all riddles, was this one. For the medicine man had simply called for an oath that no Blackfeet would follow either of them into the fight, and no Blackfeet were there. Instead, he had merely applied to some roving Crows. Would they not be delighted, for no other reward than the chance of counting coup upon his body, to have the hero of the night battle, the Iron Hand, delivered up to them? The matter could not have been clearer, and the hollow into which he had blundered so blindly and trustingly was simply rimmed with Crow warriors!

Now another and another puff of smoke bloomed like little translucent white flowers on the edge of the hollow, north and south. But by this time, he was running, and those good marksmen missed each time, although so narrowly that he always heard the whistling of the bullet.

They had him most hopelessly trapped. There was nothing for him then, except to take what shelter he could find in the open nest of the rocks. There he could at least lie down and gain some shelter.

He reached them, and flung himself flat just as another ball sung past his shoulder. He was safe, but safe for no more than a moment. Sooner or later, they would get the accurate range, and then they would surely get at him through the wide interstices of the stone, or with a plunging fire from either side. He lay there, panting, and heard the ringing hoofs of his horse as the animal galloped to a distance.

There was the river water as a possible means of escape.

He might run to it and throw himself in, trusting his life to the speed of the currents. But when he ventured a glance in that direction, he saw the water churning among the rocks, heard it roaring, and knew very well that he could not live ten seconds in that sweep of water constantly set with rocky teeth.

What could he do, then? There was nothing except a desperate charge. But a charge was the most foolish thing of all, for the sharp slope all around him would be sure to stop him to a crawling pace, and he could be shot down with consummate ease.

Then the firing stopped for a moment, and he heard a high-pitched voice with a wailing note in it, that called out: "Iron Hand! Iron Hand!"

It was in the Blackfeet tongue, and he thought surely that he could recognize the unforgotten accents of the medicine man.

"Iron Hand!" went on the other, his notes cutting clearly through the air and reaching the ear of the boy. "Now you have ridden on your last trail. Now you are lost, and the Blackfeet forget you like a dream. Iron Hand, stand up, and walk out into the sun, leaving your rifle and your pistol behind you. We will let you become a prisoner. Do you hear me? The Crows who are with me will let you become their prisoner, fool, lean dog, stupid rat!"

Messenger listened, and smiled a little to himself, but a shudder followed, for he could hear the high-pitched laughter of the medicine man floating over the hollow like the triumphant screaming of a bird of prey. He did not answer.

If the stones about him had been a foot higher, he could have found a secure shelter among them, but, as it was, a bullet beat with a heavy stroke against the face of the stone where he was lying. Another tore the heel off his shoe. So he wriggled across to the other side, only to have his face filled with rock splinters as a shot from the opposite direction clipped under his head.

He was lost!

Chapter Forty-Three

They would torture him to death, the bullets striking him again and again, until one of them reached a vital spot. But perhaps he could exact some retribution from them, and, staring through a gap in the rocks, rifle in hand, he saw a dark form appear suddenly beside one of the rocks at the eastern side of the rim of the hollow. He could thank his teachers of the old days for their long instructions in the estimation of distance. It might be 200 or 180 yards, and instantly his gun was at his shoulder. He saw the little puff of smoke and heard the bullet sing close above him. The Crow stooped toward shelter, and at that instant the boy drew his bead and curled his finger gently with a pressure of his whole hand over the trigger.

The explosion kicked up the muzzle of the weapon a little, and then, with a savage grin of satisfaction, he saw the brave straighten, make two or three staggering steps, and finally topple headlong from the rock. The body struck the sloping side, bounded like a thing made of rubber, and then tumbled head over heels to the bottom of the slope where it lay, a still and shapeless heap.

There was some meager satisfaction in this. Let them show themselves with more care, if they expected to hunt him to the death. Aye, now they would be wary how they so much as showed a head or a hand above the surrounding rock. The yell of rage and sorrow that came wailing over the hollow was the sweetest satisfaction to him.

There were many feathers in the headdress of that warrior. A chief, perhaps? Aye, but those feathers were not of the Crow mode. They were far more familiar. They were Blackfoot, in fact.

The boy almost leaped to his feet. It was Summer Day. It could be no other. An almost chance shot had accomplished his mission for him in the midst of the fight. The others were by no means giving up the struggle, however. The rifles *clanged* in rapid succession. Something ripped across the calf of his leg like a red-hot iron.

Then a great voice boomed across that shallow valley. It was a language that he did not understand, akin to the Blackfeet dialect, in fact. Then he could see the speaker, mounted on the top of a high rock, just to the south of the hollow. He was a tall Indian, one arm close to his side—yes, it was bound there with a bandage, and in another moment the boy had recognized Red Feather.

It seemed that the chief was haranguing the empty air, for all the answer he got, but never was Messenger so glad to hear any voice, for he knew that those words from their famous war chief—doubly famous now that he was delivered alive from the deadly hands of the Blackfeet—were sending back the Crow warriors who had come into the cañon of the Mighty Voice to win a cheap scalp and strike a celebrated coup.

Messenger stood up. Not only had the certainty of death been removed from him, but a new joy ran suddenly through his veins. Staring toward the rock rim where the chief stood, he saw Bray and Lessing come suddenly out from among the boulders. They waved down to him, and he laughed happily and waved back.

They were the shadows who he had truly felt following

him down the ravine. But they had been friends, and not enemies. In the very nick of time they had come secretly up behind him, and one shout from Red Feather was enough to scatter the Crow rascals. There was Straight Arrow, also, perched on another rock, and shouting, his voice sounded like the crowing of a rooster, and the movement of his arms was like the flapping of a rooster's wings.

He waved back to these doubly welcome friends, and then crossed the hollow to the place where the medicine man lay. He remembered, then, that this fellow, brute as he had been, belonged to the same tribe as War Lance. So he turned the body properly on its back, and folded the arms across the breast. The face of Summer Day had not been injured in the fall from the height, and the same leering smile that it had worn in life was on it now. His rifle lay not far off, and the boy put it beside the fallen warrior. Touching the body with instinctive horror, he closed his eyes, and a breath of wind stirring the feathers at that moment gave Messenger a ghostly feeling that the dead man had nodded, as though in acquiescence to his fate.

The stallion was then soon caught, and, zigzagging up the slope, brought Messenger again to the rim of the hollow, where he found the whole group around him—Red Feather, Straight Arrow, Bray, Lessing. He shook hands with them; he tried to speak out his thanks, but gratitude swelled in the hollow of his throat and choked him. Then the sound of a horse, galloping down the rocky ravine, reached his ears, and he pointed after it with an inquiring air. Had one of them lost his horse?

They merely smiled, and looked wisely at one another.

"There goes the man who you must thank," said Red Feather. "There he runs away from your words . . . the man who brought us all together and explained that, since we were not Blackfeet, we had a right at least to go behind you and guard your back."

"Who is he?" asked the boy eagerly.

But they only smiled again, and, since at that moment the echoing of the hoof beats rang clearly up to them along the valley, he drove his heels suddenly into the flanks of the stallion and made the good horse fly in pursuit.

Who could it be that had done the thing? Well, whoever it was would have to ride hard and brilliantly to escape from his pursuit, for the stallion went like a racer, swerving among the rocks, and striking up ringing echoes that boomed back from the cañon walls like the report of a rifle.

It was not long before he had a vague glimpse of the fugitive. A small man, he would say. He threw his weight forward, and, jockeying the stallion to the utmost speed, he swept into the last stretch that led toward the lofty gates of the ravine. And there, just before him, urging a swift pinto to its top gait, was Yellow Antelope!

She threw a frightened glance behind and shouted to her horse, but the big stallion swept easily up beside them, and the hands of Messenger pulled the pinto to a stop.

The panting horses faced one another; the panting riders stared at each other.

"Yellow Antelope," gasped the boy, "you have run away from me, but I think that after today you will never be able to escape from me again."

Suddenly her glance wavered, and she began to laugh, although there was a tremor in her voice. At that, he leaned from the saddle and took her in his powerful hands and held her before him on the stallion.

"Now look at me," he sternly commanded.

"Yes," she said, but still her glance wavered away toward the leaping and the thunder of the water.

"Tell me, Yellow Antelope, why you said no to me that other day by the river?"

"Because," she answered slowly, "I am a Blackfoot, and I cannot be a white man's wife. I knew that you only had come to us in order to find Summer Day and kill him because of a cruel thing he had done many years ago."

"Then why," he persisted, "do you let me hold you in my arms, and why do you smile at me?"

"Because," she said, "even after you had killed that wicked man, you came so swiftly after me that I began to think that perhaps it was not only Summer Day, after all, who kept you here with the tribe, but that you might stay even for the sake of your friends . . . such as War Lance, and all the young braves. And even a little for my sake, also."

He smiled down at her with a sort of stern joy.

"Shall I tell you something?"

"Aye," she said.

"The white man who came with Two Buffalo is waiting for an answer to take back to a man who once filled up the whole world for me. He was the greatest thing under the sky. The answer I was going to send back is this . . . 'My friend, all the evil things you have done for me have turned out to be good things in the end. You sent me out to kill a murderer. He is dead. So is my old self dead. Because I have found my people, and my wife among them.' Can you believe that?"

"Ah," she said, "but your wife for how long? For a year? For two years? Well, it will have to be enough. I shall close my eyes to everything except today and tomorrow, and never dare to look ahead."

"My wife forever," said the boy in answer.

"And all the friends of your life as white man?"

"I have no friends," he answered her. "I have killed Summer Day. Nevertheless, he had strong medicine, and I am dead, also. I am so dead, Yellow Antelope, that I have lost my other name, and I have nothing to call myself except the Iron Hand. And that is only in good Blackfoot!"

The stallion began to move forward slowly as the boy spoke, and he carried the girl and the Iron Hand quietly through the great rude pillars of the gate to the Mighty Voice. Once they were past it, that voice drew instantly back and seemed thundering on the rim of the sky with a deep rich music that filled all the heavens and made them tremble. They came out on a hill where the westering sun caught them in a warm tide. The Iron Hand looked over a glorious green sea of trees, and of rolling, grassy hills, and the gleam of the river went swiftly among them, like a saber stroke. He looked over this great and lovely country and began to laugh, although he was almost as close to tears as to mirth. But the girl, looking constantly up to his face, understood, and was content.

About the Author

Max Brand is the best-known pen name of Frederick Faust, creator of Dr. Kildare, Destry, and many other fictional characters popular with readers and viewers worldwide. Faust wrote for a variety of audiences in many genres. His enormous output, totaling approximately thirty million words or the equivalent of 530 ordinary books, covered nearly every field: crime, fantasy, historical romance, espionage, Westerns, science fiction, adventure, animal stories, love, war, and fashionable society, big business and big medicine. Eighty motion pictures have been based on his work along with many radio and television programs. For good measure he also published four volumes of poetry. Perhaps no other author has reached more people in more different ways.

Born in Seattle in 1892, orphaned early, Faust grew up in the rural San Joaquin Valley of California. At Berkeley he became a student rebel and one-man literary movement, contributing prodigiously to all campus publications. Denied a degree because of unconventional conduct, he embarked on a series of adventures culminating in New York City where, after a period of near starvation, he received simultaneous recognition as a serious poet and successful author of fiction. Later, he traveled widely, making his home in New York, then in Florence, and finally in Los Angeles.

Once the United States entered the Second World War, Faust abandoned his lucrative writing career and his work as a screenwriter to serve as a war correspondent with the infantry in Italy, despite his fifty-one years and a bad heart. He was killed during a night attack on a hilltop village held by the German army. New books based on magazine serials or unpublished manuscripts or restored versions continue to appear so that, alive or dead, he has averaged a new book every four months for seventy-five years. Beyond this, some work by him is newly reprinted every week of every year in one or another format somewhere in the world. A great deal more about this author and his work can be found in *The Max Brand Companion* (Greenwood Press, 1997) edited by Jon Tuska and Vicki Piekarski. His next Five Star Western will be *Bad Man's Gulch*.